# POWER'S
# PRICE

## THE ARBOUR ARCHIVES: BOOK TWO

Printed in Australia

Cover and internal design by Shawline Publishing Group Pty Ltd

First printing: June 2024

Shawline Publishing Group Pty Ltd

www.shawlinepublishing.com.au

Paperback ISBN 978-1-9231-0197-5

eBook ISBN 978-1-9231-7108-4

Hardback ISBN 978-1-9231-7120-6

Distributed by Shawline Distribution and Lightning Source Global

*Shawline Publishing Group acknowledges the traditional owners of the land and pays respects to the Elders, past, present and future.*

 A catalogue record for this work is available from the National Library of Australia

# POWER'S PRICE

## THE ARBOUR ARCHIVES: BOOK TWO

# SAM BAKER

# ALSO BY SAM BAKER

## The Arbour Archives
*Portrait of a Princess*

*This book is dedicated to the people here who got me through*

*Not all of them gave me their genes, some sheltered me while in my teens*

*Yet each of them were parents still, my empty heart they helped to fill*

*So thank you, each and every one; I'm proud to be some kind of son.*

*J a M i e*
*P e n n Y*

*S t e P h e n*
*A d r i e n n e*
*G R a e m e*
*H a z E l*
*D o m e N i c a*
*P e T a*
*C h a r l e S*

# Prologue

It was dark in the tunnels when Wendelmar fled, running as fast as his legs would take him. Or, at least, what remained of his legs. He could hear the wind howling on the other side of the wall; freedom seemed just centimetres from him as he navigated each turn from memory, having studied the layout before coming to the house upon his master's tasking. A tasking that would have made him a hero, had he not failed.

Each movement was agony. His eyes narrowed and his mouth formed a permanent knot as his body reacted to each jarring step that pounded the hard wooden ground below him. The opening that he had found so easily from the outside only a few hours ago now seemed much further away, obscured in the darkness of the night, as if to taunt him further.

Occasionally, he would rest against the wall, every part of his body pleading for him to stop, his mind encouraging him to continue despite his wounds. *I must get home*, he would think, before urging his body to shamble further along the tunnel.

After what felt like an eternity, the chill of the outside wind brushed his few remaining whiskers. The cool breeze wrapped itself around his body and embraced him as he followed its touch, caressing his few patches of remaining skin.

The moving air brought attention to the wet spots on his face and body.

*Is it water? Or is it blood?* he thought. *I mustn't stop to find out.*

As he rounded the last corner, running against the wind, his heart stuttered. The faint light of the glowing moon pierced through an opening up ahead, like a beacon in the night. Unable to restrain himself, Wendelmar began to cry tears of joy. He felt as though an immense weight had been lifted from his shoulders. Upon entering the tunnel, he had not known whether his injuries would mean his end within the abyss-like darkness, and as he stumbled out into the cool night air, elation began to dull some of the pains in his limbs. With newfound vigour, he decided that he was not going to die this night.

He limped his way out of the opening and slowed to a stop on the roof's edge, surveying the land before him. It was a stark contrast to the view from earlier, before the sun had finished its long journey from one side of the sky to the other. He recalled seeing several manicured hedges surrounding a well-kept lawn. Beyond the hedges, there were trees as tall as buildings, and taller still, spotting the landscape all the way to the horizon, upon which stood rolling hills and dipping valleys that broke the line between land and sky.

The sights that he remembered stretching out beyond the house were now hidden beneath the dark blanket of night. Small reflections of moonlight danced and gleamed from the distant stream, which cut through the land, and flowed towards his home.

After he had allowed himself a moment to compose his mind and body, he gently wiped the tears from his eyes, careful not to aggravate the hypersensitive patches of skin that now covered his face, and felt around for the vine he had used to climb the walls of the house.

Sudden movement appeared and disappeared within the depths of the night. He froze in place, scanning the distance, moving only his eyes to avoid detection.

It appeared again. This time, he locked onto it and noticed a bright light drawing closer, which flashed as it moved between the valleys and trees. He remained like a statue in the shadows, watching and waiting while the light turned towards the house, splitting into two beams.

The beams seemed to float, creeping their way around unseen obstacles, getting larger and brighter as they steadily approached the house. The crackle of gravel filled the silent air. Wendelmar kept his body as rigid as he could manage, his muscles stiffening and cramping, though he willed himself not to falter, fearing that the slightest movement could reveal him in all his vulnerability.

Just as his body began to shudder in protest, the lights came to a stop, pointing towards the house, and basking the previously unseen hedge in a piercing cone of light.

It was silent for a moment, and Wendelmar gently released a raspy breath upon realising that he had been holding it in. His ears remained standing at attention, listening for the slightest sign of movement, when suddenly the lights turned off, and everything was dark once more, save for the two red spots that had burnt into his retinas.

There was a *thud*, quickly followed by a second, which echoed from within the darkness where the lights had been, and then muffled voices. Wendelmar blinked frantically, trying to clear the spots from his vision. The voices spoke quietly for a little while, one man and one woman, from what he could make out, before a third and final *thud* rang through the valley and the voices ceased. The only sound that remained was quiet, crunching footsteps on the gravel, making their way towards the house.

Wendelmar turned his head, angling his ears to keep silently following the footsteps. As they got nearer, the steps changed from the crunching of gravel to the hollow sound of concrete.

A cold sweat enveloped Wendelmar when the footsteps tapped the solid ground directly below him. He knelt down and grasped the ledge with his hands and feet, careful to not falter, as even the slightest sound now would surely reveal his position.

Metal ground against wood, and a sliver of light filled the courtyard. Two elongated shadows, undoubtedly human, stepped into the house. One appeared to be carrying something in its arms, and while Wendelmar strained his eyes to try and identify the unusual shape, the sliver of light grew thinner, until the door clicked shut. The courtyard was once again quiet, save for the muffled conversation coming from behind the door.

*This is my chance,* he thought, grabbing the vine he had seen in the light from the front door and scrambling down it as quickly as he could, taking care not to fall, which would surely mean his end.

He reached the bottom of the vine, dropping the last few centimetres onto the gravel. The jagged edges of the small rocks caused him to shriek, but he threw his disfigured hands up and wrapped them tightly around his mouth to stop the worst of the sound from coming out.

After regaining his composure, he began to stagger towards the wall of hedges opposite the doors. The image of the small gap in the branches he had travelled through earlier, which would lead him back towards the stream, was now burning in his mind, acting as a compass through the dark. He stood on his two hind legs, his arms outstretched to maintain his balance, as he tiptoed his way through the gravel. It was agony to be sure, and extremely slow going, but limiting the pain to only two of his limbs would ensure that his arms remained refreshed for their upcoming trial. That could mean the difference between his survival and his death.

The grass couldn't have come quickly enough. The cool, soft blades immediately sent waves of relief upwards through his feet, beginning to soothe the cuts and burns on their soles and up his legs. For a moment, he lay down in the grass. The euphoric feeling that the cool caress of the wind and the damp touch of the grass provided him could not be explained in words, and for the duration, his mind quietened, and he felt no fear.

The moon was almost directly above Wendelmar now. Its faint glow distorted the world and made the tall hedge before him resemble an endless wall of hands reaching out towards him, beckoning for him to remain with them forever, but he could not. He had to get home. He needed to survive.

Groaning, he pulled himself back to his feet. His body felt slightly refreshed, and he had conjured newfound motivation, certain that he would make it back to his family at all costs.

Without much effort at all, he pushed his way through the small gap in the hedge. The valley now stretched out in front of him, and it seemed far larger than when he had peered down onto it from the roof of the house. The stream at the bottom of the valley looked like a silver serpent in the night; it wriggled its way from left to right, the wind caused small ripples on its surface, and when the light caught those ripples, it appeared as though it were covered in scales, and very much alive.

Wendelmar shuddered at the thought of a serpent so large, and with only the slightest hesitation, took off towards the base of the valley. He tried to slow himself as he approached the stream, but his footing gave way. He rolled headfirst down the last few metres of grass, coming to a sudden stop on the bank, his hands splayed out wide beside him to support his fall. His head came to a sudden stop, hovering just above the mirror-like surface.

His breathing stopped once more as he peered at the stranger reflected in the water just below him. He had not seen his body properly since he'd been injured, and what was revealed in the haunting moonlight caused pained shivers to run from the tip of his snout to the end of his tail.

The first change that caught his eye was his distorted whiskers. He had previously flaunted a thick tuft of whiskers on either side of his nose, an impressive feat indeed for such a young Malum. All that remained now were several short and charred hairs, hanging limply from his cheeks, which were certainly nothing to be proud of. Had he not already been partnered for life and started his family, he would surely have feared that this would scare off prospective mates, and ensure his life was spent in painful isolation.

He got to his feet and stood further over the water, inspecting the rest of his body. The silvery hair that had covered it was gone. His body was as bald as his nose, weeping in places from the severe burns he had received earlier in the night, when he had been thrown into the piercing tongues of flame. His tail, once of formidable length and strength, was now nothing but a stump. It made him think of a tree that had just been cut down, once so full of life, now nothing more than an inconvenience and an eyesore.

Wendelmar fell to his bottom. Tears began filling his burnt eyelids, as he held his head and wept silently. His mind filled with the thought of returning home to a family that might not even recognise him, and his stomach felt sick.

After a short time pondering how he would reveal himself to his family and what they might think of him, Wendelmar pulled himself to his feet and shook off his shame, at least for now. He focused on only one thing, which was that he wanted to live, and to do that, he needed to be strong.

Inspecting the tunnel in the rock wall to his right, he pictured his home, Mundus, an indeterminate distance downstream from where he now stood. The journey here in the daylight had been a long trek across the land, but fate seemed to agree with Wendelmar's will to survive, and for his return journey, he would have to do nothing more than walk into the stream, where he would be carried gently home.

He waded into the depths of the stream. Each step sent chills deep into his flesh, but gradually, his body adjusted and found the temperature of the water to be quite refreshing. Once he was able to, he lay on his back, gently waving his arms and legs alongside him, and he allowed the current to pull his body towards home.

He stared at the moon. Its large, round surface always inspired his imagination, and he smiled, thinking of how it was always changing, new marks seemingly appearing from nowhere, yet everybody still recognised it as the moon. This filled him with hope that his family would still recognise him, despite the grotesque appearance he now lived with.

The white orb of the moon disappeared from view for a few seconds as Wendelmar floated under the rock wall, which passed over him like a silent giant in the night.

He was completely at ease for the first time since he had left home that very morning. The water made his body feel just as it did before the attack; it felt relaxed, it felt whole, it felt like him. Whether it was the sheer exhaustion, the pain catching up to him, or the relaxing setting he now found himself in, he couldn't be sure, but he closed his eyes and drifted to sleep, just as his body drifted further from danger and closer to the safety of his home.

* * * * *

'Wake up!'

A bucket of water, alongside the unfamiliar stern voice, shocked Wendelmar back to consciousness. He coughed up the water that had lodged itself in his throat and rubbed his eyes as they adjusted to the light.

'Wh... Where am I?' he asked, feeling hard ground under him, and not the stream of water that he was expecting to still be floating down.

He could hear someone on either side of him, but the one to his left spoke first.

'You're home, Wendelmar. We found you in the stream in the early light of dawn and pulled you out. We debated leaving you, as from all appearances you looked to be dead.'

Wendelmar turned to the voice, and his eyes began to focus on the figure before him. It was indeed one of the guards from his home. The shield and spear were the familiar design of his master's army.

The other guard on his right spoke next, with a bitter tone to his voice. 'Well,' he said, snickering, 'it's your home for now, assuming you completed your mission. Guess we'll just have to wait and see what the master has to say.'

A lump formed in Wendelmar's throat. He knew the time was almost upon him and his master would soon learn of his failure. He had tried his best, and that was all he could have done. In his heart, he hoped that his master would pity his new deformities, but he was not naïve.

He shrugged off the cruel statement as just a jealous comment from the guard. There were indeed many people whose jealousy had grown after Wendelmar was chosen to complete the master's vital mission. It was not something he had any memory of volunteering for; in fact, the days leading up to the attempted assassination appeared as nothing more than a blur in his mind. He wondered if, perhaps, there were higher powers at play, but who was he to question his fate?

Pulling himself to his feet, he was rudely reminded of the pain throughout his body. His mind instantly flashed with images of the night prior and the events leading him home. It seemed almost unbelievable, and he wondered if other Malum would accuse him of exaggerating his adventure so to win favour.

After a quick survey of his surroundings, Wendelmar realised that he was indeed in Mundus, but not somewhere he had spent much time before. He was inside the throne room. It was still very early in the morning, so the room was only dimly lit by the climbing sun, which had begun to penetrate the small holes in the side walls. Faint shafts reached down to the compressed dirt floor, like lines of rain falling from the clouds.

At the far end of the room hung the balcony from where his master and king, Azul, often addressed the subjects that entered his chamber. A large sheet of tattered fabric flowed from the ceiling above the balcony in an attempt to conceal whatever lay behind it. The king hadn't been seen outside of this room for quite some time, since his rise to power and crowning, a terrifying ceremony that had trapped many a Rat King within these walls.

Wendelmar's eyes fixed upon the curtain as he noticed it moving in places, an indication that the king would be appearing soon. The guard on his right, who addressed him with more bitterness than the one on his left, spoke first.

'The king will be here soon; he ordered that you be brought here first. You know how important this mission was to him.' He fidgeted where he stood, speaking more softly as he did so. 'To all of Mundus.'

With what little energy remained in Wendelmar's body, he pulled a chair from a nearby table and sat, waiting for his master to arrive, wondering what would happen to him when he announced his failure. The faces of his children and wife lingered in his mind as the tortuous silence continued.

Wendelmar dozed off again, and one of the guards nudged him. The touch on his burnt skin caused him to jump awake, and he stood at attention as the curtain rose slowly, just enough for the king to walk out to the ledge, lowering again before the shadowy mound behind him could come into full detail.

Azul was a large Malum, twice the size of any other in their home. His face was scarred on one side; the scar ran from his neck all the way up to the middle of his head, tracing a path through his right eye, which was now nothing more than a milky orb. His unsettling grin was a permanent feature on his face. Atop his head was an extremely small golden crown, simple to some, but everything for this Malum king.

Azul's eyes traced Wendelmar's figure from head to toe. The grin on his face shrunk slightly.

'Well?' The deep, booming voice penetrated Wendelmar's very being as it echoed through the hall. 'Did you complete your mission? Did you kill the girl?'

Drool started to pool in the gaps between his teeth. He leaned over the balcony, his black eyes piercing into Wendelmar.

'My king...' Wendelmar fell to his knees, focusing on the ground as he spoke of his failure. 'I went to the house as you ordered. The girl was there, alone, as you said she would be, and I attacked her from the darkness...'

'And?' Long, silvery trails began to fall from Azul's fetid mouth as he leaned further over the balcony.

'...My king.' Wendelmar's voice faltered slightly as he braced every muscle in his body and mind. 'She defended herself well. She brandished a weapon of steel and cast me into a fire as I jumped at her for the kill.'

Azul turned sharply away, his back now facing Wendelmar, his shoulder muscles tensing.

'And how is it that you survived, Wendelmar? Fire would have consumed you in mere seconds.'

Wendelmar could sense the anger radiating from his master. He chose his next words carefully, hoping not to aggravate Azul.

'It was by the same hand that cast me into the flames, my king. The girl cared for me as she addressed my failure, before freeing me into the night.' His voice shook and his stare bored deeper into the ground, trying to avoid his master's imposing figure.

There was silence for a long time before Wendelmar spoke again.

'Please, my king. The pain fills my body, and I only wish to see my family.'

At this, Azul sneered, snapping back around with such ferocity that globules of hot saliva flung themselves around the room and splashed onto the compressed dirt floor. 'Failures do not get to see their families, Wendelmar. This you should know.'

A pit began to form in Wendelmar's throat, and he forced himself to speak through it.

'Have mercy, my king, I beg you.'

Azul stared down at Wendelmar for a long while, which felt like an eternity to the cowering and wounded Malum. A sneer began to spread across Azul's cracked lips, before he addressed his audience with a disturbing level of pride.

'I think I shall tell them you are dead and you brought great shame upon them. Meanwhile, you can rot in the dungeon and think on your failure until I feel you are worthy of being put out of your misery.'

Azul stormed off and pushed his way back through the curtain, which rippled from floor to ceiling as he disappeared into it.

Wendelmar jumped to his feet once more and screamed after his master. 'King Azul! Please, I beg of you, tell my family I am alive! Let them see me!'

At this, Azul ferociously rushed back through the curtain and threw himself at the balcony ledge, signalling to his guards with a wave of his hand, who threw Wendelmar to the ground, right at the base of the balcony.

'You dare call me by my name?' Azul screamed, as saliva dripped on Wendelmar from above. 'Your family would be disgusted at the very sight of you. Anyone would. My guards are going to make sure that nobody can ever see the monster you have become. It won't even be possible for you to see your own reflection ever again; this is the only mercy I will afford you.'

Azul nodded to the guards, who stepped forward and picked up Wendelmar by the arms, dragging him off to the side of the hall, into a purposely dark tunnel that led to the sprawling dungeons below.

'Please, my king, please!' Wendelmar screamed, as Azul once again shoved through the curtain. Out of pure desperation, Wendelmar turned his attention to the guards. 'Please! You must let me go!'

The guards ignored his pleas for help and, after a short time, came to a stop at the furthest end of the dungeon. They turned a key in an ancient lock and threw open the door to the cell. The hallways were faintly lit by tiny peepholes in the roof; however, no light penetrated the blackness within the cell. It was true dark.

The guards threw Wendelmar in, quickly pulling the door shut and sealing him into his living tomb.

'Now nobody will ever have to see such a hideous monster,' one of the guards said, before they locked the door and marched back down the hallway.

'AZUL! LET ME GO! AZUUUUUL!'

Wendelmar's cries reverberated in the dungeon as he fell to the cold, hard ground, not able to see even his nose in front of him. He screamed until his throat was bloody and each cough triggered sharp pains throughout his body. He wept to himself, silently accepting his failure and thinking of his family, and of the girl who was compassionate enough to save him, even though he had tried to kill her at the order of his cruel master, the wicked king, Azul.

# CHAPTER ONE

Much had changed in the weeks since Amelia was crowned as the new Princess of The Arbour in a small bird's-nest ceremony atop the tree that she now considered to be home. The sky was no longer the deep sapphire blue it had been over spring and summer, now appearing a darker shade of grey with each passing day. The small fluffy white clouds that had dotted the atmosphere with a beautiful weightlessness now transformed together to create large hulking masses of grey, which appeared to be bigger and darker as the days floated by. The hovering monoliths looked as though they might crush the very ground should they fall from the atmosphere, and blotted out much of the sun as they journeyed from one end of the sky to the other.

The rainy season was well and truly upon the land, and soon would come the snow. Millions upon millions of tiny flakes of ice, each uniquely different, would fall from the sky, a slow and treacherous journey. As with the clouds, each flake would join piles of others, forming large mounds that would blanket the countryside and eliminate all greenery, at least for a short time.

For now, the land around Amelia's family home was stuck in that middle point. The point between the rainy season and the snow season, when everything was just starting to change colour and die off, before resurrecting with newfound vibrancy in the spring.

Along the driveway, every fruit tree now looked thin and unhappy. The last of the fruit had fallen for the year, and the leaves had gone from an emerald green to the colour of a pumpkin. The tall hedge that surrounded the house no longer appeared as an impenetrable wall. Its leaves were varying shades of brown, orange, and red, and there were many gaps in its length. Even the grassy hills in the distance had turned different shades of yellow and brown, now looking more like sand dunes. All the changing colours together made the landscape resemble one of William's finger paintings, each colour swirling into the next, blending to the point where it was often hard to differentiate the end of one hill from the start of the next.

There was one tree on the horizon that still maintained the healthy green of its leaves, only just beginning to show the signs of discolouration on its highest branches. This was the yew tree that housed The Arbour.

It was no longer hidden amongst the surrounding foliage. The shrubbery and small trees that once blocked all but the slightest view of its top had wilted and greyed. The white fence surrounding it was clearly visible; even from the house, you could see specks of white through the intertwined branches of the shrubbery, just below the ancient yew's prominent trunk.

The gaping hole that Amelia's father made when he had tried to poison the tree had all but disappeared from the outside. If you were to look closely enough in the right spot, you would make out a few small dents, but in time they too would disappear, healed by countless hours of magic and chanting from Ealdor and Losophos.

Despite the dying world outside, inside The Arbour, things were more alive than ever before. Amelia's coronation had restored a level of morale and purpose in the citizens that had not been seen for some time. As Lady Ashlyn had sensed her imminent end, although she cared for nothing more than she had for The Arbour and its people, her focus had shifted from royal duties, and her every waking moment had been dedicated to finding her heir.

Amelia had now been a princess for eight weeks. In that time, she had been busier than ever before in her life.

The first few days were the easiest. Her family had quickly settled into the castle that stood in the centre of town, choosing to remain in The Arbour part-time, and in their 'real-world' home a couple of days a week. Her parents now had a large room with plenty of light; it was quite high up in the castle and allowed them to see everything happening on the streets below. It also allowed them to keep a close eye on William, as his room was attached to theirs, at least until he was old enough to have his own space.

Amelia's round room was the biggest of all. It stretched almost the entire width of one of the higher floors in the castle, allowing space only for the staircase that encircled the room as it crept ever further into the tower, passing her door on the way.

As she'd walked through the large wooden doors for the first time, she'd been unable to believe her eyes. It was easily three times as large as her bedroom back at home, and equally beautiful. Stretched across the furthest wall from the door was a huge stained-glass window. Much like the window in her previous room, it depicted the yew tree, but in greater detail and size. Just in front of the window was a large bed covered by a canopy.

To the right was a fireplace inlaid with timber, which appeared to be made from the yew tree, as with most wooden things inside The Arbour. On either side of the fireplace stood tall shelves, each lined with the various colourful spines of books written long ago in many strange and unique languages. Just beside one of these bookcases was where Amelia had requested a small desk be placed. She used it to draw late at night when she had the chance. The soft glow of the fire helped her to see, while it also warmed the chill air, which was growing increasingly bitter as the nights passed.

On the left of the room was one of Amelia's favourite things. There was an exceptionally large wardrobe filled with the most beautiful gowns of all sizes, each one uniquely intricate and flawlessly designed.

She had stood in front of it for hours on her first night, trying on many of the dresses within and seeing what they looked like on her, using the mirrored doors. She was pleasantly surprised to find that quite a few of the dresses shrunk down to size when she put them on, obviously enchanted to fit the wearer perfectly. After all, nobody would respect a ruler whose clothes were all ten sizes too big.

After Amelia and her family settled into their new home, the visits to their old one became rarer and rarer as the weeks continued. Her parents now returned to their other home only once a week, to collect mail and shop for things that couldn't be sourced within the tree. They rarely took William or Amelia, opting instead to spend some time alone together and leave their children in the care of the castle's many staff, whom they had grown to trust deeply.

They would leave first thing in the morning, usually on a Tuesday. The children would wait with them on the tallest spire as the morning sun approached the mirror and opened the portal, hugging them goodbye before they stepped through. When the portal closed, Amelia and William would often shout in excitement. With their parents gone, they could get away with just about anything, and it offered them a whole twenty-four hours to explore and do whatever they wanted. As Amelia's responsibilities grew within The Arbour, though, she became less excited when her parents left, and more excited for their return.

The items that their parents brought back were often life-changing for The Arbour. Amelia's mother was always bringing new and exciting seeds to diversify the town's food selection. Over the last six weeks alone, she had brought through at least three types of pumpkin, several varieties of potato, and one sample from each of the fruit trees that lined the driveway, along with cucumber, watermelon, bean, and carrot seeds. Much to Keaton's delight, she'd also brought an apple seed. It hadn't been planted yet, as Keaton and Amelia were still deciding on the perfect place. She had just been too busy lately to join him in the search.

All of the new produce that her mum had introduced had rapidly been worked on by the local farmers, and now The Arbour had an abundance of fruits and vegetables, no longer needing to rely so heavily on the ruby fruits of the tree itself. There was so much food that the farmers couldn't eat it quickly enough, so Amelia's dad had planned, and assisted in building, The Arbour's first produce market.

As her first royal decree, Amelia had allowed her dad to build the markets in the town's main courtyard, which was previously only an empty space used when farewelling a deceased person, as she had found on her first day there. She allowed her father to select the prominent location not only because it provided the most central position and the most foot traffic, but because she could see in his face whenever they walked the grounds together that he was still pained by the damage he had caused to the tree, and nearly to its inhabitants. She would wince every time she passed the spot where her head hit the ground after she was offered up by Deckard, so it was an easy decision to cover it with a market. The once-empty square was now a permanent hive of activity as farmers traded their food to other villagers for items or services. Of course, even if a person had nothing to barter, they would not go hungry. Amelia had included a clause in her decree that any villager requiring food without the means to trade for it would be given it without payment.

Amelia was very popular in the town, and her days were often spent walking from place to place, listening to the villagers' problems if they had any, and offering solutions. She was a princess of the people, and they loved her for it.

When she wasn't communing with villagers, Amelia would be busy in The Archive, studying various topics under Ealdor, including diplomacy, history, and, when she really outperformed, just a little bit of magic. She hadn't attempted any magic on her own yet and only knew a bit of theory behind it, but Ealdor had promised to in time teach her more exciting spells.

William hadn't settled in quite as well as Amelia. Sometimes it was a little too much for someone so young, and he would disappear for hours at a time, often to be later found hiding in the tunnels that lined the trunk, or running amongst the fields. He had been put in the town's school, which was very small, only housing a dozen or so children at various levels in their education. Ealdor had agreed to take him one day a week and teach him chemistry and science, which William seemed to react positively to, regularly coming home at the end of the day with his clothes covered in some new colourful concoction.

Life in The Arbour was going exceptionally. So well, in fact, that all talk of the Malum threat had ceased, even from Losophos. Amelia was pleased. His previous lessons had included tactical diagrams of The Arbour, maps of the Malum city, which was named Mundus, and in-depth looks at the Malum physiology. Lately, lessons had turned to topics that interested Amelia more, like the stories from the first people in The Arbour, or the thousands of uses for yew wood and how not to get poisoned when handling it.

Today's lesson was almost over, and Amelia was distracted by thoughts of her upcoming afternoon with Keaton. It had been almost a week since they had been able to spend time together outside of her royal duties and his responsibilities as advisor. She missed his face, and as she stared into the column of light that pierced through the pond above The Archive, pointing to a spot on the floor just in front of her, she thought back to the days before she was princess, when she'd spent time with him here, in the rows of books and relics, looking for something exciting.

Keaton quietly opened the double doors into The Archive and stepped to the right side of the room, where he could see Amelia sitting at her desk and Losophos' thin figure hunched over a book in his hands.

'Princess...'

His voice broke the silent air. Losophos closed the book in his hand and peered to the side, flashing a smile at Keaton.

'Princess,' he said again. Still nothing. Amelia was trance-like, staring into the distance, the glistening spouts of light from above reflecting in her unblinking eyes.

He was now close enough to touch her, and as he reached out his hand and rested it on her arm, she jumped high into the air, a pile of notes falling from her desk.

'Sorry, Princess.' Keaton laughed. 'I guess you were pretty deep in thought.'

She turned to look at Keaton as he bent down to collect her fallen notes, smiling at the sight of him. His clothes were no longer those of a poor street kid, as they were when she had first met him. She had ensured that when he was appointed advisor, he would have the finest clothes, and a new room in the castle spire opposite hers.

She picked his room specifically because if she felt lonely, she could lean her head out one of her windows and see it across from hers, nothing but air between them. If the candlelight in his window was flickering, she would know he was awake and hope that he was thinking of her. On more than one occasion, she had gone to the window to find that he was also standing in his, looking towards her.

'They were happy thoughts,' she said, as he stood up and gave her the fallen notes. 'Thank you for collecting those.'

'Anytime, your highness.' Keaton gave an exaggerated bow, his hair almost brushing the top of his shoes.

Amelia pushed him gently on his shoulder, causing him to stumble and chuckle. 'How many times do I have to tell you? You don't need to call me by my title when nobody's around. You know I prefer Amelia.'

He stood back up and met her eyes, a cheeky smirk spread across his face. 'I know, but I like to annoy you.' He poked out his tongue to highlight that he was joking. 'Quickly now, I've decided on a spot to plant the apple seed, and I want to take you there!'

At this revelation, Amelia jumped out of her seat, placing her notes from the day into her backpack, and shouted to Losophos, 'Thank you for today. I'll see you soon!'

Losophos snickered as he watched the two children run out the door, hand in hand. And in a voice that he knew only he would be able to hear, he whispered, 'Oh, to be young and in love.'

\* \* \* \* \*

It was a particularly cold afternoon as Keaton and Amelia rode to the place where the seed was to be buried. The cart that Amelia's dad had built for them was much smaller than the one Keaton used to ride for Ealdor, but it was far more comfortable, and significantly quieter than the old market cart whose countless glass vials rattled with every movement. Rather than just a wooden plank, the seat had been covered in a soft material that didn't hurt their bottoms as they jumped up and down over the dirt paths and cobblestone roads. The seat was a little bit smaller, to be true, but they didn't mind this; it ensured that they would sit right next to each other, sides touching, as they journeyed. This proved especially important on cold days like today, when they would huddle together for warmth. Keaton became well-practiced at having one arm wrapped around Amelia, but still maintaining control of the reins in both of his gloved hands. The marvellous white horse, Samson, pulled the cart. He was chosen specifically, as Amelia had fallen in love with his personality the moment he'd shared in Keaton's apple.

They were riding back along the main road towards the castle, and Amelia was beginning to wonder where in the city Keaton had found a dirt patch large enough to plant a tree when he veered sharply off the road and angled the cart towards a small hill on the outskirts of town. Amelia was unfamiliar with the area, but looking around, she could see there was a small pond hidden amongst some unremarkable boulders. Keaton pulled the reins and the horse whinnied to a halt.

'Just over here,' Keaton said, as he grabbed Amelia's hand and walked her around a few small rocks. They came to a boulder large enough for them to sit on, which lay just above the pond and looked towards the town.

'This is where my mum used to come to think, before she had me,' Keaton said. His voice sounded enthusiastic, but there was a pain hidden in his words that Amelia noticed whenever he spoke of his mother. Amelia knew that he had been learning all about her from Deckard, who was now proud to have his son as a permanent part of his life.

He peered into the distance. Amelia joined him on the boulder, her head finding a comfortable spot in the curve of his neck.

'I've been coming here almost every day since I found out from Dad,' he said, the pain still clear in his voice. 'He told me that the first time they ever saw each other, he was running laps around the town to keep fit before his testing for the royal guard. He saw her sitting here. They were both young, and he thought that she was the most beautiful thing he had ever seen. He decided to run the same path every day after that, just to see her, until one day she wasn't there.'

'Well? Then what happened?' Amelia asked.

Keaton pointed towards the small pond just in front of them. The sun was low in the sky and didn't shine directly on its surface, but small ripples still reflected indirect light all around.

'Dad came running over to this rock to see where she was. He found some clothes in a pile next to it and saw that she was swimming in the pond. He tried to walk away quietly, embarrassed that she would think he was a creep, but she saw him and told him to jump in too.'

He released a small laugh. Amelia could feel it, as his body jerked before he continued.

'He wasn't sure what to do, but it had been a really hot day and he'd worked up a sweat, so he jumped in with her. They started talking and getting to know each other. Every day after that, when he ran to that side of the town, he would stop by the pond and they'd spend time together. Eventually, they fell in love, and you know the rest.'

His voice grew quieter as he finished his sentence. Amelia hugged him tight.

'I think this is a perfect spot,' she said, smiling up at him. 'Let's plant it now, and before long, we'll have an apple tree to sit under when the weather turns hot.'

They stood from the boulder together and walked over to a small mound of dirt just beside the pond. Amelia dug a hole with her hands and stood back as Keaton placed the seed inside and covered it over. He then took a step towards the pond and bent over it, filling his hands with water, before twisting back to where the seed was buried. He watered the dirt around it, patting his hands dry on the legs of his pants and breathing hot air into them.

'I can't wait to see it fully grown,' Amelia said, wrapping her fingers around Keaton's in an effort to warm them.

'Me too!' he said. 'But I think it will be a while yet before I get to eat some fresh apples from this tree.' Leaning into Amelia's embrace, he kissed her lightly on the cheek, before guiding her back to the boulder. They sat together once more, enjoying the view and the company.

'I suppose we'd best head home for dinner,' Amelia said, standing from the boulder and pulling Keaton back to the cart. 'We can ask Ealdor about an acceleration potion for the apple tree when we get there!'

At hearing this, Keaton perked up and nodded in agreement, jumping into the cart seat beside her. 'I hope he has one to spare. I can't wait to sit here and eat apples all day!'

Amelia giggled at the thought of Keaton, his belly as round as an apple from eating far too much.

'You'll have to start going on runs to keep fit, like your dad used to,' she said, as she poked him in the stomach. 'And I might quite enjoy swimming under the shade of the tree while you do.'

They both laughed as the cart lurched forward, focusing on the town almost within reach, and the warmth of the air coming from the many chimneys and fireplaces below them.

As they rode into the castle's front courtyard, they were greeted hurriedly by one of the castle workers. Amelia hadn't yet managed to learn all of their names, but she thought that this one might be called Eliza.

'You're very late, Princess!' she exclaimed, breathless from rushing over to greet the cart.

Amelia jumped down as Keaton released the horse into its pen.

'Late for what?' she asked, wondering what she had forgotten this time.

Eliza looked her in the eyes with surprise and a little bit of concern.

'Your brother's birthday dinner.'

# CHAPTER TWO

The castle's main hall was a blur of moving colours and noise when Amelia burst through its doors. The middle of the room was filled from end to end with long banquet tables, each one covered in a rainbow of fruits, drinks and decorations. Each seat was occupied by a smiling guest, many of whom were so engrossed in conversation that they hadn't noticed Amelia rush in through the doors. Those who did notice stopped what they were doing, offering a small bow in her direction, to which she waved her hand, indicating for them to forgo the formalities.

She had grown to dislike the townsfolk bowing in front of her or trying to kiss her hand every time they met. It was unconventional for them to not acknowledge their princess with the proper marks of respect; however, it made Amelia much more comfortable to be treated like a normal person. After all, she wanted them to see her as more of a friend than a superior.

Stretching along the far end of the room was the table where her family sat, along with the most important members of the community. At one end were the chairs for Losophos, Ealdor and Keaton. The closest of those three seats to Amelia was always taken by Keaton, offering up the excuse that her advisor should always be close at hand. Everybody else knew that the pair were infatuated with one another and this allowed them to be close at all times. At the opposite end of the table were the chairs for Amelia's parents, and, of course, the one who tonight's celebrations were all about, her little brother, William.

Amelia's chair stood taller and more prominently than any of those around it. Its wooden frame was composed of fine white branches, much like the ones that formed the crown she wore atop her head. The seat was a lush purple colour, with the softest stuffing stitched into it. It always made Amelia think she was sitting on a cloud, and on more than one occasion, the comfort it provided had caused her to doze off during dinner. This, of course, would only happen after a particularly long day.

Amelia approached the family table, heading straight over to William, who was picking at the assortment of treats that graced his plate. There was a large pile of wrapped gifts on the ground before him. She knelt next to his chair, wrapping him in a hug. He jumped slightly as she did so.

'Happy birthday, baby brother,' she whispered into his ear, before pulling away and waiting to see his response.

He looked at her, appearing displeased, and crossed his arms.

'You're late,' he mumbled, 'and I'm not a baby anymore.'

Amelia's heart sank a little. She had not intended to be late, which did happen more often now than she thought it would, but she also didn't expect someone as young as William to understand why. No matter the excuse she offered, it would not ease his disappointment.

'I... I'm sorry, William. Something came up, and I had to see that it was resolved.' She hoped that he wouldn't see through her fib. She had noticed a change in William's attitude towards her since they had moved into The Arbour, and often detected hints of jealousy from him, something she could only imagine was normal between siblings, though for them it had been greatly exacerbated by her current position of power.

Their mother, Amity, who was sitting next to William, leaned closer towards them.

'Will, my darling boy, you have to understand how much

responsibility your sister has now. She is loved and needed by many more people than just the three of us.' Amity motioned from William and Amelia to her side, where their father Lyall sat, enjoying his meal as he listened in on the conversation.

The frown on William's face grew deeper and he slouched further into his chair, his arms remaining crossed over his chest.

'She's *my* sister, though. I should be more important than any of these people, especially today.'

A pain formed in Amelia's chest. William was right; he was her only brother, and they had always been closer than most. It was William, after all, who had gifted Amelia the ruby brooch that now held so much more meaning to her. She would not have been able to complete even half the trials she had faced in her journey to the throne without it.

Amelia stood between William's chair and her mother's, turning to take in the crowd of faces that stretched out before her. It was quieter than when she had first walked in, as most of the guests were watching her, speaking in low voices between bites of food, or sips of wine from their goblets. She felt awful that her new role had contributed to her forgetting her only brother's birthday, but she was grateful to Amity for trying to defend her and defuse the situation.

With a deep breath, Amelia forced a smile for the crowd, and conversation sparked back to life from the depths of the hall. She gently squeezed her mother's shoulder, who reached a hand up and met hers, squeezing it in response, as if to say *I understand.*

As she turned away and walked towards her own chair, Amelia was met by Deckard.

'Good evening, my lady.' He bowed deeply, the top of his thinning hair now level with her face. The tip of the sword that was permanently sheathed on his hip gently scraped the ground.

Deckard was one of the few people Amelia still allowed to address her with complete formality at all times. It made her feel powerful, a complete change from when they had first met, but it also kept him comfortable. As the head of the Royal Guard, he was always being watched by scrupulous eyes, and from what she understood of military men, routine was everything.

'Good evening, Deckard. Please rise.'

He stood to attention for a brief moment, then resumed his position in the shadows behind her ornate chair.

Before Amelia had managed to sit down, Losophos rushed in from the side. He pushed an arm towards her and unfurled his enormous fingers, like the opening petals of a flower in bloom, to reveal a small, neatly wrapped cube, which sat delicately in the centre of his palm.

'Princess, you left in such a hurry today that you forgot to grab the present you picked out for Master William.'

Amelia made no attempt to hide the confusion on her face, as the only people close enough to make it out were Deckard, Keaton, Ealdor, and of course Losophos himself. She had no recollection of selecting any present for William, let alone one from The Archive, and began to wonder if she was in fact losing her mind with forgetfulness.

'But I don't–' she stammered.

Losophos raised his other hand sharply, and held it in front of Amelia's face in order to stop her speaking. Stunned, and feeling a little disrespected, Amelia was about to let her frustration out on him when he motioned forward once more with the wrapped gift.

'You poor, forgetful thing. I know you've been so busy lately... it would be unfair to expect you to remember everything. Now, give him the present *you picked out*.' He paid particular attention to the last three words. He also made sure to speak loudly enough that everyone at the family table, including William, could hear what was being said. Then he forced the present into Amelia's hands and returned to his place beside Ealdor.

After a few long seconds of pure confusion, Amelia started to realise what was being done for her. She had never picked out any gift for William, and Losophos knew it too.

*He probably heard much of my conversation with William, and in the hopes of protecting my relationship with my brother, he gave me the present that he himself had brought.*

Amelia turned back around to face William, who had twisted in his seat to look towards her. The scowl that had previously featured upon his face had been replaced with a small smile. His faith in his sister had been restored slightly.

Walking around the table, Amelia placed the present on top of the pile that had already accumulated. It was only a small box, and quite light. She would have to speak with Losophos at the next opportunity to find out what was inside, so she could pretend to know all about it if William asked.

Amelia returned to her chair and, finally, with no more interruptions, managed to sit down. The plate of food in front of her caused her stomach to rumble as she eyed a particularly plump roast potato. It felt like she hadn't eaten in days, and she reached for the fork in front of her.

As she was just about to pierce the potato, Deckard stepped forward from the shadows, shouting into the room, loud enough that even the furthest corners could hear him over their conversation.

'ALL RISE FOR PRINCESS AMELIA!'

All conversation disappeared as every person in the room stood from their seat and turned to face Amelia. Trying her best to conceal her fatigue and annoyance, Amelia rose, water glass in hand. With her free hand, she indicated for everybody to sit down, and with the last of her energy, delivered an impromptu birthday speech.

\* \* \* \* \*

The hour was late when Amelia returned to her room. The castle was dark, with only a few dim candles glowing in their holders on the walls to guide her way, and the air made itself known with a heavy bitterness that only the winter could bring. The festivities had carried on for some time, and she had grown extremely tired, quietly excusing herself from the party in order to get some space.

This had, unfortunately, become the new normal for Amelia. Much of her time was no longer her own. The days were often filled from start to finish with royal duties, and the opportunities to get some time alone and sketch had grown few and far between, but she remained hopeful that this would change once she had settled in more, and the town would once again survive autonomously.

Pulling off her gown, she threw on a pair of her pyjamas from what was now known to them as 'the outside world'. She hung the gown back up in her seemly infinite wardrobe, and pulled out one of her hooded jumpers, slipping it on. For a moment she stood, welcoming the comfort of her casual clothing, before she shuffled over to her desk, where some pencils and a sketchpad awaited her.

It had been a few days since she last sketched anything, and the pad still lay open on the image she was previously working on. A picture of the castle she now sat in stretched from one end of the page to the other.

Turning to the next blank page, Amelia picked up a pencil and began to draw, not focusing on what she was drawing, instead letting her hands do all the work. As she sketched, the image of a small pond surrounded by rocks appeared on the page, the same pond where she had just spent the afternoon with Keaton. The only difference between the image in her memory and the image on the page was that she added a fully grown apple tree to her sketch, with two shaded figures lying underneath it.

She smiled to herself and sat staring into the smouldering fireplace across from her until a gentle knocking at her door brought her back to reality.

'Come in!' she shouted. Her room was far too large for anybody at the door to hear her if she spoke normally. She had learned this in previous days, when visitors knocked three or four times, not hearing her responses, until she rushed to the door in frustration and opened it for them.

The door slowly creaked open, and William stepped from the dark hallway and into the warm glow of the room. He was also sporting some very comfortable looking pyjamas, and he grinned at Amelia as he closed the door behind him.

'If it isn't my *seven*-year-old brother,' Amelia said, standing from her chair. William hurried towards her, falling into her arms, and the pair shared a lengthy embrace.

Amelia pulled back from William, smiling at him. 'I thought you would be down there for hours more, opening all of your presents.'

His head drooped. 'There's so many... it's going to take so long I thought I'd leave it until tomorrow.'

Amelia shook her head fondly, thinking that William must be the only boy on planet Earth to complain about having too many presents.

'Well,' she began, as she walked over to her bed, taking a seat on its edge. 'What brings you all the way up here?'

William followed her, jumping up onto her bed and lying on his back, his eyes focusing on the fabric that stretched between the four posts, arms outstretched above his head. He let out a long sigh, before rolling onto his side and looking at her once more. 'I don't like my room. I still hear weird noises at night, and I miss sleeping with you.'

Amelia's heart filled with warmth. She was pleased to hear that her baby brother still found comfort in her, and that her busy schedule hadn't yet ruined their relationship, something she hoped would never happen.

She fell down on her side beside him, so they were facing each other, and placed a hand on his shoulder. 'You're welcome to sleep in my bed whenever you want, even if I'm not here... After all, my bed is big enough for the whole family.'

They both giggled.

'Tell me about your day, William. I want to hear everything.'

He sat up excitedly, beginning to talk her through all he had done since waking early that morning in anticipation of his big day. She listened for as long as she could, unable to stop her thoughts from trailing off as he spoke, though she still made sure she nodded occasionally and appeared as though she were paying attention. Her mind turned to what she had planned for the next day.

Their parents would be leaving first thing in the morning, heading back to the farmhouse to bring back some more of the outside world. They had held a community meeting just yesterday in the market square, where there had been several requests for "exotic" items. As usual, the farmers requested new varieties of crops, specifically winter crops, as the climate was growing increasingly cold. Due to the inclement weather, the town's tailor had also requested thicker fabrics to assist with creating a new winter line for those who could afford his hefty prices. As compensation, he would, of course, be making matching winter gowns for Amelia and her mother.

William was planning to spend his day opening gifts, and once he had finished that, he would head to The Archive to continue searching its infinite shelves for artifacts he deemed "cool" enough to place in his private collection. Amelia and Losophos allowed him to do this on the condition that he never removed anything from The Archive without running it by them first.

Amelia's day would also end in The Archive. However, before that, she would need to make it through another of Ealdor's chemistry lessons, followed by a tactical update from Deckard.

Her relationship with Deckard had certainly improved since their first encounter, but she remained wary of him. Being so close with Keaton gave her a very personal, albeit biased, perspective on who he was. He had impressed her with his defensive plan, which he'd initiated in the event of an unalerted attack from the Malum, and he was making every effort towards fixing his relationship with his son, something she was growing to respect him for.

'–and then I came up here to talk to you.'

Amelia came back to reality as William finished his recount of the day, almost like waking from a dream. The two of them yawned in unison, a sign that it was time for bed.

William crawled further up the mattress, towards the pillows, as

Amelia walked to the candles that lined the walls. The quiet of the night was the perfect time to practise the one spell she had been taught so far. She was still very weak in terms of magic, but she could feel herself getting stronger every time she used it.

Raising her hand to the first candle, she focused on the flame and whispered the word.

'*Ventus.*'

The flame flickered into nothingness. A thin wisp of smoke floated to the ceiling, like a slow rocket heading to the stars.

She proceeded to each candle around the room, extinguishing them one by one, ending at the candle closest to her windows, as she always did. This had become a regular ritual, although tonight was the first time she had been brave enough to extinguish the candles using magic unsupervised. After putting out the last candle each night, she would peer across to the spire where Keaton slept, spending a few moments gazing at his window, sometimes staring into his eyes as he looked back.

Tonight, his room was dark, save for the soft glow of his fireplace from somewhere deep within the space. Amelia had stayed up later than usual to spend time with William, and Keaton had also had a big day, meaning he was most likely already in bed.

She blew a kiss towards his window, before turning back to her own bed and climbing under the blanket on the left side, whispering a goodnight to William, who was already fast asleep.

\* \* \* \* \*

The world outside was bright when Amelia was awoken by the sound of William stirring next to her. In a panic, she shot straight up, rubbing the sleep out of her eyes and confirming through her window that it was indeed well into the morning.

'Will!' she shouted as she jumped out of the bed and raced to pick her clothes for the day. 'Will! Get up quickly, or we'll miss saying goodbye to Mum and Dad.'

William stirred again for a moment, before his eyes shot open. He leapt out of the bed and raced to the door, throwing it open without a word, the sound of his footsteps echoing through the staircase as he descended.

'I'll meet you in the throne room!' she shouted after him, gently closing the door.

Once she was dressed, Amelia made her way down the twisting staircase, passing many closed doors. Some were open, with the noise of people working emanating from within.

When she reached the hall where William's party had taken place only hours ago, it almost appeared to be a different room. The tables were all gone, the floors were sparkling clean, and the pile of presents had been relocated, no doubt into William's room, so he could open them privately.

Amelia approached one of the castle helpers, a small girl who was so busy dusting the high walls that she hadn't noticed her approaching. Amelia cleared her throat, which caused the girl to jump and utter a small squeal.

'Forgive me, Princess,' she whispered as she bowed before Amelia. 'I didn't hear you.' She looked terrified, as though she may have offended Amelia, and her eyes began to glaze over with tears.

With a sympathetic smile, Amelia placed her hand on the girl's shoulder, helping her back up into a standing position. Inspecting her closer, Amelia realised she was nothing more than a very young child, possibly around William's age. Amelia felt a pang of guilt for her having to work away in the castle, but knew that it was what the townsfolk were used to, and what they enjoyed.

'Please don't get worked up over the formalities. I know how easy it is to get lost in the moment and block out the world around you, especially when you work so hard.'

The girl smiled, brushing the wetness from her eyes. 'Thank you, Princess Amelia.'

Amelia released the girl's shoulder, her expression changing to a friendlier grin. 'What's your name?'

'T... Tilly, Princess.' She lowered her head slightly, appearing shy.

'That's a beautiful name. I was wondering if you could help me with something, Tilly.'

'Anything, Princess!'

Just as Amelia was about to ask her question, William came running into the room. Amelia and Tilly both turned to look at him, laughing at his appearance.

In his haste to get dressed, he had thrown his shirt on inside out, his laces were still undone and he was only wearing one sock. Amelia brushed her fingers through his hair, flattening out the tangles that had formed while he slept.

Amelia turned back to face Tilly, William now by her side, and asked as politely as she could, 'Have you seen our parents this morning?'

'Yes, I have,' she replied. 'They didn't want to wake you, and they left for the mirror at first light.'

William and Amelia looked at each other. Without a word, they took off towards the entrance, hoping to make it to the mirror before their parents stepped through, both knowing it was probably already too late.

# CHAPTER THREE

By the time the pair reached the tallest spire, it was too late. They had used the shortcut they found when exploring the castle, climbing through its towers until they were just below the highest ledge where the mirror stood, finding the small, well-hidden staircase that snuck its way up through the floor.

This was much quicker than scaling the inside walls of the trunk. However, they still didn't make it in time to see off their parents. The sun was well past the point at which the mirror opened, and their parents had a good head start on them. Amelia was disappointed that she wasn't able to say goodbye, but William saw it as an opportunity for mischief. Without their parents around, he would be free to do almost anything without consequence, at least until they returned the next morning. And so, after a brief hug goodbye, William and Amelia went their separate ways for the day.

As Amelia once again found herself walking through the throne room towards the exit, she noticed that Tilly was still dusting, a task that seemed trivial, as the room was already sparkling. Stopping in her tracks, Amelia called out, 'Tilly?'

Again, Tilly turned around to face Amelia. However, before she could bow, Amelia raised her hand and spoke. 'Tilly, I think you've done a fantastic job cleaning this room, and I want to show you my appreciation.'

Tilly's jaw hung open in shock.

'I want you to take the rest of the day off. Go get changed into some comfy clothes; if you don't have any, you can see the tailor and tell him I sent you. Then, if you please, you can go and play with my little brother, William. I'm sure he'll appreciate the company of somebody of similar age.'

Tilly's face turned so pale it almost blended into the walls behind her, but after a few seconds of quiet contemplation, she curtsied and began to walk backwards. Running now, down a side passage made for the staff, the sound of a faint giggle reverberated along the stone walls, back to where Amelia still stood.

Amelia smiled to herself, pleased that she was able to at least help one person today. Then, with a skip in her step, she hurried out of the main doors, to where Keaton was waiting for her.

'Good morning, Amelia.' Keaton greeted her with a large smile as she hopped down the steps towards where he stood.

'Good morning, Keaton,' she responded, taking his hand as he helped her climb into the cart's passenger seat.

The urge to greet each other with a hug each morning had led to them having a discussion in the days after Amelia's coronation. Both agreed that it might be best, for now at least, if they kept their romantic lives out of the public eye as much as possible. This had made it difficult for them to express their true feelings, but behind closed doors, when they had a moment to spare, they enjoyed their time together, drawing, talking, and exploring the upper parts of the tree.

Keaton would often ask what the outside world was like, curious as to how it differed from the one within. Amelia would describe the planet as she knew it, a vast orb of unimaginable size where one could drive for days and days, but still not even reach the edge of one of its many continents. This detail had proven the hardest for Keaton to imagine, given that his world could be circumnavigated in less than a day if you knew which route to take.

They often spoke of the technological differences between The

Arbour and the outside world. A place where you could communicate with anybody on the planet from a tiny piece of glass in your pocket, as long as you kept it charged with electricity, a resource that you could obtain freely from the sun. Keaton suggested on one occasion that electricity must simply be a form of magic that the outside world had evolved over time, but after explaining the science behind electricity, Amelia convinced him that no magic could be so easily monopolised.

As Keaton urged Samson forward, the immaculate cart shuddered to life behind the equally immaculate equine creature. It was quiet today, not unnaturally so, but enough that Amelia noticed the wind through the leaves high above the town, something she couldn't normally hear over the bustle of the townsfolk, and the songs of happy birds that frequently visited the tree's upper layers.

Keaton, who had apparently sensed the same quiet in the world, began to speak, his familiar voice helping to take Amelia's mind off the busy schedule ahead of her.

'How did things go with Will yesterday?' he asked. 'I noticed your room was still well-lit when I went to bed, so I guessed you had another late night.'

Amelia slumped deep into the cushioned chair of the cart. 'Yes, I did. He wanted to tell me about his day. The poor kid... he must've known I was distracted. I just couldn't concentrate.'

Keaton was keenly focused on the road ahead, but still made the effort to gaze at Amelia momentarily. She could see in his eyes that he felt bad for her.

'Amelia, you know it's not your fault, right? You have a lot of responsibility now. A lot of people look up to you for help and inspiration. Losophos and Ealdor are training you hard because they can see something coming that nobody else can, or nobody else wants to.'

He took one of his hands off the reins and placed it on hers, squeezing gently. 'One day he'll see that you're doing all you can. Until then, he'll just have to wait.'

Amelia straightened up in the seat, squeezing Keaton's hand in return. 'Well, thanks to Losophos, William doesn't think I'm quite so terrible a sister.' She giggled, looking up to Keaton's face. He was so occupied with driving the cart he didn't notice her stare. 'That reminds me, I must ask Losophos what was in the present before William tells me all about it and I have to pretend to know what he's talking about.'

Keaton chuckled, looking at Amelia, the two of them locking eyes for just a few seconds. 'That's probably a good idea. I bet it's something cool from The Archive.'

The cart took Amelia and Keaton through the winding streets to the far side of the castle, where Ealdor's workshop was located. As they slowed to a stop before the courtyard steps, Keaton jumped down from the cart, the gravel offering a satisfying crunch as he landed. He tied the reins around the wooden beam purpose-built for a horse to rest at. A bathtub-sized watering trough was built in below it.

Once he had secured Samson, Keaton offered his hand up to assist Amelia out of the cart. She took it and stepped down just before the stairs, which she climbed without much enthusiasm. After a few steps, she turned, realising that Keaton wasn't walking up with her.

'Aren't you coming to the workshop today?' she asked, trying not to appear too disappointed. Having Keaton in her classes made them all the more interesting.

'I overheard you speaking with Tilly this morning, so I thought I'd put her mother's mind at ease and escort her out to the bird's nest on the cart.'

Amelia retraced her steps down to where Keaton stood, wrapping him in a hug. She kissed him on the cheek and whispered a quick thank you, before racing back up towards Ealdor's workshop, where he was sure to be waiting patiently.

She smiled to herself as she hurried through the halls and towards the laboratory, feeling very lucky.

\* \* \* \* \*

The hours passed slowly as Ealdor tried to teach Amelia some advanced principles of chemistry. She usually found it hard to focus during his lessons, but today was particularly difficult. The weight of her responsibilities was starting to press down on her; the last twenty-four hours alone had proven how complacent she was getting.

Ealdor could see that Amelia was not her usual self, gazing off into space every few minutes and fumbling with jars of various powders and liquids. He knew too well what she was going through. He had seen it before with Lady Ashlyn, and he knew exactly what was required to take her mind off things for a short while.

'Princess.' He waved his hands in front of him, and the vials and books that covered Amelia's desk began to float back to their spots on the shelves.

'Princess Amelia...' Again, he tried to gain her attention, but she was deep in a daydream, stuck in that place between reality and sleep.

'*Fulgur*,' he whispered. A small cloud appeared, hovering over the desk between them, as dark as the night and swirling wildly. It circled faster and faster until there was a blinding flash of light, and with it, a large clap of thunder.

Jumping at the sound, Amelia's boredom changed to bemusement as she watched the cloud dissipate. Ealdor had her attention once more, and he knew how he was going to keep it.

'Well now, I think that's quite enough of the boring stuff for one day.' He smirked, reaching deep into the right sleeve of his tunic, and produced a small blue book.

Amelia's eyes widened. She had seen that book before, when Ealdor first began to teach her how to control her magic. He placed it on the desk in front of him, his hands resting on top.

'How has your progress been on the wind spell I taught you?' he asked, beckoning with his hand to some candles, which floated towards them and rested on the table close to Amelia.

Amelia jumped out of her seat, pushing it backwards with her foot, so she was standing over the candles. 'It's getting stronger,' she remarked excitedly. 'I don't have to concentrate quite so hard anymore.'

Ealdor grinned. 'That's good to hear. Show me.' His hand hovered over the three candles, all of which produced a bright orange flame simultaneously.

Amelia leaned in close to them, her right hand hovering just beside the first candle. '*Ventus*,' she whispered, its flame flickering out moments later. She repeated the process with the second and third candles, then grinned at Ealdor, her arms resting at her sides. She much preferred these lessons.

'Well done,' Ealdor said with a tone of cheerful surprise. 'You have indeed gotten quicker and more confident...'

Amelia couldn't help but smile. She'd never once dreamed that she would be able to use magic; it still felt unreal.

'...but you can do better.' Ealdor waved his hand over the candles once more, and they flickered to life, just as before. 'This time, I want you to put out all three at the same time.'

Amelia's smile contorted to a look of sheer concentration. She closed her eyes and raised her hands so they were pointed towards the flickering candles.

'Feel the power around you, Amelia. Let "The Great Tree" flow through you. Clear your mind and concentrate on your goal. Picture those three flames in front of you and speak the word.'

Amelia stood for a moment, focusing on the noises around her, the bubbling liquids on the many tables throughout the room, her own breath as it escaped her mouth and nose. She still hadn't experienced the flow of power that Ealdor spoke of, but she felt something, a tiny, easily missed sensation like a tingling in her fingers.

Picturing only the three small flames in her mind, Amelia took a deep breath and muttered the word. '*Ventus*.'

As she opened her eyes, she saw that two of the three candles had indeed gone out, which excited her deeply. This was the first time she had been able to extinguish more than one at a time, and it confirmed that she was indeed slowly getting stronger.

'Not bad for your first try.' Ealdor smiled. 'Continue to practise before you sleep and show me when you've achieved all three.'

With a wave of his hand, the two smoking candles floated back off towards the far end of the room. He blew out the third and opened the blue book, flicking to the page he was looking for.

'As a reward for your hard work today, how would you like to learn a new spell?'

Amelia immediately perked up.

'Oh, yes please, Ealdor! I would like that very much.' She clapped her hands together and smiled wider than she had in days.

'Well, my dear, putting out the flame is already quite impressive, but lighting it is even more so. The steps are the same; clear your mind, picture the object and imagine the flame appearing, while speaking the word, *Ignis*.'

Immediately, a small orange flame covered the candle's wick. It seemed to have cost Ealdor no effort at all.

Amelia closed her eyes and held her hand up to the candle, concentrating hard and muttering '*Ventus*' to first extinguish it. Peeking through one eye, she saw that the flame was gone, and smirked to herself as she focused on the new word. For a silent moment, she played with it in her mind, picturing a small flame. When she began to feel the familiar tingle in one of her fingers, she uttered, '*Ignis*.'

Before the word fully escaped her mouth, Amelia was distracted by the sound of the door opening. She turned her head slightly towards it as she finished.

A gasp came from across the table where Ealdor was standing. Amelia opened her eyes to see what had happened, as Keaton walked further into the room, indicating it was time to move on to the next lesson in The Archive.

She had managed to conjure a flame on her first attempt. However, it was not burning atop the candle as she'd expected. It had sprouted on one of the pieces of paper she had written her notes on during the lesson, causing Ealdor to panic slightly, before he regained his composure and put it out with a wave of his hand.

'A good first attempt, Amelia. However, it is much harder to create than it is to destroy, so it may take a bit more practise. Preferably in a place with minimal distractions.'

Amelia had no intention of waiting in Ealdor's dark workshop any longer than she needed to and quickly gathered her notes, jamming them into her dress pocket. She rushed out the door, Keaton following closely behind, and shouted a quick thanks to Ealdor as she left.

Ealdor followed the pair into his courtyard, where they had quickly jumped aboard the cart, preparing to leave for The Archive, where Losophos awaited them.

'Amelia, don't forget to practise your spells. You must do so carefully and often. Tomorrow's lesson is cancelled due to your parents returning, but we will begin a new topic the following day. I know chemistry bores you, though you're too polite to say it.'

Amelia tried to suppress her grin. 'Thank you, Ealdor. Will I see you later for Deckard's tactical update?'

Ealdor looked from Amelia to Keaton, as though not sure how to answer. 'Yes, I suppose you will,' he said. 'I have one thing to do first, so please start without me if I'm late.'

Amelia waved at him as Keaton cracked the reins, causing the horse and cart to lurch forward once more. This time, they were bound towards The Archive, and a teacher who Amelia could more easily distract, as he loved to ramble on about history and magical artifacts... things that interested her far more than chemistry.

# CHAPTER FOUR

The castle was quiet as William returned from seeing off his parents with Amelia. The halls that were bustling with guests only the night before were now empty, with no sound but his own footsteps echoing from wall to wall.

William counted each step as he climbed the winding staircase up to his room. One hundred and thirty-nine steps, each meticulously carved from some fancy stone, never to be truly appreciated by the eyes of their visitors, hidden under the blanket of dim light.

To get to his own room, William had to first go through his parents', which was big enough for a large bed, three wardrobes, some lounge furniture, and several windows. After pushing through the door tucked away in a corner, William was back in his own little room, a dark, dusty, cramped space. It had been selected for him by his parents, who didn't think he was old enough to have his own huge room, for fear that he'd fall into his fireplace, or out a window.

He didn't mind having protective parents; that wasn't the issue at all. The thing that really bothered him was the lack of attention he had received since moving into The Arbour. All anybody ever spoke about was Amelia, the girl who fulfilled a prophecy and was now worshipped like a hero. He missed the simple days of playing with her in the mud, or crafting with his family around a well-thought-out afternoon tea.

The worst part of William's room wasn't the darkness, nor the size. Much like the room he had picked in their farmhouse when they moved only months ago, it was plagued with strange noises in the night. When he brought it to the attention of his parents, or the staff who cleaned around the castle, nobody seemed able to hear what William frequently claimed to, so it was dismissed as just a means of seeking attention. He liked to pretend that it didn't affect him, but the truth was that it had begun to make him paranoid; he was losing countless hours of sleep each week.

There was something in his room today that made him smile, though. In the dim light, he could see a very large pile of presents stacked neatly at the foot of his bed. Almost as tall as he was, at first it had looked like some shadowy figure waiting for him, but the reality was much better.

Wasting no time at all, he began to dig through the presents, moving all of the small ones over to the side, so he could start with the largest ones at the base of the pile. The first and biggest present that he opened was a bicycle in a box, something that had clearly been brought through from the outside world by his parents. It wasn't yet constructed, and he placed it on his bed so that when his dad returned, they could make it together.

William opened present after present, revealing beautiful clothes, a quilt with the tree stitched into it that must have been from his mum, and wooden toys, including a small sword and shield. There were even some gifts of precious gems and metals, which he didn't have much use for.

As he got to the smallest of the presents, William recognised the one Amelia had given to him the night before, a relatively plain wooden box wrapped in a vine that was fashioned to look like a bow. He ripped the vine free and opened the hinged lid, revealing a beautiful gold-banded ring with three small rubies on its face. Inside the lid was a small note written in beautiful cursive writing, which William was able to decipher after concentrating really hard.

*"William, for the Brooch of Protection you gave me, I gift you
this ring. May it do the same for you."*

William's heart stuttered as he stared into the deep red rubies,
picturing the brooch he had found back in the farmhouse. The ring
was indeed a perfect copy, only smaller.

He pulled it from the box, inspecting the gold band more closely. It
looked far too big for his tiny fingers, but when he placed one inside,
the band shrunk to perfectly fit him. When he waved his hand in the
air to see if the ring would slip off, it didn't.

Pleased with his new haul, William selected a few of his favourite
items, placing them into a new leather satchel that he had also been
gifted. He flung the satchel over his shoulder and raced back down
the one hundred and thirty-nine steps, making a quick stop at the
pantry.

It was quiet as he entered, heat emanating from the hearth. The smell
of freshly cooked treats hit his nose like an unexpected punch to the
face. Spying an assortment of cookies and tarts, he threw a selection
of the still-warm treats into a nearby napkin. There were already some
missing, so he hoped nobody would notice a few more as he folded up
the napkin and placed it carefully into his satchel. Hearing footsteps
approaching from one of the many corridors that led to the pantry,
he raced back out the way he came, heading towards the nearest exit.

As he followed the streets that twisted and turned their way around
the town, William was greeted pleasantly by all who noticed him.
Shopkeepers would poke their heads out of open doors, ladies would
wave from the windows above, children playing in the street would
stop what they were doing to greet him while he silently walked
towards the outskirts of the village.

He was relieved once he had stepped out beyond the last layer of
houses and shops that surrounded the town. Nothing lay before him
but fields and, stretching high up into the sky in the distance, the trunk
of the tree.

Having travelled this path many times before, William continued without hesitation, eyeing the staircase in the outer wall that went up to the bird's nest. It would take a couple of hours to get there by foot, but his parents wouldn't let him ride a horse alone yet, and he enjoyed the journey, listening to the sounds of nature around him. He rarely was made to walk home at the end of the day either. Deckard or some other guard often found him as he worked his way back down the trunk and delivered him to the safety of the castle via horse or cart.

He smiled as he thought on the bicycle waiting for him in his room. Once it was built, he could use it to ride to the outer walls and cut his travel time in half, but for today, he relished the long walk.

It was a relatively uneventful journey from the town to the outer wall. The wind was slightly stronger today than in previous weeks, so most of the noise that filled the trunk came from its dancing leaves and branches. As he got to the inner wall, he inspected the road that ran the entire inner edge of the tree. It was clear to the left, and on the right side, in the distance, there was a small cloud of dust left by something travelling the opposite way. It was clear for him to cross.

As he climbed the carved wooden stairs and passageways winding through the trunk, William almost encountered one guard, but due to his small size, he was able to successfully hide in a small tunnel as the guard walked past. If he got caught now, he would be in trouble and taken back to the school, where he was supposed to be during the day.

He didn't care for any of the other students there, as few as they were. They were all far too snobby, or boring, or loud. He preferred the quiet, and while his parents were away, he intended to take advantage of it.

Finally reaching the branch that held the bird's nest, William crept out along its length. He firmly held onto the new tether that ran along it, a long rope that his parents had installed so that if he did continue to visit such a dangerous spot, they could at least relax a little knowing that he wouldn't fall.

Pushing through the leaf layer, William spotted the edge of the bird's nest. A smile spread across his face, and he hurried towards it.

The sun was high in the sky by this point, so the sticks and feathers that made up the nest were warm to the touch. It felt comforting as he hugged it close and climbed the edge, kicking his legs over and rolling down into the middle.

He lay in the sunlight for a moment, his eyes closed, listening to the leaves and basking in the soft warmth of the sun's touch on his face, when something unexpected disturbed him.

A giggle came from the opposite side of the nest. As he opened his eyes, allowing them a few seconds to adjust to the sunlight, he spotted a young girl sitting in wait.

'Good morning, Master William.' She stood and curtsied to him.

William blushed, embarrassed that he had so carelessly rolled into the nest, not knowing that a stranger would already be there.

'Good m... morning,' he muttered, looking between the ground and the girl.

She had a plain face with not much colour, but a beautiful smile, and she appeared to be around his age. He thought he might have seen her cleaning the castle before, but her dress appeared far too new and fancy for a worker's.

'My name is Tilly, Master William. Princess Amelia asked me if I could come and play with you today.' She smiled at him, a little nervous.

They sat in silence for a moment, neither speaking, until Tilly produced something from a large pocket on the side of her dress, holding it out to William.

'I snuck some treats from the pantry for you while the matron wasn't looking.'

William smiled, reaching into his satchel and producing his own horde of treats, which was wrapped in an identical napkin.

'So did I!' he exclaimed, and the pair laughed loudly, before sitting down in the middle of the nest and sharing the assorted treats.

\* \* \* \* \*

The sun's glow was barely visible in the sky when Keaton arrived to take Tilly and Will back to the castle. When he came upon the bird's nest, he could hear them yelling at one another, though not out of anger. It sounded like excitement.

Peering over the edge of the nest, he could see that they were playing with two of Will's new birthday presents, the wooden sword and shield. Will was cowering behind the shield as Tilly pretended to strike it with all of her might. They laughed every time she struck him.

To the side of the nest were some napkins covered in crumbs and jam stains. Keaton smiled to himself, knowing that the cheeky pair must have pinched some treats for the day, just as he used to when he snuck into the castle to meet Lady Ashlyn.

'Master Will!' Keaton yelled, causing both young fighters to jump backwards and fall into the softness of the nest. 'I see you're enjoying the present my father got for you.'

He smiled as he said it, but deep down, he felt a little hurt that he had never received anything of the sort from his father while he was growing up. They had since begun to repair their relationship, which brought him comfort.

'Keaton!' Will shouted, excitedly leaping forward and jumping over the side of the nest to give him a hug.

Will had grown close to Keaton, looking up to him as though he were a big brother. Keaton was the only person in The Arbour who would regularly visit Will and play with him when he asked for it.

'Well, it looks like you two have had quite the day. I hope you didn't ruin your appetite for dinner.' Keaton eyed the pile of crumbs in the nest while Tilly and Will giggled to each other as though they shared some mischievous secret.

'Come now, you two. It'll be dark before long, and we still have to pick up Amelia on the way home.'

Keaton turned and started to walk back along the branch. From behind him, he could hear Will and Tilly packing up their things into

Will's new satchel, before scrambling out of the nest and following him back along the branch.

It didn't take too long for them to reach the bottom of the trunk. Keaton was the first to the cart; Tilly and Will were a little slower, busy playing tag on the way down.

'Quickly now, up you jump.' Keaton groaned as he lifted Tilly onto the passenger side of the cart, followed by Will. Finally, Keaton unhitched Samson and leapt up himself.

The sun had completely set by now, meaning that the inside of the tree was very dark. The inner trunk was spectacularly lit by thousands of eternally burning torches, spiralling their way up the inside walls, though the glow was not bright enough to spread along the floor.

Tilly and Will were quiet as the cart pulled along the road towards The Archive. It was only a few minutes before Tilly's head lowered and began bobbing up and down with the cart's movements. Her heavy eyes closed as she recovered from what must have been an unusual day for her.

Keaton smiled and whispered to Will, 'That's probably for the best. I didn't want to have to use this.' He pulled a small biscuit from his pocket. 'This was mixed with a special potion, so anyone who eats it falls asleep. We still have to try and keep the location of The Archive a secret, just in case.'

Will nodded, understanding the importance of The Archive, his second favourite place in The Arbour.

'Keaton,' he whispered. 'Can I ask you a secret question?'

Keaton looked at Will, whose eyes seemed sad, or confused, or a mixture of both. It was hard to tell in the dark.

'Anything, Master Will. Anything at all.' He loosened the reins, letting the horse and cart move more slowly down the road, making the journey quieter and smoother, so as not to awaken Tilly.

'Well... you like my sister, don't you?' Will stared directly at Keaton, looking for any sort of response.

Keaton was immediately embarrassed. A hot wave shrouded his

body, and he could feel his face going red as he struggled to find the right words.

'Yes... I do.'

Will continued to stare into Keaton's face.

'I mean, you really like her, don't you? Do you love her?'

Again, Keaton felt a wave of heat flow through him. This time, though, his heart pounded harder, and the reins grew sweaty in his hands.

'I... I think so,' he whispered. 'I may be older than you, but I'm still young too. So is your sister. It's hard to know for sure, but it feels like love.' He turned his head to meet Will's gaze, and they held that eye contact for a moment before Will nodded, then faced away.

Keaton could see Will playing with the ring on his finger, twisting it from side to side, before he asked his next question.

'What does it feel like?' he asked, his eyes fixed on his ring.

Keaton remained quiet for a few moments.

'It's the best and the worst feeling in the world.'

Will snorted before looking to Keaton in confusion. 'What do you mean? How can something be the best and the worst at the same time?'

'Well, when I look at Amelia, no matter how sad I am, I can't help but smile. That's the best. But when I'm not with her, I worry about her and overthink everything. That's the worst.'

He paused for a moment, taking a deep breath in before continuing.

'It's like when we're together, the rest of the world goes quiet. The sounds of birds and conversation fade; all I hear is her breathing and her voice. I can't feel anything around me, but I feel everything inside me. It's like I've swallowed the biggest thunderstorm you've ever seen, but rather than being scary or imposing, it's warm and comfortable. It's like I've known her my whole life, but only because my life never really began until the day I met her.'

Choking on his last few words, Keaton turned away from Will to hide the tears forming in his eyes, something that had only happened to him previously when speaking of his mother.

Will looked at Tilly, who was sleeping peacefully. Her face was calm, and although plain, just as it was earlier, the evening shadows danced around it, making it seem more alive than before. He searched himself as he watched her, trying to feel anything that Keaton had just described, but there was nothing there. He shed a tear.

Seeing this, Keaton grabbed Will's shoulder.

'William, don't be upset if you don't feel anything like that. You're still so young. You have so much time ahead of you for stuff like that, and sometimes, a good friend is just as important as someone to love.'

Will smiled up at Keaton, before wiping the tear from his eye. 'Thanks. I'm glad I can talk to you.'

'Anytime, buddy.' Keaton smiled to himself.

A short while later, they reached the lake that hid The Archive. Keaton brought the cart to a stop as gently and quietly as he could, Tilly remaining asleep throughout, before he carefully jumped out onto the grass.

'I'll run in and grab her. You stay here and look after your friend.' He brushed his hand through Will's hair and rubbed side-to-side, so it looked dishevelled. 'Don't worry if I take a little bit of time. They might still be busy in their lessons.'

Will watched as Keaton ran over the small crest of the hill and towards the hidden door in the trunk. After checking there was nobody around, he looked at Tilly again and smiled, happy now that he finally had a friend in this new place. He sat deeper into the bench, staring up into the dark sky, spotting stars and occasional glimpses of the moon through the leaves.

For a few moments, he was happy and calm, eager to see Amelia and thank her for the birthday present she had gotten him. And then strange voices began to speak from the darkness.

# CHAPTER FIVE

I t had been hours since Amelia had arrived at The Archive. Losophos
had taken her through many topics, but had relaxed the schedule
a bit, knowing that the constant high-tempo study routine was
dragging her down emotionally.

They spent a few hours reviewing the more recent years of The
Arbour, before Losophos suggested that they walk around The
Archive's many rows of bookshelves and display cases, talking about
some of the artifacts that lay there. This indeed interested Amelia more
than studying history, especially after a day of chemistry with Ealdor.
Losophos followed Amelia as she navigated the labyrinthian rooms
that made up The Archive, stopping at random intervals, whenever
something interesting caught her eye.

'How about this one?' she asked, pointing to a dazzlingly shiny
silver helm inlaid with fine lines of gold. From its top sprouted a single
feather, almost as long as Amelia's forearm, and a deep blazing red in
colour.

Losophos inspected the item for a moment, grumbling quietly as he
recalled its history.

'Well, this is The Helm of The Windwalker. It's said that the wearer
could jump through the air as though large wings sprouted from their
shoulders. It dates back to the earliest days of The Great Tree, though
its magic was lost long ago.'

They continued on in silence for a few minutes, until Amelia picked another item.

'And this one?' she asked, pointing towards what looked like a glove, though its fingers were long and sharp, and it was covered in layers and layers of golden scales.

'Well.' He grumbled to himself. 'This is The Hand of Simmeon, once again belonging to a warrior from the earliest days of The Arbour, cleaved from his arm in the heat of battle.'

Amelia leaned in closer to the glove, now seeing the bone protruding from it.

'Gross!' she exclaimed. 'Why is the shape so abnormal? I thought you were all of human origin.'

Losophos clicked his tongue and spoke with an envious tone. 'As with much of our magic, this too was lost to time. In the very earliest stories of The Arbour, there were magic users so strong that they could seemingly alter their body shape at will, an ability that proved most useful when in combat, or when competing in athletic trials.'

Amelia tried to picture herself changing shape to resemble the hauntingly disfigured glove, shuddered at the thought, and continued to walk down the row of shelves.

'I don't know how you manage to remember all of this, Losophos. It's surely too much for one person. I can't even manage to remember something as simple as my brother's birthday.'

The footsteps behind Amelia stopped. She turned to look at Losophos, who had a familiar look of pity on his face.

'My princess, you mustn't be so hard on yourself. I've had hundreds of years to become good at my craft; forgive me, but you are still just a child learning to take up the mantle that has presented itself to you. It is only natural to stumble sometimes. How you pick yourself up is what's important.'

'Thank you,' Amelia said, smiling. 'I'm lucky to have you to assist me. If you hadn't shown up yesterday with a gift for William, he might never have forgiven me.' She paused. 'Actually, before I forget again, what was it that you gave him?'

Losophos walked further down the aisle, beckoning for Amelia to follow. As they twisted and turned through makeshift walkways and dimly lit rooms, Amelia began to recognise her surroundings.

They reached the Tablet of Sunt Vitae, something that had been crucial to Amelia's success only weeks ago, but was now nothing more than a table. Upon it lay a small book, which Losophos pushed towards her. She gazed down upon the open pages.

On the left was a small drawing of a ring, emblazoned with the same symbols as Amelia's brooch. The other page was covered in magical script that Amelia still didn't know how to read.

'Princess Amelia, when you told me how William decided to give you the Protection Brooch rather than keep it for himself, I thought it fitting that he get his own Jewel of Protection, something that the both of you could relate over, something that would make him feel safe.'

Amelia beamed at Losophos. 'What an absolutely wonderful idea. But what do all these inscriptions say?'

He turned the book back around to where he could read it. 'Well, it being so small, I could only place a few spells over the ring, and this lists the ones I chose. Let's see here... This one means the ring will grow or shrink to fit the wearer's finger, no matter how large or small. The three gems protect the wearer from limited elemental and physical damage. Being rubies, they protect best against fire.'

Losophos continued to trace his fingers down the page. 'And this last one connects his ring to your brooch at all times. It's unclear exactly how it works, but in theory, you should be able to sense his direction to some extent.'

Amelia looked down at the brooch pinned to her chest, having reclaimed it from Keaton after she had a replica made for him as her advisor. Her fingers touched its surface, trying to see if she could sense anything. She concentrated for a short while, until she felt a sudden pull of energy, as though something was willing her to go in a specific direction. She spun around slowly several times, trying to feel the perfect spot. When the pull felt strongest in front of her, she guessed she was pointing the right way, and a slight tingle in her mind, accompanied by a flash of colour, confirmed what she had suspected. When she opened her eyes, she found that she was facing the castle, and she smiled deeply, knowing that William was safe at home.

Losophos watched on, pleased. 'It seems I have now successfully mastered the art of creating magical jewellery. Something that may come in useful to you, should the battle with Azul come to pass.'

Amelia released her focus on the brooch, the tingles fading as she did so.

'You never cease to amaze me.' She grinned, approaching Losophos and hugging him tightly, as thanks for his gift not only to William, but to her also.

They sat in relative silence for a while, Amelia skimming through the pages of some books on the table, as Losophos dusted the tall shelves nearby. Before long, the familiar creak of the front door bounded through the main room, and Keaton's smiling face appeared in the opening.

'Good evening, Losophos, my princess. Are you ready to return to the castle? I heard you talking as I came down the stairs, so I waited for a while until all was quiet. I hope I didn't interrupt anything.'

Amelia moved from the desk to Keaton as quickly as she could.

'Amelia,' Losophos began, 'might I suggest we postpone the tactical update until tomorrow? You have once again had a very long day, and I think an early night would do you all well.'

Looking from Keaton to Losophos, Amelia nodded, knowing that he wanted to help her relax, if only for one night.

'Very well,' he said as he bowed low. 'I shall inform Captain Deckard.'

Amelia and Keaton pushed back through the doorway, shouting a goodnight to Losophos. Halfway up the stairs, when they knew they were completely alone, they stopped and embraced, a routine that they had practised regularly over the past weeks. This was one of the only places they could get privacy.

'I missed you today,' Keaton whispered in her ear, placing a delicate kiss on the side of her head.

'I missed you too,' Amelia whispered back, pulling him in tighter and relishing in his warmth.

A few minutes passed as they each told the other about their day, and the two separated, climbing up the remainder of the steps, hand in hand, in no rush at all.

'It seems Will made a friend today,' Keaton said as they walked out of the hidden doorway, following the small hill that ran alongside the lake.

'I'm glad.' Amelia smiled to herself. She knew William had been struggling, so was relieved to hear he had somebody he could relate to. 'You must've had a busy afternoon in the cart if you've already dropped him at the castle and come back for me.'

Keaton looked to Amelia. 'No, I only collected Will and Tilly a short while ago. Why would you think he's already at the castle?'

Amelia was just about to explain how Losophos had enchanted William's ring, and how it must be faulty, when the cart appeared within view. Her words froze as she studied the shadowy outline of the cart and its only occupant, a shape that Amelia didn't recognise to be William's.

Together, they hurried towards the cart. Their fears were confirmed. There was only one person resting on its bench, sloping slightly to one side. Tilly sat, still asleep, with no sign of William.

'Where could he have gone?' Amelia asked, quickly scanning the empty fields. 'Surely he didn't go back to the nest.'

Keaton rushed around to the driver's side as Amelia bounded up into her usual spot.

'He was here when I left, I swear it. He was going to stay and watch over Tilly. He didn't seem strange at all. If anything, he seemed happier than I'd seen him in days.'

A pit grew in Amelia's stomach. She knew that he couldn't have gone too far, and nobody within The Arbour would want to hurt him, unless they were somehow working with the Malum.

'Return to the castle,' she told Keaton. If he wasn't there when they arrived, she would once again use the brooch to sense his location. The cart lurched forward at speed, which caused Tilly to jolt awake. Realising she had been leaning on Amelia, she apologised profusely, her cheeks quickly turning a deep shade of red.

Trying not to appear concerned, Amelia commented on the beautiful dress that Tilly now wore, mentally telling herself that she would have to go and personally thank the tailor for his efforts in the next few days.

After the initial shock of leaning on Amelia subsided, Tilly realised that William was missing.

'Where's William?' she asked, looking from Amelia to Keaton, and back again.

Amelia didn't know what to say. Luckily for her, Keaton interjected with an excuse.

'Master Will was so eager to get home that he didn't want to wait for me to collect the princess, and he decided to make his own way there. I'm sure he's safely within the warmth of the castle walls as we speak, enjoying a hot meal.' Keaton glanced at Amelia as he spoke, trying to calm her at the same time. Amelia relaxed slightly, her tightly closed fists opening as she stretched her fingers.

When the cart rolled through the castle's main entrance, there were a few people standing outside, waiting. The stablehand was there to collect Samson, take him back to his pen, and feed and groom him before he went to bed. The matron was also there, ready to command the staff to serve Amelia's meal in the hall. The third person was Tilly's mother. The expression on her face turned from concern to relief as she saw Tilly safe and well between Amelia and Keaton.

The cart came to a stop, and the stablehand helped Amelia down from the cart, followed by Tilly, who was immediately whisked up by her mother.

'My, what an exceptional day you must've had. And look at that beautiful dress!' She turned her attention to Amelia. 'I can't thank you enough, my princess.' She bowed, Tilly holding her hand and bowing beside her.

'It's quite alright. I hear that your daughter and my brother have become good friends. I do hope to see them playing together in the future, if that is okay with you, of course.'

Tilly's mother began to blush, bowing again. 'If it would please you, my lady.'

She retreated into the castle with Tilly, who could be heard reciting everything she had done that day. Her mother wasn't sure whether she should be more proud or embarrassed. It was, after all, quite improper.

Keaton and Amelia walked towards the main door, hoping to find Will eating his meal at the table near Amelia's chair.

'My lady, my lord, would you like your meals served now?' the matron asked politely.

'If you could please tell me first, has William returned yet?' Amelia asked.

'Yes, my lady. He returned shortly before you arrived. He appeared to be in quite a sweat, and his breathing was rapid, as though he had run from one side of the tree to the other, although he claimed he wasn't hungry and headed up the stairs towards his room.'

Amelia and Keaton simultaneously sighed a breath of relief, before thanking the matron and pushing further into the castle. Amelia raced ahead, eager to see William, pushing through his door, closely followed by Keaton.

The room was dark. They both saw a shape on the bed, shrouded in shadows. Amelia approached, sitting on the side of the bed and placing her hand on it, expecting it to be William, sleeping peacefully.

To her shock, the shape was not that of a person, but a large box. As her eyes adjusted, she saw that it was one of his presents, a new bike, placed on the bed.

'He's not here,' she whispered to Keaton, who was still standing in the doorway.

'Maybe he's gone to your room again?' Keaton suggested.

They rushed down the steps and through passageways that led up to Amelia's tower. Walking into her room, it was a stark contrast to William's. The space was warm, and gentle light danced about the walls from the waning fireplace and the several candles that ran around the perimeter.

Amelia did a lap of her room, searching every nook and cranny for William, but once again, he was nowhere to be seen. She poked her head out to tell Keaton the news, as he didn't feel it was proper to enter her room when they were alone, regardless of the situation.

'Wait here a moment,' Amelia said. 'I'll try to use magic to find him.'

She closed the door once more and walked to the centre of the room. Placing her hand on the brooch, she focused her thoughts on finding William, picturing the ring that he was hopefully still wearing. Again, her body felt the irresistible pull of energy, and she turned herself around again and again, trying to find the strongest point. With the confirmation of a colourful flash in her mind, Amelia knew that she had found him, although his location sent a cold sweat through her body.

Bursting through the doors, Amelia raced past Keaton, yelling as she jumped up the steps, 'He's on the roof!'

Keaton remained still for a moment, before chasing after Amelia.

'What?' he shouted back. 'What's he doing there?'

Racing up the staircase, he quickly caught up to her.

'I don't know,' she said into the darkness in front of her. 'Perhaps he misses Mum and Dad.'

The two didn't speak again until they pushed through the hidden trapdoor above them, which came out directly onto the castle's highest peak, where the mirrors stood permanently in silent reflection.

The moon portal faced Amelia as she climbed out of the hatch, its surface still an unmoving blank slate, as the moon was obscured by heavy clouds.

When she walked around the mirror, her heart stopped for a moment. William's small body was huddled up against the sun portal, shivering in the cold night air.

'William!' she shouted. 'What on earth are you thinking?'

William appeared to snap out of a trance as he heard Amelia's voice. Turning to face her, his cheeks wet with tears, he jumped to his feet and ran towards her, hugging her waist as tightly as he could.

Amelia hugged him back. Keaton rounded the mirror, spotting the pair and coming to a stop, leaning on the side of the mirror as he watched them.

'What happened?' Amelia whispered into the top of William's head. 'Why did you run away?'

William said nothing for a moment, until his soft voice broke the silence from within Amelia's arms.

'I was scared.' He whimpered. 'The voices guided me here. I thought it might have been Mum and Dad coming back somehow.' His body started to shake as he once again began to cry.

Amelia shifted her gaze to meet Keaton's, concern clear in her eyes.

'You know there's no way they can return until the sun comes up,' she began. 'I don't know what you think you heard, but it wasn't them.'

She lowered herself onto her knees, so that she was level with his face. 'You mustn't do that again,' she pleaded, tears beginning to fill her eyes. 'You gave me such a fright.'

William and Amelia hugged once more. Keaton signalled to Amelia that he would leave them alone for now, so they could spend some time together, retreating into the darkness of the hatch.

After they had finished hugging and wiped away their tears, Amelia and William climbed back through the trapdoor, closing it behind them and carefully stepping down the staircases that led to Amelia's room.

Along the way, they held hands. Amelia asked to hear all about his day with Tilly, of which he spoke with some excitement. She could feel the ring on his finger, stroking it gently with one of her own, grateful that such a thing existed, happy that it had already proved its worth and hoping that she wouldn't have to use it again quite so soon.

'Why don't you stay with me again tonight?' Amelia asked, once he had finished recounting his day. 'I learned a new spell today, if you'd like to see it, and I can arrange for us to be woken early to meet Mum and Dad.'

William smiled up at Amelia for a moment, before looking back down the passage ahead of them.

'I would like that.'

# CHAPTER SIX

Amelia decided not to leave William's side until their parents returned. They shared a meal in the dining room. Keaton was fetched by a castle worker and ate beside them, dismissing himself after he had finished.

Before returning to Amelia's room, they stopped by William's. They grabbed several of the birthday presents strewn about the place so they could play together for a while, something they hadn't really done since moving into The Arbour. Amelia made sure to request an early morning wake-up from a castle worker, so they could meet their parents as they came through the mirror.

They played late into the night, Amelia showing off her new magic spell once they had decided it was bedtime. She extinguished the candles, as was her normal nightly ritual; however, she could now manage two at a time. Once all the candles were out and the room was sufficiently dark, she placed one in the centre of the stone floor and sat on the bed with William, focusing on the candle and muttering the new word she had learned that morning.

'*Ignis*,' she whispered, with her arm outstretched towards the cold wick.

Before she opened her eyes, William's reaction told her that she had been successful. 'Wow!'

She had done it, more successfully than with Ealdor. She had managed to light the wick on fire, perhaps due to the lack of distractions in her room, allowing her to focus more clearly on her target.

Focusing once more, she spoke the other spell. *'Ventus.'* The flame dissipated, and the room once more returned to dark.

Stepping to the window, she checked the opposite spire, seeing Keaton's window was also black. She blew a kiss through the night towards him and returned to her bed, where William was already buried deep in the endless pile of blankets that adorned it.

'Good night, William,' Amelia whispered as she climbed in, leaning over towards him and kissing his forehead.

'Night, Mealy,' he replied, before rolling over into a more comfortable position.

\* \* \* \* \*

The world outside her window was still fairly dark when Amelia heard the knock. Climbing out of her bed, she stumbled to the door, opening it to find the matron standing there, a kind smile on her face.

'Good morning, my lady. The sun will be up soon,' she said politely. She curtsied and retreated back down the stairs.

'Thank you,' Amelia responded, before closing her door and returning to the bed to wake William.

He was still fast asleep when she sat down beside him, placing her hand on his shoulder and shaking him gently. Leaning in close to his ear, she whispered, 'William, Mum and Dad will be here soon. It's time to get up.'

He stirred under the blankets before opening his eyes slightly, looking at Amelia with a groan.

'Come on. Go bathe and get dressed, and I'll meet you up there.' She shook his shoulder again. This time, he stretched his arms and legs as far as he could, his mouth gaping wide as a yawn escaped it. Rolling out of the bed, he tiptoed across the cool stone floor towards the door, opening it just enough to step out and closing it gently behind him.

Amelia sat on the edge of the bed for a few moments, staring out the window, looking to the tower where Keaton probably still slept, and the world beyond that, which sprawled out to the edge of the trunk. The autumn crops were waning, the colour fading from the world inside The Arbour as the cold winter season continued to set in. She'd been told that the seasons didn't affect the inside world quite as much as the outside. This so far had proven true, but it was only a matter of time before the snow found its way down the inside of the trunk, painting the usually colourful world a dull palette of whites and blues. A smile broke her tired face as she pondered whether the snowflakes would shrink once they entered the boundaries of The Arbour, much as the rain did, or if they would remain untouched as they glided to the floor of the tree like giant powerless aircraft.

As the world outside continued to grow brighter, Amelia picked out something to wear. Her usual wardrobe of dresses had begun to change to more appropriate seasonal attire, and she opted for long pants and a lightweight sweater.

She stepped into the bathroom tucked away in the far corner of her room, bathing quickly, which not only helped her wake up, but also cleaned off the stress from the day that had passed. After taking some time to brush her teeth and hair, she felt she looked presentable enough to be seen by anyone, placing her crown atop her head and stepping out into the corridors.

Taking her time as she went, Amelia followed the passages and winding staircases that took her to the small hidden room at the top of the tower. She carefully climbed the secret steps, pushing open the hatch and climbing out into the fresh air of the morning world.

She didn't have to wait long for William to show up, closely followed by Keaton, who closed the hatch and joined them on the other side of the mirror, hoping to prolong the secret of the staircase for as long as they could. He smiled at the siblings and handed them some pastries from the pantry, which William and Amelia bit into, grateful for the warmth they provided.

As they sat, they could hear loud, clunky footsteps approaching from the other side of the mirror. Somebody was walking down the bridge that connected the platform to the spire. They waited for the person to appear, as the footsteps changed from the wooden panels of the bridge to the stone floor of the spire.

Deckard's hulking figure rounded the mirror, bowing at the sight of Amelia and nodding to William and Keaton.

'Good morning,' he grumbled. 'I thought I would come and wait for your parents and offer some help. No doubt they have many things to carry back to the castle. I didn't see any of you climbing the staircases up the tree trunk, so I assumed I would be alone, though I'm sure there must be some trickery or magic involved.'

The three children shared cheeky smiles and continued to pretend that there was nothing suspicious going on. Even if they did tell Deckard of the secret hatch he was almost standing on top of, it would serve him no use, as his broad shoulders would not fit through its limited width.

Minutes passed as they all watched the portal's surface, waiting for the sunlight to simultaneously hit the mirror in front of them and the mirror in Amelia's old room. Once it did, the surface of the portal began to ripple like a pool standing on its side. They'd expected two figures to step through, but only one came.

Amity appeared, carrying a large basket filled with fabrics and seeds, smiling widely as she saw the three children waiting for her under Deckard's watchful eye.

'Good morning, my loves,' she exclaimed, placing the basket on the ground and meeting William and Amelia, who ran towards her, wrapping them up in a hug.

'I missed you too.' She laughed. 'I hope you didn't get up to too much mischief.' She poked them both on the nose.

'Where's Dad?' Amelia asked, looking behind her mother, towards the mirror.

Amity knelt down so her face was closer to theirs. 'Well, your father came up with a wonderful idea yesterday, and the both of us are going to be working on it today. I'm afraid we won't be back again until tomorrow morning.'

Amelia and William lowered their heads, sad that they would have to go another day without their parents around.

'But,' Amity said excitedly, 'you'll be able to see us from the branches all day, if it makes you feel better. We'll be working around the tree. I'd tell you all about it, but I haven't got much time before the mirror closes, so I have to say goodbye quickly, my dears.'

She hugged the pair tightly again. William and Amelia both placed a kiss on her cheek, before she stood up and addressed Deckard.

'Captain Deckard, could you please see that these supplies get to the markets?' She picked up the basket and handed it to Deckard, who bowed slightly.

'It would be my pleasure, ma'am.' Without another word, he turned away and walked around the mirror, once again making his way across the bridge.

Before either of her children could say another word, Amity stepped back towards the mirror, blowing them each a kiss.

'Love you!' Amelia and William both shouted after her, as she disappeared into the watery surface.

\* \* \* \* \*

By the time Amelia, Keaton and William had returned to the castle and eaten a proper breakfast, the day had changed. What little wind there was had completely disappeared, and the ceiling of clouds had finally broken, making way for the deep blue sky and the warmth that the sun provided to the freezing earth.

They piled onto the cart waiting for them in the courtyard, placing a hamper of fruits and treats in the back, and the three of them were on their way. They didn't speak much on the ride over to the trunk. Each relished the relaxing moment they had earned, hoping that the quiet wouldn't end anytime soon, although knowing that it would. Amelia sat next to Keaton, taking the opportunity once they exited the town to shuffle up next to him, resting her head on his shoulder as he steered the cart.

After making the long climb up the inner wall of the trunk, they stepped carefully out onto the branch that held the bird's nest. Amelia and William held hands, Keaton carrying the basket, as they pushed through the thinning leaf layer. They climbed into the bird's nest and lay on the soft surface, until sounds from underneath the tree drew their attention.

Hearing the faint voices of her parents, accompanied by the sound of metal on wood, like someone was hammering something large, Amelia crawled to the edge of the nest that hung out over the ground. The unobstructed view allowed her to see what they were working on. Over near the white wooden fence that surrounded the clearing, her father pounded stakes into the ground with a large mallet, while her mother stopped him every few swings to take measurements, ensuring that whatever they were working on would be constructed perfectly.

Keaton and William joined Amelia on the edge of the nest, passing around food and little bottles of cold, fizzy liquid. Each of them ate their fill, before tossing the rubbish over the edge, watching as it reached the ground and disappeared from existence.

Finally, their parents' handiwork became clear. From outside the gate, Lyall walked into the clearing, carrying with him a large solar panel. He rested it on top of the small platform he had just built, which angled it towards the sun. Below the panel was a small, enclosed compartment, obviously some sort of battery, from where the cables ran. A much longer cable was coiled on the ground, waiting to be connected to whatever the panel was meant to power.

'Hey, Keaton,' Amelia said, putting her arm around his shoulder, 'do you remember that electricity thing I told you about?'

He looked at the sky for a moment, recalling the conversation they had shared about this magical thing that powered communication and entertainment devices.

'Kind of,' he said. 'Why?'

Amelia smiled, pointing down to the small structure that had just been completed by her parents, who were now also sitting down on the comfort of the mossy ground, enjoying a small snack.

'That shiny black square creates electricity from the sunlight, and judging by the length of the cable connected to it, I think Dad must be planning to provide power to The Arbour.'

'Wow!' Keaton said, still confused about how this non-magic thing worked. 'Why would we need power? We've gotten by for so long without it.'

This question was one that Amelia could not yet answer. Shrugging her shoulders, she offered a simple, 'I'm not sure, but it must be important.'

The three spent the next few hours watching from above as Amity and Lyall played with various lengths of cable, very discreetly running a length of it up the tree, its frayed copper ends hanging limp over a branch high off the ground.

'Children!' Lyall shouted into the air. 'If you're there watching us, tell the guards not to worry about this cable. We'll explain it all tomorrow when we return.'

He waited for a moment, as though expecting some sort of response, before turning back to Amity. The pair left the fenced enclosure hand in hand, smiling at one another.

'Well,' said Keaton, breaking the silence after a short while. 'I suppose we'd best attend the tactical brief today. I'm sure we've put it off for long enough.'

Amelia slid down into the nest, coming to rest on her back.

'Yes, I suppose we'd better. I imagine Deckard won't be too pleased if we postpone it again.' She chuckled, as Keaton rolled back into the nest beside her, William finally giving in and joining them on the ground.

'What will you do, William?' she asked. 'Would you like to come with Keaton and I to The Archive, or would you like to do your own thing?'

William thought quietly for a moment, pondering his options. On one hand, he loved roaming The Archive, finding exciting artifacts and learning all about them, but he had also made his first friend in the tree. He might have more fun exploring the town with her, without the supervision of older people.

'I'll return to the castle,' he said.

'Okay, then, but we won't be able to give you a lift back. Keaton and I both have to attend this meeting, and we could be there for a few hours, so you may be asleep by the time we return.'

William picked himself up, hugging Amelia and Keaton a quick goodbye.

'It's okay,' he said, a small smile on his face. 'I'll go back across the bridge and down the secret hatch. I'll be back in no time.'

He climbed over the edge of the nest and waddled along the branch towards the trunk.

'Be careful!' Amelia shouted after him, leaning over the side of the nest to watch him leave.

After he was gone from her sight, she turned back to Keaton, who had packed up the picnic basket and was ready to leave.

'I really worry about him sometimes,' Amelia said. 'He hasn't been the same since we moved to the farm. I hope he finds what he needs to make him happy soon.'

Keaton wrapped his arm around her shoulder as they stepped out of the nest and back along the branch.

'He'll be okay, he's just had a difficult few months. Trust me. It mustn't be easy to suddenly share someone you love with a thousand strangers. He just needs time.'

Keaton kissed the side of her head. Amelia raised her hand to meet his, which was dangling just over her left shoulder, bending her head and kissing his palm in response.

'I hope you're right.'

\* \* \* \* \*

By the time Keaton and Amelia arrived at the lake near The Archive, the sky was filling with colours as the sun began to set in the mountains. Once Samson had been hitched near the water, they walked together, taking the opportunity to hold hands. Rather than going straight to the hidden door, they strolled down to the shoreline and lay down on their backs, taking some time to watch the sky as it darkened.

Without saying anything to Keaton, Amelia placed a hand over her brooch and closed her eyes, focusing on locating William's ring. She searched for a few moments, eventually feeling the pull of energy, the flash of colour, and the tingle in her fingers. She found herself drawn towards the castle in the distance. She breathed a sigh of relief, quietly enough that she didn't disturb Keaton's thoughts, happy that William was safe at home.

Once the sky was dark, they stood, the grass now flattened in the shape of two small humans, and walked towards the cascading vines that hid the secret door. Descending the dimly lit steps, they saw that the door into The Archive was slightly ajar, light spilling out onto the base of the stairs. The sound of a few faint voices arguing filled the air, a sign that everybody was here already. Everybody except for Amelia and Keaton.

# Chapter Seven

William followed the edge of the trunk wall until he reached the bridge that hung freely between it and the castle's tallest spire. Normally, the bridge was a dangerous, floating path, swaying from side to side as it got caught in the gusts of wind that lapped over the top of the tree. Today, however, the air remained calm. Not even the slightest breeze dared to shake the path as he journeyed across its length.

It took up a good chunk of the afternoon, his journey home, and as he reached the relative safety of the castle spire, the sun was well on its way out of the sky. Ahead of him, in the direction of their house in the outside world, the sky was still ablaze with a deep red. Behind him, the mountains were shrouded in shadow as night crawled its way across the landscape, a faint light on the horizon indicating the moon had begun to rise.

William walked one very slow lap of the mirror, placing his hand on the cold, flat surface of the moon portal, dragging his fingers along behind him as they curved around the side of the mirror, now gliding along the surface of the sun portal. He missed his parents.

After a moment of silent contemplation, William located the crack in the brickwork underneath him. Wedging his fingers in, he lifted with all his might, the secret hatch flinging open to reveal the unlit tunnel below, the top steps only just visible in the darkness.

Carefully, he climbed down, closing the hatch behind him. He jogged down the winding corridors, back towards the hall. As he stepped into the room, the matron spotted him.

'Just you tonight, Master William?' she asked politely, wiping down the wooden table.

'I'm afraid so,' he mumbled, taking his seat, looking around him at the empty room and feeling truly alone.

The matron gently laid an empty plate in front of him, as well as a knife, fork, and glass, before waddling back towards the kitchen.

'Matron Isabella!' he called out. She turned to face him.

'Yes, Master William?'

William cleared his throat, embarrassed to ask his question, but in need of company.

'Is Tilly around? It would be nice to eat with a friend.'

The matron's expression changed from shock to pity. 'I'll go fetch her for you now, my dear,' she said with a motherly smile, receding into a side passage.

A few minutes passed as William played with his knife and fork, the matron returning shortly to place a second set of dinnerware across from him. The faint sound of footsteps skipping down one of the side hallways began to echo through the room, amplified by the confronting silence. The skipping slowed and then stopped, the footsteps returning to a regular pace, as William spotted Tilly appearing out of a doorway, a toothy grin on her face.

William was happy to have some company, and the two enjoyed a roast dinner together while they spoke and laughed about anything they could think of. William laughed so hard at one point that he narrowly missed spraying the sip of water he'd taken all over the matron as she cleared their plates.

Once they had finished their meal, William and Tilly said a quick goodnight. William asked if she'd like to join him in the bird's nest later in the week so they could play together again, and she agreed enthusiastically.

William was sure to thank the matron before he headed for the stairs. Climbing them quickly, he burst into his room. He stripped off his clothes, grabbing the pyjamas that he had thrown on the bed earlier that morning, his boxed bicycle still lying in wait for his dad to return. Stealthily peering out of his door, he checked his parents' room to make sure nobody was there and ran as fast as he could in the nude to the bathroom opposite. Bathing speedily, he dried himself off and pulled on his long pyjamas, stepping into a pair of slippers.

Looking back towards his room, William stared into the darkness that grew behind the door, deciding he would sleep in Amelia's room again tonight, wondering how much longer it would be before she returned home.

He climbed the winding staircase to her room and threw himself into the pile of blankets covering her bed. Wrapping himself in a warm cocoon, he closed his eyes, thinking happily about his new friend.

* * * * *

Deckard's tactical update wasn't quite as boring as Amelia had expected. She had spent some time thinking on it in previous days, worrying that it would be a mix of boring statistics and militaristic orders that she wouldn't understand.

Instead, Deckard had managed to provide a brief that clearly outlined the defensive capabilities within the tree, using various diagrams and blueprint-style plans to get his message across. Each entrance and exit was represented on a scale map, crudely drawn, but accurate enough that each person knew where it was located. The largest exit, Beersheba's cave, currently had a large red cross drawn over it, as the entrance was still sealed by a thick layer of silken web.

The number of guards, both in service and in training, was just shy of one hundred, with numbers expected to increase following any attack on The Arbour. Much like in the outside world, the people of The Arbour would rally together when needed most, in order to defend their home, the only home they would ever have.

Being born in The Arbour could be seen as both a blessing and a curse. On one side, you were born into a place with a good level of protection, plenty of resources to go around, and a strong, happy community. On the other side, you were, by definition, trapped. You could never leave The Arbour, even if it was conquered. There was no escape that wouldn't end in death.

This precarious balancing act was why Deckard had suggested these meetings go ahead as soon as possible. To avoid their world toppling over and falling into chaos, strict, almost regimental plans would need to be followed.

Once Deckard had completed his discussion of military numbers, available equipment and any possible entry and exit points, Losophos presented his prediction of the moon cycle.

'The seasons are changing quickly,' he began, his monotonous voice perfectly enunciating every rehearsed word. 'We should expect to see the arc of the moon begin to alter. On a clear night, its light will once again activate the moon portal.'

Ealdor clicked his tongue in disapproval, inspecting the moon chart that Losophos had laid out on the table.

'I too have felt this change coming with the cold air.' Deckard groaned. 'I have already increased the patrols along the upper walkways, and plan to post a larger, permanent team of sentries by the moon portal once they complete their training. For now, two men will guard it on clear nights. My men will give their lives before allowing any foul creature from that portal to enter our city. Not again.'

Amelia looked at Deckard, seeing the pain in his eyes. She had heard the stories from Losophos, during their history lessons, of the last few times the Malum had managed to sneak through the moon portal, wreaking havoc amongst the city, before being brought to an end by those brave enough to face them.

Wanting to break the sombre silence, and show that she had been paying attention, Amelia spoke directly to Deckard.

'How long will it be until the new patrols are trained? I've seen the moon arcing higher into the sky each night. What if we aren't ready?'

Ealdor looked between Amelia and Deckard. 'A good question,' he said, flashing a quick grin at Amelia, as Losophos grunted in agreement.

Deckard thought for a moment.

'I will have them ready in three days.' He nodded to himself. 'Three days.'

'Let us hope that is enough,' Losophos said, standing and rolling up the moon chart.

'Are there any further points to discuss?' Ealdor asked, looking to Amelia, Keaton, Deckard, and finally Losophos.

Nobody brought up anything. They had already been talking for a few hours, and fatigue had begun to set in.

'Then without further ado, I call this meeting to an end. We will convene again in three days, or following the successful training and posting of the new guards, whichever should come first.'

When Ealdor had finished speaking, Amelia stood, all the other members rising after her, waiting for her approval to carry on.

'Thank you all for attending,' Amelia said.

She, Keaton, Deckard and Ealdor all bade Losophos a good night, before proceeding up the straight staircase and out of the hidden entrance. Amelia's cart stood exactly where it had been left, over the small hill near the lake. Samson began neighing excitedly, as though in conversation with the other two horses hitched there, one belonging to Deckard, the other to Ealdor.

Deckard and Ealdor mounted, bidding the young lovers farewell as they rode off into the night. Amelia watched their shadowy figures grow smaller on the horizon.

As Keaton reined Samson in, he tapped his hooves in response, and began to trot gracefully down the dirt road, following the path home. Amelia and Keaton huddled together on the cart's bench, the castle and surrounding town growing before them, bathed in the soft glow of moonlight.

When they were only a few kilometres outside the town perimeter, they saw a cloud of dirt forming on the road ahead, rapidly travelling towards them. Keaton slowed the horse to a gentle trot, ready to swerve off the path if whatever was causing the cloud continued to head in their direction.

The cloud grew larger, and the silhouette of a single figure on a horse emerged from within it. When it got closer, Keaton identified the figure as Ealdor.

'Why is he coming back?' Amelia asked. 'Did he forget something?'

Keaton's gaze remained on Ealdor. 'I'm not sure that's the reason,' he said, unsuccessfully trying to mask the concern in his voice.

Amelia and Keaton stepped out of the cart as Ealdor approached, slowing rapidly just before them. He appeared out of breath, sweat dripping down his face. It was the most alive either of them had ever seen him.

'Amelia!' he shouted. 'Get on my horse!'

Amelia looked at Keaton, fear spreading across both of their faces.

'What's wrong?' Amelia asked. 'Did something happen to Deckard? Why is he not with you?'

'There's no time!' He guided his horse forward and reached out to her. 'Get on, we need to get to The Archive. Keaton, you meet us there with the cart, and don't dawdle!'

In a display of strength that shocked Amelia, Ealdor swung her up onto the saddle behind him in one smooth motion. Cracking the reins, he raced the horse back towards The Archive at a speed she had only ever felt before in a car. For only a few minutes, they galloped along the road, reaching their destination in record time. Ealdor's horse was obviously imbued with magical powers that could make it run faster than normal.

Ealdor dismounted right next to The Archive door, removing the horse's reins and smacking its hind leg, allowing it to run freely. 'I'm sorry for being so forward, Amelia,' he huffed, as he pushed open the door and clattered down the dark stairs with Amelia close behind. 'I'll explain everything once we're inside.'

Large piles of books crashed down on either side of them as Ealdor and Amelia burst through the main doors of The Archive. Waving his arm above his head without turning around, Ealdor commanded the great doors to close, and they sealed the pair inside the room with a resonating *thud*.

Losophos was sitting at the table they had met around not too long ago, the chairs still warm from body heat. Looking at Ealdor, he stood, a sombre look on his face. In a voice that almost sounded scared, an emotion Amelia had not yet seen in the otherwise stoic man, he muttered four words.

'I felt it too.'

Ealdor looked to the ground between them, only offering a guttural hum in acknowledgement.

Amelia stood alone in the centre of the entrance, the moonlight beaming down through the lake above and the illusory roof. Enough was enough. She had been ripped off the ground and dragged back here with no explanation, and it was time to find out what was going on.

'Well?' she said, her eyes locked on the back of Ealdor's head. 'Are you going to tell me what's happening?'

Ealdor turned slowly towards her, his face completely red and wet. He went to the table where Losophos was seated, pulling out a chair for Amelia before sitting in his own. Producing the long pipe from his sleeve, he lit it and inhaled sharply a few times, encouraging the flame to spread within the bowl of his pipe.

'Before Deckard and I made it inside the town walls, we could hear the screams,' he began.

The hairs on Amelia's neck and arms stood at attention almost immediately as she thought of her subjects, her friends, William...

'When we rode through the gates, we spoke to a group of villagers.'

He took a long, deep breath from his pipe. 'They told us they had seen shadowy figures climbing down the castle walls. Inhuman figures. Lots of them.'

'The Malum have returned,' Losophos whispered, staring through the roof at the moon that peered over the leaves.

'And what of Deckard? What of William?' Amelia asked, her eyes filling with tears as she spoke her brother's name.

'Deckard rode on into the castle to join his men in the fight. As for William, I can't say. Protecting you was my priority.'

Amelia began to sob uncontrollably into her hands as Keaton burst into the room. He ran to her side, throwing his arms around her.

'What's happened?' he asked. 'Why is she so upset?'

'The castle is under attack; your father fights for us. As for William, his fate is currently unknown.' Ealdor took the longest breath of his pipe yet, blowing a seemingly never-ending trail of sweet-smelling smoke into the air above him, obscuring the moon.

'There is one thing you can do while we sit here and await more news, dear Amelia,' Losophos said in a soft voice.

Amelia shot upright, remembering the new ability she now had, and placed her right hand over the brooch on her chest. She closed her eyes and focused harder than ever before, searching through the darkness in her mind to locate William.

Minutes passed. No feeling or image pierced through the darkness of her mind. No comforting tingle told her where he was.

Again and again she tried, until finally, she opened her eyes and stared into the ground before her, her right hand dropping into her lap, a stream of tears again cascading down her face.

'I can't feel him.'

# CHAPTER EIGHT

The sounds of battle filled the air in the distance. A cacophony of screaming women and children, men shouting, weapons clanging. Deckard sat ever taller on his mount as he and Ealdor rode at a furious pace. Never in Deckard's lifetime had he witnessed such a brazen attack on his home. Never had he seen the streets so deserted as when he and Ealdor had finally arrived within the town's perimeter. The doors and windows within view of them had been shuttered, and the scared citizens were hiding in the dark confines of their homes.

'Go!' he shouted to Ealdor, over the commotion and screams that came from the centre of The Arbour, within the castle walls. 'Get the princess back to The Archive and wait there.'

Ealdor did not wait around for further orders. With a tug on his horse's reins, he about-faced and galloped back into the night, the *crack* of leather straps against its hide driving it faster.

Deckard took one deep breath and urged his own horse forward, screaming 'Ya!' and standing in his stirrups as he raced towards the roaring cacophony.

What lay before Deckard as he rode in through the castle gates was a scene of pure chaos. He was forced to dismount and run towards the main doors on foot, as the crowd of fleeing workers was too dense and chaotic, and his horse was unwilling to go any further.

'Step aside!' he yelled, as his wooden armour was bumped several times by the panicked citizens. 'Calm yourselves!'

Pointing to one of the two guards who stood watch over the courtyard from atop the main stairs, he screamed over the crowd, 'You there, with me!'

The young guard locked eyes with him, and with spear and shield in hand, ran down the steps.

'Sir,' the guard shouted, when he arrived before Deckard and stood at attention.

'What happened here?' Deckard asked, his voice returning to a more normal level as the shuffling of feet and muffled screams faded beyond the castle walls.

The young soldier looked Deckard in the eyes with a fear he could not remember seeing for many years. The hairs on the back of his neck stood on end while he peered into the soldier's soul.

'The Malum are here. They came from the roof. They're everywhere, sir, looking for her.'

Heat filled Deckard's body, and with all his might, he grasped the pommel of his sword and ripped it from its sheath.

'Compose yourself, lad,' he said to the trembling soldier.

Just as he had finished speaking, a piercing crash filled the air.

Deckard and the soldier both looked high up to the main spire of the castle. Sweat dripped into Deckard's eyes as he beheld countless glass shards falling from Amelia's window, the coloured flecks filling the dark air like a million deadly stars plummeting to the earth.

Without wasting a second, Deckard seized the shield from the soldier's hand. 'Get down!' he shouted, crouching over the cowering soldier and throwing his arms above his head, using the shield to cover them both from the shower of sharp flakes that wanted to tear them to shreds.

Within seconds, the shards reached them. A ringing filled the air as the countless projectiles bounced off or stuck within the wood of the shield, many thousands more reaching the stone floor around them and shattering into an unimaginable number of smaller pieces.

Once the sound had ceased, Deckard threw the shield to the side. It slid, grinding along glass fragments, until it came to a stop a few feet from them, large shards protruding from its surface. If not for the shield, their blood would have spread amongst the glass that now covered the courtyard like a blanket of winter snow.

Filled with a blind rage, Deckard leapt up the stairs, taking several at a time, until he found himself at the doorway. Without pause, he muttered to the remaining soldier, 'With me,' and together they marched into the hall.

The interior of the castle now mirrored the town streets, as a deafening emptiness filled the large space. Seeing no movement, Deckard raced towards the passage at the side of the hall and followed it up the central spire, stopping before the door that belonged to Amelia's parents, and to Master William, who he hoped had remained hidden inside.

'Wait here,' he commanded the soldier, as he pushed through the door with his sword extending out in front of him.

The room was cold. The fireplace had not been kindled that day, as there was no point in heating an empty space. Seeing this, Deckard turned left, and aided by the moonlight, found his way to the small door to William's bedroom.

The door was ajar. Deckard paused by it for a moment, listening for any movement from within.

There was nothing.

'Master William?' he whispered, not wanting to frighten the boy, who would no doubt be cowering in fear. 'Master William, it's me, Deckard.' With his free hand, he gently opened the door, which groaned on its hinges.

The room was black. A deep black that made it impossible to see, hiding any secrets that lay within, like an impenetrable cowl of night.

A thought occurred to him.

The princess's room.

He had heard that William often stayed with his sister. *Could he be there now?*

Deckard's gut twisted as he remembered the window shattering. Silently praying that he was wrong, he raced back out, surprising the soldier standing guard in the passage, and charged up the stairway to his right, faster than he previously had, hoping by whatever gods may exist that the boy was alright.

When the stairs levelled out, Deckard and the soldier slowed their steps. A thin haze filled the passage as hot smoke from the fireplace within the room met the bitter winter air through the smashed window, and spilled out of the open doorway into the hall.

An unfamiliar feeling gripped Deckard, which he tried hard to suppress, grasping the hilt of his sword with both hands, as hard as his fingers would allow.

*Is this fear?*

Inhaling deeply, only once, Deckard burst through the open doorway, closely followed by the spear-wielding soldier, who gasped at what he saw.

The room before them was a mess. To the right, the fire's hot coals spilled out onto the floor, as though something had been thrown into them and found its way back out again. The small drawing desk that normally sat by the fireplace had toppled over. Sheets of paper, both blank and filled with art, lined the floor. To the left, the tall, imposing wardrobe had been wrenched open, and its contents spilled through the room like the guts of a felled carcass.

The most shocking sight of all, however, came from straight ahead. The window that took up much of the wall had indeed been destroyed. Jagged chunks remained in its corners, the only evidence that it had existed in the first place, other than a few shards that had been flung inside the room. Amongst the smaller shards were large, bloody footprints that led from the bed to the window. Not human footprints, but those of a Malum.

Beside the window stood the bed. Its blankets and sheets were flung across the floor. One hung limp over the ledge, half out in the cold night air. Feathers were strewn across the mattress, the hollow shells of the pillows barely visible amongst their insides.

A sudden pain filled Deckard's chest as his eyes moved to the foot of the bed. Standing there, untouched, was a small pair of brown slippers. Slippers that did not belong to the princess, nor to this room, but to William.

\* \* \* \* \*

It took Deckard more than an hour to leave the castle. Finding the matron huddled in a corner of the pantry, he ordered her to collect the staff who had fled and coordinate a clean-up.

Along with six of his best soldiers, Deckard journeyed to the tree's outer wall. Crossing the bridge towards the tip of the castle spire, he could see the moon portal, its surface rippling gently under the bright moonlight. At its feet were two huddled figures, which he knew would be the lifeless corpses of the sentries who had been posted there earlier in the evening.

As his boots connected with the solid roof, his fears were confirmed. The two soldiers were indeed dead, a spear sticking out from each of their backs. Clearly, they'd been attacked from within the mirror, as they stood watch over the bridge, their blood now filling the gaps between the stones.

'Get them out of here,' he said to the older soldier behind him.

When the last of them arrived at the end of the bridge, they witnessed the bloody figures, their friends. The youngest soldier, who Deckard thought could not have been older than sixteen, grasped the rope that ran the length of the bridge, leaned deep over it, and vomited.

'Listen here, and listen well,' Deckard began. The five soldiers who had not been tasked with removing the bodies stood to attention; even the boy who vomited forced himself into composure, bile still glistening on his lips. 'What you have witnessed tonight is unprecedented within these walls, but if you don't come to your senses now, there will be countless more lives lost. The Arbour will run red with the blood of your friends, your family, and your people.'

As the older soldier picked up one of his fallen comrades and hobbled back towards the inner wall of the tree, Deckard knelt. Removing the glove from his right hand, he dipped his fingers in the pools of blood before him, and wiped the warm fluid across his face.

After a moment of silence, he continued.

'While this portal remains open, we remain in danger. I beg of you, as your commander, and as your fellow man, do not falter tonight. Watch this portal, and allow nothing through. Kill any that may try. Do not surrender to the tiredness in your eyes, because one mistake up here may mean the end of all of us.'

Returning to his feet, Deckard picked up the second corpse. He threw it over his shoulder, ruby drops of blood leaving trails down his perfectly polished armour, and started back along the bridge.

While the five soldiers standing sentry were still within earshot, without stopping, Deckard spoke with defeat in his voice, his previous failure in the loss of Lady Ashlyn ringing through his mind.

'I must report to the princess. Good luck to you all.'

# CHAPTER NINE

Hours had passed since Amelia had returned to The Archive with Ealdor. She had tried several times to locate William using her brooch, every time with no success.

'What does it mean?' she asked Losophos, hoping that he would have some unrelated explanation as to why it wasn't working.

He pondered for a time, while she continued to reach out to the ring, breaking his silence when he had narrowed down the possibilities.

'There are three potential reasons I can think of why you can't find Master William,' he said glumly. 'None of which you are going to like, I'm afraid.'

Amelia broke her focus, listening now to Losophos.

'The first reason, with the best outcome, would be if Master William took the ring off, or had it taken from him. The abilities only work when the ring is worn by something living.'

Amelia nodded in silent consideration.

'The next reason, and the most complicated, could be that he is too far away for you to sense.'

'What do you mean, too far away?' She shook her head, anger and sadness clouding her logical thinking. 'I sensed him just fine the other day when I was here and he was in the castle. How much further could he be?'

Ealdor spoke this time, knowing that he had the best information regarding the attack so far.

'I think what Losophos is suggesting, Amelia, is that if the attackers infiltrated The Arbour using the moon portal, it's possible they took William back with them. Although for what purpose, I can't comprehend.'

Amelia's eyes began to fill with tears again. Choking on her words, she said what she dreaded most.

'You said the ring only works on living things, right?'

Losophos nodded silently in response.

'So, let me guess. The last of your reasons is that he's dead, isn't it?'

'I'm afraid so.'

Amelia lay down in a ball on the cold stone floor, hugging her knees to her chest and sobbing loudly. Ealdor and Losophos slumped in their chairs, silently wishing that there was another option they hadn't considered. Keaton sat beside the shaking body of the girl he loved, placing his hand on her shoulder, silently letting her know that he was there for her.

The hours continued to pass with no news. Amelia cried herself to sleep, her head resting in Keaton's lap as he stroked her hair. Ealdor and Losophos continued to sit at the table in silent contemplation, Ealdor smoking a seemingly endless supply of flavoured tobacco, while Losophos fingered through a register of books, collating all of the information in The Archive's many shelves regarding the Malum kingdom.

A noise broke the silence in the chamber after a time. However, it did not come from within, instead seeming to originate from the stairwell outside the main door.

Losophos and Ealdor sprung into action, jumping to their feet and taking their places in front of the door, readying combat stances.

'Hide her, quickly,' Ealdor hissed at Keaton, who gently shook Amelia awake and guided her down a dark row of bookshelves.

The noise from outside became more rapid, getting louder and closer as the seconds passed. It came to a stop just before the door, silence once again resonating through the chamber as Keaton and Amelia held their breath, peering over a low shelf.

With a creak, the doors pushed open slightly, a thin crack of darkness revealing itself between them, before vanishing as they closed with a *thud*. Again, they separated, creating a larger gap. Something could be seen standing in the gloom. For a final time, the doors pushed open, this time swinging wide enough to allow the figure to pass through. Deckard stepped into the faint light of the room, collapsing to his knees as Losophos and Ealdor rushed forward to assist him.

'Dad!' Keaton shouted, running out of the row he'd been hiding in and approaching his exhausted father.

Amelia followed slowly behind, inspecting Deckard. He looked like a man defeated. His face was sticking out of his armour, a swollen, red visage, dripping with sweat and blood.

Inspecting him further, Amelia saw that his hands were empty. The fingers of his gloves were scratched and torn, his dirty nails protruding from the leather. His sword was sheathed by his side, and he sat on his knees, breathing heavily, clearly exhausted. There were drips of blood on his torso and legs, although Amelia couldn't see any injury on him. A sign, perhaps, that it wasn't his blood.

Sensing what Amelia was going to ask, Losophos placed his hand on her shoulder, not taking his eyes off the pained man before him. 'Give him some time to breathe,' he whispered. 'There's a carafe of water on the table. Bring it for him. Please.'

Amelia had gotten used to giving orders, not following them, but she knew that the quickest way to find out what she needed to know would be to do as Losophos said, and provide Deckard with as much comfort as she could, at least until he was able to compose a sentence. She grabbed the carafe, the water only centimetres from the top, sloshing from side to side as she carried it towards her captain.

Losophos and Ealdor made quick work of removing Deckard's outer armour, taking care to check for any injuries as they removed each piece. Keaton watched on in horrified anticipation as he knelt by his father's side, one arm around his back, keeping him upright.

When Amelia reached Deckard, he looked at her, still breathing heavily. Unable to use his words, he grabbed the pitcher from her hands, raising it above his head and pouring most of it through his hair and down his shoulders.

He appeared to relax for a moment, at least a little bit, steam rising off his hot skin. After gulping down some water, he began to regain his breath. The speed at which his chest was rising and falling slowed, a more normal tempo returning to his body.

With difficulty, he forced out a few brief words, sucking down air between each one.

'They... took... him...'

He didn't need to say any more.

Amelia's heart sank.

*They got William.*

*They got him, and I wasn't there to help.*

She silently stood up and began to walk backwards, looking to each of the faces before her. She began to think of her parents. *How am I going to tell them? They don't know!*

Her mind was racing, her body filled with anger, confusion, disappointment, fear. Her breathing became more rapid, the room spinning before her eyes. The corners of her vision began to fill with an expanding darkness. She could see white spots in what remained of her sight, dancing and twinkling in her eyes as though the room was filled with shooting stars.

As her vision closed, she fumbled backwards, her foot catching on a crack between the tiles. She could feel herself falling. Momentary weightlessness, then a sudden impact to her head, followed by blackness.

\* \* \* \*

The bag that sat over William's head had grown wet with tears, the scratchy material sticking to the damp spots on his cheeks. He didn't understand what was happening. One moment he had been sleeping peacefully in Amelia's bed, wrapped tightly in the warmth of her blankets, waiting for her to return. The next, he was awakened by an explosion of shattering glass, the window scattering all over the floor. Unfamiliar arms snatched him up, dark figures shoving a gag into his mouth and yanking a bag over his head before he could see what was happening, or who was there.

He wasn't sure how long they had been carrying him. He'd felt the cold air as the intruder jumped out the window with him slung over their shoulder, dangling precariously as they appeared to climb up the very walls of the castle.

Hearing screams from the town below, William knew that something was very wrong. When they climbed to the top of the tower, he felt the intruder steady themselves on the solid ground. A few voices from either side appeared to hiss words at him enthusiastically, but he was unable to make out anything particular.

The intruder began to walk again, and in an instant, the echoing screams disappeared and were replaced by thunderous applause and cheering. The air felt different here. It was almost sticky, and putrid smells filled his nostrils, causing him to cough.

'Silence!' the intruder hissed into his ear, smacking him on the shoulder so William knew they weren't messing around.

They continued to carry William for a few minutes, the cheers and applause quieting as they stepped into a large room, footsteps echoing high into the ceiling. The room was far from empty, though. William could hear whispers from several others as they proceeded deeper into the space.

'They got her,' he heard one of them say. 'They did it.'

The intruder carrying William stepped up a few stairs before slowing to a stop, gently pulling him over their shoulder and laying him on the ground. They took a moment to tie William's wrists and ankles together, before shuffling back and standing silently, waiting for something.

The whispers in the room grew. The words from one person overlapped with those from the next, making it impossible for William to identify exactly what was being said. As the voices continued to rise in volume, there was a sound above him, reminding him of a curtain being drawn. The voices immediately stopped, and the room returned to silence.

'Brave soldiers!'

William jumped as a deafening voice boomed through the room, bouncing from wall to wall, originating from somewhere up above him.

'Tonight, you've made your people, and your king, proud!'

The room filled with thunderous applause once more, eventually slowing to a hush as the voice spoke again.

'Once I take the crown from this undeserving girl, we will inherit what is rightfully ours, stopping anybody who dares to stand in our way!'

Applause again filled the air, this time allowed to carry on for some time before receding back to quiet.

'Remove the mask!' the voice bellowed. 'I want to see the fear in her eyes.'

The person who'd placed William on the floor approached him again. This time, they turned him to face the voice and ripped the hood from his head.

There was a collective gasp from the crowd. Whispers began to creep amongst their ranks as they saw the boy who sat before them, cowering in fear.

William inspected the dark, dirty room. In front of him was a large balcony. Tattered curtains lined its sides and one large sheet hung from above, obscuring whatever lay behind it. Before it, leaning over the banister above William and peering down in embarrassed anger, was a large rat. One side of his face was scarred, his yellow teeth razor sharp and sticking out of his mouth in all directions, their colour almost matching the tiny crown atop his head. Without turning around, William knew that all those voices behind him belonged to many more rats. He must be inside that place Amelia discussed occasionally with her staff when she didn't think he was listening, the Malum kingdom.

'What is the meaning of this?' the large rat screamed at the one who had just uncovered him.

The rat behind William began to breathe rapidly. 'There must be some mistake, my king. He was in her bed.'

From beside the king came the sound of fleshy footsteps. A smaller rat walked to his side and spoke into his ear.

'My king... we know who this young creature is. He is the one we have been working on for some time now. I can see it in him.' The rat waved one of his gnarled paws towards William, his eyes glowing as he stared deep into William's soul.

William froze, not even breathing for a moment, the sound of the rat's voice triggering something deep within him. Something distant, yet familiar.

The king's angry expression changed to one of elation. 'But of course.' Drool cascaded from his deformed snout as he grinned, showing many spots where teeth once stood, now pink, fleshy bumps. 'Perhaps there is hope yet. Take him to the dungeon and work on him. I predict they will come for him soon, and he needs to be ready by then.'

The smaller rat looked at William with a grin that was somehow more sinister than the king's, causing William immediate discomfort.

'You heard the king!' he shouted. 'Take him away!'

For the last time, the room erupted into a celebration of gnashing teeth and clapping paws, as the same rat who'd stolen William from Amelia's bed now carried him into the depths of the Malum kingdom.

William heard the smaller rat shout once more. 'All hail King Azul!'

To which his audience began to chant, 'Azul! Azul! Azul!'

* * * * *

When Amelia opened her eyes, she saw The Archive's familiar glass ceiling, through which the moon and stars continued to glow. She looked to her right, where Ealdor, Losophos and Deckard all sat at the table. Keaton remained by her side, asleep. Someone had taken the time to place something soft under her head, a courtesy that she felt grateful for.

Slowly, she pushed herself onto her feet, grabbing Keaton's hand and squeezing it gently until he woke up, yawning.

'How are you feeling?' he asked, standing and wrapping her in a hug.

'I'm okay,' she whispered. 'Just tired.'

'Come on.' He motioned towards the table. 'There's things you need to hear.'

Together, they walked over, Keaton pulling out a chair for Amelia. Once she was seated, he took his own, the two still holding hands.

'How are you, Amelia?' Deckard asked. She wasn't sure how long she had been unconscious, but it was enough time for him to almost fully recover. His face was no longer swollen and red. Instead, it had returned to its usual gradient, his skin now dry, no longer caked in sweat, dirt and blood.

'Never mind me,' she said, offering him a self-pitying smirk. 'How are you?'

Deckard shifted slightly in his seat. It was strange seeing him without his wooden armour on; however, he still maintained a large and imposing figure.

'I'm fine now, my princess, but I have much to tell.'

Amelia crossed her legs and settled into a more comfortable position, preparing her body to hear what Deckard had to reveal.

'Please go on,' she said, squeezing Keaton's hand to remind herself that he was still there. He squeezed back.

Deckard recounted the story of what he had encountered earlier that night.

'We lost two men tonight, two new trainees who were patrolling the bridge.' He bowed his head, his face twisting as though he might cry. 'I still have to tell their families.'

'Did the Malum come through the moon portal?' Ealdor asked, eager for confirmation.

'They did,' Deckard said. 'We've posted a permanent sentry of my six finest guards while we decide what to do. I suggest that we destroy the moon portal, shatter it while we can to avoid future bloodshed.'

Amelia leapt out of her seat. 'No!' she screamed. 'We mustn't destroy it until we get William back!'

Ealdor stood, raising his arms at both Amelia and Deckard. 'Let's not have this talk now. Deckard, you need rest.' He pointed at Keaton. 'Take him home, and ensure he gets there safely. I will stay with Amelia until her parents return at dawn.'

Keaton looked at Amelia as though searching for approval.

'Go.' She nodded, kissing him on the cheek and watching as he helped his father stand and limp out the door.

Once the sound of their footsteps had quietened, Ealdor placed his arm around Amelia's shoulder and guided her towards the door. 'Come now, let us go and wait for your parents. We can discuss what to tell them on the journey over. The sun will be rising in a few short hours.'

As they rode towards the castle, Amelia could not stop thinking of William. Was he okay? How would they get to him? Was it a trap? Those worries, and more, filled her head as she fell into a brief slumber, conserving her energy for the talk she was about to have with her parents.

# CHAPTER TEN

First light was peeking over the mountains as Amelia and Ealdor pushed through the secret hatch at the top of the tower, startling the guards who now maintained a permanent watch over the platform, just as Deckard had described.

'Forget what you saw just now,' Ealdor said to them, closing the hatch behind him.

Amelia stepped around to the moon portal, gazing into its surface, her head and one hand resting against it as she placed her other over her brooch. Focusing as hard as she could, through the exhaustion that the near-sleepless night had bestowed upon her, she searched for William, finding no light in the darkness. She wasn't sure if she had felt the beginnings of a tingle, or if it was just her imagination.

Her head still rested on the surface of the mirror when she opened her eyes, spotting a collection of bloodstains at her feet. Ealdor saw her expression change and realised what she had seen.

'We'll get that cleaned up soon,' he said, once again placing his arm around her, guiding her to the side of the mirror that her parents would shortly be stepping through.

They watched and waited, silently eyeing the mirror's surface. Amelia focused on how exhausted she looked. There were bags under her eyes, which were red from the tears she had shed. Her hair was dishevelled, and she was still wearing the clothes she'd put on the morning before. They would no doubt be smelling ripe soon.

The surface of the mirror began to ripple, jolting Amelia back to reality as she mustered all the courage she had left.

Her parents stepped through, grinning from ear to ear. Their smiles were replaced by furrowed brows as they saw the despair on Amelia's face. She began to cry, running towards her mother and wrapping both arms around her waist, sobbing into her bosom.

'Oh, dear.' Amity tutted. 'Whatever is the matter? Where's William?' She looked around to see only Ealdor and several guards.

Before she could jump to her own conclusions, Ealdor cleared his throat, and began to share the story of what had happened that night, as Amelia continued to sob in her mother's arms.

Amity and Lyall looked on in shock. Her expression had changed to one of pain and confusion, while he'd managed to maintain his composure slightly better, although his eyes had begun to glisten and turn red.

'You mean there's another portal?' she asked, her voice became louder as worry for her missing son continued to grow inside her heart. 'And he was taken through by an enemy? What are we doing about it? Why are we still standing here?'

Lyall put his arms around what currently remained of his family, trying his best to calm everyone as he contemplated what they could do.

'Well,' he began, 'what steps have you taken to get my son back? And how can I help?'

Ealdor was surprised by Lyall's steadiness, the respect he had for Lyall deepening.

'We will be discussing our options after lunch in the castle hall. You are most welcome to attend, sir.'

Nodding, Lyall loosened his grip on Amelia and Amity, walking towards Ealdor and shaking his hand.

'Thank you for taking care of my daughter,' he said, his voice wobbling.

Ealdor bowed slightly. 'It is my duty and my pleasure. Now, if I can make a recommendation, I would suggest you take young Amelia here down to your room to get some rest before lunch. She's had quite the long night, and her room won't be ready for some time yet.'

Ealdor moved over to the hatch, waving his hand over it, causing it to rise and reveal the stairs down into the tower. Amelia and her parents stepped into the space one by one, closing the hatch behind them and making their way to their quarters, where they were met by the matron, relief filling her face.

'Oh, thank goodness you're alright!' She smiled sympathetically at Amelia. 'I've left some fruit on the table for you. I've also filled the bath with hot water and some aromatic salts, to help you relax and clear your mind.'

'Thank you, matron,' Amelia mumbled, following her parents into the room, the matron shutting the door behind them.

As her parents sat on the lounge furniture in the corner of their room, the reality of what had happened finally set in. Amity was deeply upset, Lyall comforting her as best he could, while they spoke quietly about what they could do next.

'I... I think I'll just have a bath,' Amelia said.

'We'll be right here if you need us,' Lyall called.

Amelia stepped into the bathroom, gently closing the door behind her and turning the lock. She slid down the door, ending in the foetal position, silently sobbing onto the stone floor.

The scent of eucalyptus and lavender filled the air. Her nose cleared, and her head stopped throbbing. A few moments passed before she mustered the strength to lift herself back onto her feet, her arms trembling as she pushed up off the ground. Slowly, she slipped off her clothes and climbed into the bath, warm water enveloping her whole body as she sunk into it.

She lay in the water, part floating, part sinking. A few times, she pushed her entire body under, water covering her face and filling her nose and ears while she held her breath, imagining she was in a bad dream, and this was what she had to do to wake up and escape it.

The bathroom was lit entirely by candles. She counted them, looking from one corner to the next. Three on each wall, making a total of twelve.

She closed her eyes, envisioning nothing but those twelve candles in the darkness of her mind, using her pain and anger to channel as much energy as she could into focusing.

'*Ventus*,' she whispered.

She opened her eyes, and the room was dark, all twelve candles extinguished. Once again, she continued to grow stronger.

\* \* \* \* \*

Amelia was awoken by a gentle knocking at the door. She wasn't sure how long she had been asleep, but as she moved her body in the water, feeling her fingers, she noticed they were very wrinkly.

'Amelia,' her mother called quietly through the door. 'Amelia, can we talk?'

A lump formed in her throat once more, but this time, she maintained control over her thoughts, the calming waters having done their work.

'One second,' she called out into the darkness, reaching for the sides of the tub.

She pulled herself out of the bath. Picturing the candles near the door, she focused her mind and whispered, '*Ignis*.' The three cold wicks once again burnt to life, providing faint light to the foggy room.

Amelia dried herself off quickly, slipping into a robe and tying it off around her waist, before walking over to the door and unlocking it, allowing her mother to step inside.

'Hey, sweetie,' she said, forcing a smile, though Amelia could see in her eyes that she had been crying. 'Why don't you go sit in front of the mirror, and I'll do your hair while we talk?'

The bench before the mirror was neatly stocked with makeup boxes and accessories, including brushes, combs and scissors. Amity stood in position behind Amelia, massaging the water out of her hair with a fresh towel.

'Before you say anything, I want you to know that William being taken wasn't your fault. Your father and I should have been here, or at least made sure you were both safer.'

Amelia lifted the towel away from her face so she could look into the mirror, spotting her mother's reflection. Her face was pained. She was staring at a blank spot on the wall as she rubbed Amelia's head and spoke of her guilt.

'It wasn't your fault either,' Amelia offered. 'It would've happened whether you were here or not, and it could've happened to anybody, although it seems they were after me.'

Amity threw the towel into a basket by the wall and rested her hands on the back of the chair, leaning in close and kissing the top of Amelia's head.

'I know, sweetheart,' she said, with a genuine smile. 'I know.'

She began to braid Amelia's hair, which was still a little damp, but workable. Her hands twisted and turned, forming a large plait down the centre of Amelia's head.

'I know your father and the people here are going to do whatever they can to get William back, but I need you to promise me something.' She stopped weaving for a moment as she looked Amelia's reflection directly in the eyes. 'I need you to promise you won't go through that mirror. I don't think I could handle losing you both.'

She raised a hand to her eyes as she started to sob again. Amelia stood in her chair so she was almost at her mother's height, placing one hand on Amity's shoulder and lifting her chin with the other, so they were looking into each other's eyes.

'You know I can't promise that, Mum,' she said. 'But we'll bring William back. Alive. As long as he's wearing the ring I gave him for his birthday, he should be safe, and you can be sure that when I go through that mirror to get him back, I'll also be well protected.'

Amity stood in silent reflection, seeing that her little girl had indeed been growing rapidly since finding this world. She pulled Amelia in for a hug, lifting her from the chair and placing her on the ground.

'I expected as much,' she said, a bittersweet half-smile on her lips. 'At least tell me that you'll be careful, and you'll take your father with you.'

Amelia thought for a moment, realising she hadn't even begun to consider putting together a team, let alone who would be a part of it. After all, the locals couldn't leave the tree's boundary.

'I will,' she said, looking around her mother, to where her dad stood in the open door. Smiling, he entered the bathroom, a neat package in his hands, and placed it on a small table against the wall.

'Ealdor sent these up for you,' he said, patting the top of the parcel. 'He wants you to wear them to the briefing after lunch.'

Amelia nodded. 'Thanks.'

He smiled at her once more, a warm smile, before taking Amity's hand and pulling her out of the bathroom so Amelia could change in private.

'Mum, Dad...' Amelia called, as they were about to shut the door.

They stopped in their tracks and turned around. Amity was wiping her face, and Lyall had one arm around her shoulder, the other on the door handle, as they looked at Amelia expectantly.

'...I love you,' she said. She focused on maintaining her eye contact with them as she spoke, so they knew just how deeply she meant it.

They smiled back at her, both of them responding, 'We love you too,' before closing the door.

When Amelia stepped out of the bathroom, her parents were no longer present. It had taken her quite a while to change into her new clothes, which were more complicated to don than she had thought possible.

There was a small note on the inside of the package that explained how to place each fine layer of fabric into position. It had been crafted using materials from the outside world, and in the note, the tailor explained how, with Losophos' help, it had been enchanted. It could theoretically stay intact whenever she exited The Arbour, as long as she didn't remove it from her body.

The foundation was a form-fitting bodysuit that ran from her toes up to her neckline. Its material wasn't something she had seen before; it was almost like metal, although it was quite flexible and charcoal grey in colour.

Onto this under-layer, many additional pieces were placed, which were composed of ultra-thin, ultra-durable wood. These pieces connected at the shins, thighs, waist, chest, shoulders, and forearms. On the chest piece, there was a small circular hole in the wood, where a loop of fabric stood from the bodysuit, just enough for her to pin her brooch into. The golden disc clicked into place perfectly once she let it go, sitting flush with the outer layer.

The bodysuit ended at her wrists, leaving her hands exposed, until she found the half-gloves. She slid them on. The tops of her hands were now protected by a series of small wooden scales, malleable enough that she could fully extend her fingers and form a fist without any limitation.

Inspecting her new outfit in her mother's full-length mirror, Amelia twisted and turned, checking out every angle, feeling the materials work with her body as she moved about the space in a few hops, skips and rolls.

Her tummy rumbled when she spied the fruit on her parents' lounge furniture. Quickly, she rushed over to it and shoved what she could into her face, realising she hadn't eaten since afternoon tea the previous day. She wasn't sure if she would still make it in time for lunch or not, so she ate until there was still a little bit of room left in her stomach, before leaving her parents' room, stopping for a moment to touch William's door on the way out.

As Amelia walked through the corridors of the castle, bound for the main hall, where the brief was shortly to take place, she noticed the quiet that had settled in since last night's attack. Where previously there were workers in many places, cleaning or mending, even just standing about having a conversation, all of them were gone. All of the castle's many passages seemed empty today, except for one.

As she approached the last corner before the main hall, Amelia saw Tilly standing alone in the corridor that stretched out before her, as though waiting for someone. Tilly locked eyes with her and quickly walked in her direction.

'Princess Amelia,' she said, curtseying deeply, before standing up again and admiring Amelia's new outfit. 'You look scary. Are you getting ready to attack the Malum?'

Amelia smiled at Tilly. Her innocent and casual yet confident way of speaking reminded Amelia of her younger self.

'That was the plan,' she said.

Tilly got very close to Amelia, glanced all around and whispered, 'My mum always says that I can do anything I put my mind to, as long as I believe in myself. I hope you believe in yourself, Princess, because I believe in you.'

Amelia looked away from Tilly, wanting to hide the tears forming in her eyes.

Leaning in close to Tilly, Amelia thought for a moment, before whispering back to her. 'Your mother sounds like a very smart lady.'

Amelia continued down the corridor. She stepped into the light spilling from the main hall, the many voices within stopping as they saw her appear within the doorway.

'All rise for Princess Amelia!'

Deckard's voice boomed from beside her throne. She took comfort in hearing him sound so normal.

Only expecting the usual attendees, Ealdor, Losophos, Keaton and Deckard, Amelia was shocked to see that quite a few of the townsfolk had turned up to the brief. She quickly glanced over the room, feeling hundreds of faces look at her, and feeling powerful in her new suit.

She walked up the centre aisle, the crowd parting to let her pass.

As she approached her throne, she smiled at her parents, who were standing just to the side. Deckard and Keaton were positioned behind her throne, and she nodded to them, before turning to face the crowd and sitting in the cushioned seat that awaited her.

From her right, Ealdor's voice echoed out into the hall, followed by a long, deafening silence.

'Let us begin.'

# CHAPTER ELEVEN

When William opened his eyes, he thought that he might still be in his little room in the castle. This space was similarly dark. A musty, wet sort of smell filled the air, and it was quiet, save for the occasional droplet of water falling somewhere within the shadow.

Maybe it had all just been a bad dream.

But as he rolled to his side, he knew that wasn't the case. This bed wasn't his comfortable mattress. It was far denser, with bits poking him in the back, as though it was filled with sticks. There was no blanket, although the ambient warmth was high enough that he didn't need one anyway.

On the wall to his left, he saw that there was an exceptionally dim square of light, about the height and width of a large door. He got to his feet, tripping over a bucket, which toppled and rolled somewhere out of sight.

He felt his way to the door, first finding a warm metal handle, which was dripping with condensation. Running his hands further around the door, he thought it might be made of an incredibly old, mouldy wood. He saw a smaller square of light above him. Standing on his tippy-toes, he was just able to peer out of what appeared to be a window, filled with vertical bars to keep whoever was inside from climbing out.

Guess it wasn't a dream, then.

To his left, there was nothing more than a plain mud wall. An old wooden torch was mounted in the centre; however, it wasn't lit. The roof also consisted of mud, tiny pinpricks of light penetrating its depths, the only source of illumination in the otherwise barren area.

To his right was a dark passageway. He could not see how far it stretched, but when he kicked the base of the door, the echo carried on down the hall for longer than he would've liked.

Directly across the thin hallway stood an identical door to his, the only difference being that the small, barred window had been covered with a rough square of wood, nailed in without any care or precision. William listened for a time, hearing nothing but his own heartbeat, and the occasional scratching or whimpering that he thought might be coming from the cell across from him.

Without anything else to do, William decided to feel his way around his own room, in an attempt to figure out how big it was, and to see if there were any hidden exits. Not that he thought he would ever be that lucky.

Before he began, he checked himself, running his hands from head to toe, making sure everything was still where it was supposed to be, and nothing was bleeding or damaged. His feet were bare. He remembered his slippers, which he'd placed at the foot of Amelia's bed before jumping into it. He was still wearing his long pyjamas, the ones with blue and white stripes, not that he could see the colour.

As he checked his face and head, he felt something hard on his cheek. His heart calmed as he realised he still had his birthday ring on his finger. The rats had either not seen it, or not bothered taking it from him.

He began feeling his way around the room, in a clockwise direction, stepping down onto the dirt floor. The wall continued for a couple of metres before he hit a corner and began following it the other way. He went on for approximately twice the length of the small wall, and as he reached the corner, his foot slipped on what felt like wet metal bars.

One... two... three... four. He felt four of them with his feet. They were covered in some sort of wet slick that didn't smell very nice. Carefully navigating the small gaps between the rods, William continued along the next wall, reaching the head of his bed after only a few steps, following it around to the other side and reaching the final corner.

When he once again reached the door, his heart sank. He returned to the bed, the only object in the room that wasn't him, not including the bucket, and sat in his silent prison. The lack of sight heightened his sense of smell and hearing. The smell, he decided, he would rather be without.

Boredom came upon him very quickly. In his room at the castle, he would at least hear the occasional sounds of the town below, or his parents talking in the next room, or even the whispers that plagued him at night. Something to concentrate on. In this place, there was just nothingness, not even the sound of the breeze, which normally travelled down passageways, no matter how deep and secluded.

Time felt like it had slowed to a crawl, with nothing to entertain him. William lay down sideways across the bed, swinging his legs over the side, kicking in time with his heartbeat.

One... two...

First his left leg, then his right.

One... two...

Again, his left leg kicked, his right leg following shortly after.

He focused on this for what felt like an impossibly long time, before a change came to the rhythm.

One... two... three...

It threw his legs off rhythm, his left leg still hanging in the air as he waited for the next beat to come.

One... two... three...

William sat upright, placing his ringed hand over his heart, trying to identify where this phantom beat had appeared from.

One... two...

He let out a sigh of relief. His heartbeat was normal, but he could still hear the third beat, which was slowly getting louder.

As he focused on the thumping, the extra beat continued to grow louder, faint echoes of it now filling his cell. He stepped up to the door, placing his head against the bars, his ear sticking out between them while the echoes reverberated from somewhere further down the corridor.

He waited and listened, as the sound grew closer and closer, realising it was footsteps approaching when he began to see something moving in the darkness. He pushed himself back from the door, missing the bottom step and falling to the muddy ground. Panicking, he felt for the leg of his bed, pulling himself under it, while the footsteps came to a halt just outside his door, the figure's shadow peering in through the barred window.

With a solid click, the door's lock flicked open, the wet wooden frame groaning as it swung inwards, coming to rest with a gentle *thump* on the cell wall.

From under the bed, William watched two large feet, covered in hair, large claws growing from their toes, step into the room, mud squelching beneath their soles as the rat moved deeper into the room.

The feet stopped directly before the end of the bed, pausing for a moment before turning towards William, the long claws only inches from his face. Without a sound, the bed began to rise into the air, slowly revealing the body of the rat that stood before him.

It appeared to be wearing a long robe, which hung loosely down its sides, sporadically gaping with holes. On its fingers were an assortment of rings, touting large gems in all the colours of the rainbow.

Once the bed had hovered to the level of the rat's head, its cold black eyes peered down to the floor where William lay. A satisfied smirk spread across its face, showing its yellow teeth.

'There you are,' Its voice was male, and slick like oil.

William had no time to react. Before he could even move, the rat waved one of his fingers and roots burst through the dirt wall behind him, twisting their way towards William. They wrapped around his arms and legs, lifting him up into the air so he was at the creature's eye level.

The rat paced back and forth, inspecting William as though trying to find something.

'Do you know me, boy?' he asked.

William thought back over the last day's events. It took him a while to remember this rat's features, as most of the rats he'd seen looked very similar. There was something about his voice that William felt connected to, though.

'You're the one that spoke to the king last night, aren't you?'

The rat snickered. 'I speak to the king often.'

He stopped pacing, standing right in front of William now, his long, wet nose almost touching William's. The whiskers that sprouted from its sides were enormously long and well-manicured.

'You know me from long before that, young William. Don't you remember?'

Chills ran down William's spine.

How does he know my name?

He tightened his lips and refused to say anything further.

Again, the rat snickered to himself. He took a step back, intertwining his fingers in front of his chest and closing his eyes, as though he were praying.

'Guess I'll have to remind you,' he said, his eyes opening suddenly, the previously black and lifeless orbs now filled with a deep green light that radiated from within him. He began to whisper. The words seemed to fly around the room, filling the space with echoes, bouncing from wall to wall.

Slowly, each word appeared in William's head, as though they could float right through him. Though he couldn't understand a single one of them, he knew exactly what they were. They were the same whispers that he'd been hearing since the first night they moved into the new farmhouse, the night everything started for both him and Amelia.

Realising that all of his paranoia and misery up until this point had been caused by this powerful rat, who was perhaps even more powerful than Ealdor or Losophos, so strong that he could whisper in William's ear across great distances, William opened his mouth wide and began to scream at the top of his lungs.

'GET OUT OF MY HEAD!'

He screamed again and again, his throat raw, his cheeks wet with the tears that dripped from his chin and ran down his neck.

Finally, the rat stopped chanting, his eyes returning to the lifeless black that had previously made William uncomfortable. Now they provided him relief, because what they did when they turned green was far more discomforting.

The rat once again waved a single finger. The roots that had restrained William began to unravel themselves and crawl back into the dirt from whence they came, William lying in defeat on the floor.

'My name is Oscuro, William. You'd best keep your strength up; we have so much work to do.'

\* \* \* \* \*

Wendelmar was awoken by the sound of pained screams outside his cell. He was unsure how long he had been in his prison; the only indication of time even passing was the one meal a day he would be thrown. A bucket of rotting scraps.

While not something anyone, even a Malum, would prefer to eat, his only choices were to eat it or die. The decision had come easily to him. He did not have any intention of dying. He had been permanently disfigured on the outside; however, he still had a heart on the inside, and a family that would no doubt be mourning him, believing him dead.

He wasn't sure how it would happen, or when, but he lived on the belief that rescue would come for him sooner or later. If he wasn't ready, he would be left behind.

Crawling his way to the door, he climbed up the wall, digging his claws as far into the dirt as he could until he had a comfortable position near the barred window. It had been covered from the outside, one last sign of disrespect, as Azul believed nobody should look upon something so ugly. The rat that nailed up the board, however, did not do a particularly good job, and thus the wooden square was wonky enough that there was a small gap.

As he peered out, he noticed that the door opposite was wide open. The king's magician stood against the far left wall, his eyes glowing green, chanting some spell into the air.

To Wendelmar's shock, the magician was not torturing one of their own. He was instead working on a young boy, a human, whose face struck dread into Wendelmar's heart, causing him to scramble towards the far corner, where he sat, huddled in the dark. It was a face that was familiar to him, a face that carried some of the same features as the young girl he had tried to kill.

He'd had all the time in the world to reflect on what he'd done, since being locked in his cell, and he'd spent a lot of it thinking back to the night that everything had gone wrong. He was a simple Malum, following the order of his king, believing he was doing his people a service.

He lost his personality that night. His mind, his body, his freedom, his people, his family. He could not remember the conversation that led him to agree to commit murder, especially the murder of a human child. He wasn't sure if he had suppressed the memory for his own sanity, or if it had been taken from him by some other means, but he pondered the thought often.

In the darkness, Wendelmar sat, waiting for the screaming across the hall to end, waiting for the evil voice of the king's magician to stop and for his footsteps to head back down the tunnel from where he came.

As he waited, Wendelmar began to feel a sense of hope. The young boy across the hall could actually be the key to him escaping with his own life, and making amends with the young girl, Amelia, who he had wrongfully tried to kill.

Wendelmar heard a gentle click, as William's door was once again locked, the villainous magician beginning to proceed back down the hallway, towards his home.

Once the footsteps had faded, Wendelmar climbed back to the door, poking the tip of his snout through the tiny crack in the window and whispering into the darkness, towards William's cell.

'We will escape here together, my friend.'

# CHAPTER TWELVE

The emergency meeting was going smoother than Amelia could ever have anticipated. Everybody seemed to know exactly what the process was. All of the attendees had their chance to speak, suggesting an option to the floor, if they wanted to. Once every person had said their piece, each option was written onto a small sign, and placed above a corresponding barrel to be voted on. The final decision was made based on the percentage of votes, regardless of the outcome.

By the end of the "suggestion stage", seven different barrels stood along the length of the room, reaching from one end of the banquet table to the other. The seven suggestions ranged from sensible to outright insane, the result of equal speaking opportunity.

Highest-ranking citizens had the first say. Amelia had been the first to speak, suggesting that a small team proceed through the moon portal and bring William back. Deckard had suggested a less subtle option, recommending that The Arbour send through every available man, woman and child that could hold a weapon. His goal was to wipe the rats from the face of the earth, which would take even longer to achieve. This also came with the complication of not yet knowing if there was a way to transport any citizens through the mirror without instant death, or if Mundus itself was also protected by a magical boundary, much like The Arbour.

Ealdor, Losophos and Amelia's parents declined to offer a

suggestion, already pleased with the options available. As the hypothetical microphone was turned to the floor, all but five of the citizens in attendance also declined to put forward a solution.

The first of the five was an older man, who looked as though he might be a crop farmer, his clothes soiled, his hands worn from years of hard work.

'Why don't we just smash the thing and be done with it?'

This received some cheers from the crowd, and the option was added to the list, which concerned Amelia.

The remaining four suggestions were not particularly popular. They included doing nothing, submitting to the new Malum overlords, finding a way to flee the tree and move to a new location, and choosing one champion from within the tree to assassinate the rat king, Azul.

Once the suggestion stage was ended, they proceeded to the voting stage. This involved each person in the room picking a coloured stone out of the barrel with their preferred option written above it. The stone would then be placed into a much larger barrel that stood in front of Ealdor, to be counted by him once each person had voted. The result would be announced immediately after the count in order to reduce any doubt.

When the voting was ready to commence, Ealdor obscured the row of barrels behind a long row of curtains that seemed to fly out of his sleeve as he waved his arms about. He directed people to form a queue. One by one, they were to walk down the length of the curtained tunnel.

Amelia proceeded through first, as was her right, selecting the blue stone that corresponded to her suggestion. At the end of the tunnel, she gently tossed it into the larger barrel and returned to her chair.

She sat and observed as her parents proceeded through next, followed by Deckard, members of the guard, and lastly the general population. For close to an hour, she watched and waited, hearing the rocks bouncing as they were thrown into the end barrel, resonating through the meeting hall while the silent mass of people waited to see what the vote revealed.

When the last of the townsfolk left the tunnel, Ealdor flourished his arms again, the curtains vanishing right back up his enormous sleeves. The small barrels now appeared empty, the signs still standing above them, the large barrel filled to the brim with hundreds of coloured stones.

One by one, he removed the signs from the smaller barrels, and placed them on the ground at the foot of Amelia's table. He ushered the townsfolk to the sides of the hall, clearing a long gap down the middle of the room.

'The longest line of stones will be the choice we use! There will be no contesting the outcome henceforth.'

Stepping in front of Amelia, Ealdor bowed low. 'Princess Amelia, with your permission.'

Amelia looked across the room. Concern was growing inside her that she may not get the outcome she wanted, but it was far too late to change it now. The votes had been cast, and there were many witnesses.

She nodded to Ealdor, who turned to face the crowd, his hands rising high into the air above him, as he closed his eyes and concentrated.

The stones exploded from the large barrel. A rainbow of different colours swirled through the air above Ealdor, as the stones began to place themselves in a line before the sign they corresponded to.

Amelia closed her eyes and held her breath, her heart racing in her chest. Her fingers curled into her palms, forming fists while she awaited the result.

After a few seconds, there was a gasp from the crowd, before applause started, prompting Amelia to open her eyes and look at the result that had unfolded before her.

Relief washed over her. Four of the lines were no longer than a couple of stones. The suggestion of submitting to the Malum was the lowest, with only one lonely stone in front of it, not far behind doing nothing, and relocating The Arbour to somewhere new.

There were three clear competitors that stretched deep into the room, two of them nearly reaching the door at the far side, so far away that Amelia could barely make out the difference in their length.

A line of purple stones stopped just short of the leading two. This line was for the voters who wanted to smash the mirror, something Amelia was glad hadn't won. There was now a chance to get William back.

The longest two were Amelia's own suggestion, the option of sending a rescue party through, and a suggestion from one of the villagers, the option of sending through a lone assassin to eliminate Azul.

Amelia couldn't make out which of the lines was longer from where she sat, so she stood to get a better look. It was still too close to tell.

She quickly pushed her chair back, rushing down the steps and walking along the lines until she reached the end, Ealdor arriving just after her.

'Curious,' he whispered.

Amelia thought on the result for a moment, before turning to the hundreds of faces staring in her direction, declaring the outcome with as much enthusiasm as she could muster.

'My people, you have all spoken to me today. Each of you have had your say by casting your stone into the voting pool, and I have promised to deliver a result.'

She bent down, picking up a stone from both her own line and the line that ran next to it. She waited for a few moments before holding her blue stone high into the air so that everyone could see it.

'We will be sending in a small team to rescue my brother.' The room erupted into thunderous applause for a moment, until she threw her other hand into the air, causing the applause to die down for a moment.

'And that team will also attempt to assassinate Azul!' she screamed as loudly as she could, feeling fierce as she stood in her armour.

The people she served all cheered in celebration and support, all but Ealdor, who remained behind Amelia, his concern at the resulting tie showing clearly on his face.

\* \* \* \* \*

The last of the villagers had only just left when Amelia next had the chance to speak privately with those she trusted most. Ealdor, Deckard, Keaton and her own parents were all who remained in the hall. Losophos had politely refused the invitation, explaining that he was working on something that would be vital to the mission's success. He instead asked Amelia to join him in The Archive the following morning, to which she agreed.

The group congratulated Amelia, praising her for the wisdom she displayed in her announcement at the unexpected draw.

'Who do you intend to send through in this team?' Ealdor asked rather glumly.

Amelia looked at the faces that sat around her, all of them eager to hear who she had chosen as her champions.

'Well, your military training puts you at the top of the list, Deckard,' Amelia said, to which Deckard nodded in acceptance.

'I would do it gladly, my princess.' He bowed. 'And who would be coming with me?'

'I have thought on it from the moment William was taken, and there are only a few that I trust enough to complete this task, with all the complications it may offer.'

The group remained silent, their eyes fixed on Amelia.

'You may require someone who can fit into tight spaces, someone you have worked with before, and someone to think with emotion, so I would also name Keaton as one of my champions.'

Keaton stood and bowed.

'I won't let you down, Amelia,' he said, before returning to his seat.

Amelia locked eyes with her father, remembering her earlier discussion with Amity.

'You will need someone who has a connection with William, someone he will listen to, and someone who won't give up, no matter how desperate the situation, so I name my father, Lyall, as one of my champions.'

Even though he didn't have to, he stood and bowed to Amelia, thankful that she had listened to their advice.

'Don't worry, sweetheart. We'll get him back.'

She smiled at him for a moment, before Deckard interjected, clearing his throat.

'Forgive me, Princess, but it is my recommendation that we have a team of four. This will make it easier to split up into pairs and achieve both tasks simultaneously. If we assassinate Azul first, they'll know we're there, and we will surely never get close to Master William. And again, if we rescue Master William first, and they notice him missing before we can get to Azul...'

'I agree,' she replied. 'Which is why I'm coming with you.'

Deckard and Keaton reacted as she had expected, both offering her looks of confusion. It was Deckard who spoke first, Keaton quickly accepting that he wouldn't be able to change her mind.

'Princess, please. Your father and I can hold our own. I can see your logic in deciding to send Keaton, but to put yourself into such a dangerous position... What if something were to happen?'

The worry in Deckard's voice reminded Amelia of the previous evening, when he had told the story of William's abduction. It gave her chills.

'Deckard, I have the ability to sense the ring that William hopefully still has with him. I understand that you don't want me putting myself in danger, but with my help, we'll be able to find him in no time at all. Besides, we aren't even sure we'll be successful in transporting you and Keaton outside of The Arbour. We may be lucky, and there may still be magic surrounding the rat city from the old days of trade, but if the worst happens, there will need to be more than one of us who can leave unharmed. Would you instead have me send through both of my parents to their potential deaths?'

Deckard played with the thought for only a moment.

'Surely another could wield this power. Please, send Ealdor or Losophos in your place. It's not worth risking your life for your brother.'

His last words took Amelia by surprise. A lump immediately formed in her throat, and she felt a deep, burning anger.

Deckard could see that he had upset her.

'Princess, I'm sorry if I caused offence, I was only–'

'It's fine,' she said, standing and striding to the top of the stairs, coming to a pause as she looked into the empty hall.

'I don't expect everybody to understand why I feel I must go with you, but the reasons are crystal clear in my mind. William is my brother. He's the only one I've got, and I love him. When I first heard that I was going to be a big sister, I was sad; I didn't want somebody else to come along and take my parents' attention away from me. I was young and stupid, and I couldn't have been more wrong.'

Amelia turned back around to face the table, walking slowly up to it as she spoke.

'The moment I saw William's face, I knew that I loved him, that I would always love him. Rather than jealousy, I felt responsibility. To make sure he was safe and happy. To make sure he was loved.'

She placed her hands on the table and leaned into them. Her eyes focused on its surface as she felt her mum's hand rest on top of her own.

'That's the thing about siblings, Deckard. They come in many different shapes and sizes. Some are always close, some grow old having spent most of their lives not talking to each other, and some... some share a bond strong enough to rival that of best friends, even soulmates. I imagine it's hard for those without to appreciate the connection siblings share, so I understand your hesitation, but this is deeply important to me.'

She pulled her hand out from under her mother's, touching the brooch on her chest, tracing its outline with her fingers as her eyes grew wet with tears.

'I would give my life for my brother. I accepted that the moment I first saw him, and I've been reminded of it every time I've seen him since. I failed to protect him, which is why I need to go and bring him back.'

Amelia wiped the tears from her eyes, looking around the table to see that her mum and dad had also begun to cry.

'You're right, Princess. I do not understand the bond between siblings,' Deckard said. 'But I understand love. If it is your wish to join us, I will not question it further. I just ask that you take some time to prepare yourself. It will be dangerous.'

Amelia nodded silently, glad that he had begun to understand.

Ealdor stood from his chair, the scraping of its wooden legs on the stone floor capturing everyone's attention.

'Don't worry; she will be prepared. I will see to it personally.' He shambled across the hall, towards the exit. 'I will see you in The Archive tomorrow morning, Amelia. Much to do!'

Keaton stood next, approaching Amelia with Deckard following close behind. He bowed, before whispering a goodbye and proceeding down the steps towards the door.

Deckard and Amelia now stood before each other. Amelia thought she could see some red in the hulking giant's eyes, after her speech.

'We will each need our own time to prepare. I suggest we make our attempt through the moon portal in two nights' time, when the garrison surrounding the mirror can be fully supported.'

Amelia took a moment to consider it, knowing that if they went through before they were ready, it might end poorly, but still wishing they could leave that very night.

'Agreed,' she said, watching as he bowed and turned away.

She felt herself relax slightly as the door clicked shut behind Deckard, knowing she was alone with her parents. She took a seat at the top of the stairs. After a moment, she heard their chairs moving, followed by footsteps approaching. They joined her atop the steps, one sitting on each side of her, placing their arms around her back and saying nothing for a time, until Amelia excused herself, returning to her room, where she sat for the rest of the afternoon, sketching drawings of William.

# CHAPTER THIRTEEN

It was another clear morning when Amelia arrived at The Archive. She had seen Keaton on her way out of the castle, though he was busy training with Deckard. Not wanting to interrupt, she decided to get into her cart and try her hand at driving herself.

It had begun rather clunkily. She had narrowly avoided a few stalls and shopfront displays on her way out of the town, but as she reached the open fields and grasslands, the empty roads gave her time and space to practise further, proving to be exactly what she needed. It helped that Samson had a mind of his own and knew where to go.

She pulled the cart to a stop near the shoreline, dismounting not quite as gracefully as usual, her body still getting used to the reasonably flexible armour. After untying Samson, she walked over to The Archive door and descended the staircase towards the main room, moving with purpose and enthusiasm. She quickly spotted Ealdor and Losophos sharing words around the table. They greeted her as energetically as they could, but she could tell that they were exhausted. The two of them had probably been in discussion, or, more likely, creative argument, for most of the night.

'Good morning, Amelia.' Losophos offered her a grin.

'Good morning.' She smiled at them both politely, before getting to the topic at hand. 'What progress have you made? Have you thought of the best way to mount our offensive? A spell? A potion?'

Ealdor chuckled quietly to himself. 'Potions and spells would certainly help, but that isn't what we've been discussing this morning, Princess. In fact, we have a bit of a problem, and we aren't sure how to go about solving it.'

Amelia pulled a chair out from the table, sitting down as she awaited the news.

Losophos was the one to speak next, Ealdor producing his pipe from his sleeve. 'Ealdor and I have been speaking through the night. We both agree that striking against Azul will be our best chance at ending this war forever, but that does come with its difficulties, the biggest one being we cannot guarantee that the moon portal will still be open by the time you've found William and dealt with the vile king.'

Amelia nodded. She hadn't foreseen this problem. She had been focused on the tasks, not escaping safely once they were done.

'And what solutions have you come up with?' she asked.

Ealdor and Losophos shared a quick glance.

Losophos continued, 'We have only identified one option that provides great promise. But you may not like it.'

Amelia grabbed the sides of her chair under the table, bracing herself for what she was going to hear, unsure exactly how bleak the odds were.

'We think that your best course of action would be to destroy the mirror from the other side, as soon as you go through. It may be the only opportunity you get.'

Amelia had expected to hear something crazy, but not quite that bad.

'And then how do you suggest we get back?' she asked. 'Dad and I can survive outside The Arbour's boundary, but we don't know how far it stretches into the rat city, if at all. Keaton and Deckard could be vaporised as soon as they take three steps in that place. Even if we could solve that problem, we don't know how far the city is from The Arbour. The journey could take days and would be extremely dangerous at that size.'

'I did say you wouldn't like it,' Losophos said, pushing a book across the table towards her. 'But we've at least solved one of the problems.'

Amelia inspected the pages that lay open before her. She was unable to read the handwritten script, but focused on the sketches, which reminded her of the three gems she wore in her crown, although these weren't in a crown. They were in rings, much like William's.

'What does this mean?' she asked, pushing the book back towards Losophos.

'It means, Princess, that we have solved the problem of getting people outside the boundary, though we can only do it for three at a time. This passage explains that if the rubies from your crown are transferred into three rings, the wearers of those rings will, theoretically, be able to proceed beyond the boundary without effect. The blood used to form those rubies was from the outside world, and it seems the spirits of the dead mean to protect us once again.'

'Well, that is good news,' Amelia said. 'But we don't need all three. Dad and I can already survive on the outside.'

Ealdor grumbled quietly, blowing a puff of smoke from his mouth before speaking.

'That is where we come across the next problem, Amelia. The mirror cannot be destroyed by brute force alone. It is a magical object and will require a great deal of magic to dismantle.'

Amelia looked confused.

'What are you saying, Ealdor?'

'I'm saying that I must be one of your champions. It's the only way to ensure the mirror's destruction.'

Amelia sat in quiet contemplation for a moment, thinking on all the news that had been laid out before her.

'Agreed,' she said. 'On one condition.'

Ealdor looked at her, wondering what condition she could possibly enforce over him.

'Once we proceed through, you should be with us while we search for William. When that is complete, you can return to the mirror with

William and my dad. If it is still open, you are to send them through, after which you will destroy it. That will no doubt get the attention of the rats, which should give us some time to achieve our secondary goal.'

Ealdor frowned.

'But, Princess, you may need my help with Azul. As soon as I destroy the mirror, every rat nearby will be upon me and I won't be able to get to you.'

Amelia smiled a sad sort of smile, not one intended to bring joy.

'The people of The Arbour need you more than we will. Once the mirror is destroyed, you are to begin your journey back to the tree on foot. We'll catch up with you later. This is my wish, and the only condition of you becoming one of my champions. Do you accept?'

Ealdor pondered the idea for a time. He drew several puffs from his pipe, blowing smoke out of his lips moments after, before he responded.

'You have my word,' he said, bowing slightly in his chair. 'Now if you will excuse me, I must prepare.'

He got up, extinguishing his pipe before placing it back up his sleeve, saying a farewell to Amelia and Losophos, and making for the door.

Once the echoing footsteps up the staircase had ceased, Amelia looked once more at the book Losophos had shown her, inspecting the illustrations.

'Will it damage them?' she asked, reaching up to touch the red stones on her head.

'Not as far as I can tell, Princess. I should be able to restore them once you return.'

This relieved some of Amelia's discomfort. She had worked hard for the rubies and the crown, and did not want to damage such precious things.

Losophos cleared his throat.

'There is one more thing, Amelia.'

She looked at him with sad eyes, unsure if she could bear any further complications.

'I will need to enchant your brooch with an additional spell to ensure you don't revert back to your usual size upon leaving the rat city. Not only would it make you a large target for the assassins' poison weapons, but you would also risk crushing any companions with you, should it happen unexpectedly.'

Amelia thought on this for a long while.

'How long will it take?' she asked, her voice quiet.

'I will need to take the crown and the brooch from you before you leave here today.'

She nodded slowly, reaching up and taking the crown off her head, placing it gently on the table between her and Losophos. She was more hesitant to relinquish the brooch, her only possible means of locating William, but eventually she removed it from her corset and set it beside the crown.

'Be careful with them, please,' she said, feeling as though she had just offered up all that was dear to her in the world.

'You have my word, Amelia. This will take most of my power and will be time-consuming; you must ensure that I am left alone in peace. I will meet you at the portal before you leave.'

'Very well,' she said. Quietly, she stood from her seat and, feeling naked and alone, walked out of The Archive and back to the company of Samson.

* * * * *

Before returning to the castle, Amelia decided to take a detour and have some time to herself, stopping at the small pond that Keaton had shown her in the days prior. She wasn't sure if she was making the right choices. Nor did she think they were wrong; she just wondered why nothing felt good.

The day remained quiet as she sat in silent contemplation, staring into the small body of water, wondering what it felt like. Deciding that she wanted to soak her feet in its depths, she removed her shoes and pulled the fabric of the bodysuit up to her knees, before sitting on a small patch of grass that sprouted beside the water. The cool liquid felt good on her legs, and she took great comfort in the gentle sun that shone down from above.

Amelia wasn't sure how long she'd been there when she was startled by a sound not far from her, the sound of someone approaching, footsteps getting clearer as they came closer to the pond.

She waited silently, following the direction of the noise, until the top of the person's head appeared over the grass. She smiled and breathed a sigh of relief as she saw Keaton walking in her direction. His face was red with exhaustion, his arms bruised and sweaty.

'Keaton!' she yelled, and he jumped at the unexpected voice.

He looked up from the ground and saw her sitting by the water, a grin forming on his parched lips as he picked up his pace, quickly arriving at the pond.

'Amelia. What a surprise to see you here! I tried to find you earlier, but you'd obviously left already. I saw the cart missing and figured you'd gone to The Archive.'

She smiled at him as he placed the bundle of gear he was carrying down on the ground, perching himself next to her.

'What brings you here?' he asked.

Amelia leaned further back, her head resting on a clump of dirt as she stared up into the sky.

'I just wanted to relax,' she said. 'Who knows when we'll be able to do this again?'

She turned her head to look at Keaton, who was gazing into the water.

'And what about you?' she asked. 'What brings you here, brave knight?'

He nudged her as she giggled at him, embarrassed that he'd been caught looking so exhausted.

'I wanted to relax too. I've been training to fight all day. I don't reckon I'm any good with a sword.' He rubbed his arms, wincing when his fingers brushed the lumps and bumps that had formed.

'You'll get better,' she said, sitting upright again and placing her hands on his arm. 'Besides, with any luck, you might not even have to fight anything.'

He continued to stare into the pond, his hand meeting hers.

'Yes,' he said, 'I hope that's true. It doesn't make it any less scary, though, and anyone who says they aren't afraid is lying.'

Amelia reached up and gave him a kiss on the cheek.

'I suppose you're right,' she whispered. 'Although there's nothing wrong with being scared. It just might save your life.'

Keaton smiled at her.

'You know what would save my life right about now?'

Amelia was confused, watching as he stood up and walked behind her.

'What?' she asked.

She heard him throw something on the ground, before his footsteps began to race towards her again. She ducked as he ran right past her and leapt into the pond in a blur of skin and cloth, showering her in droplets.

As he resurfaced, he flicked his hair back, smiling at her once more, his face rejuvenated by the pond's gentle caress.

'A swim!' he shouted, before ducking back under the water with a splash.

Once he was sufficiently cool and relaxed, Keaton swam to the shore where Amelia sat. He rested his arms on the ground beside her, laying his head down on them as he looked at her and asked the question he had been avoiding up until this moment.

'What if we get there and Will isn't... you know... okay?'

Amelia turned towards the castle. She had thought about this before, but it didn't make her feel any better hearing it come from someone else. She simply didn't know how to respond. It was incomprehensible that William wouldn't be okay, that he was now suffering, or had already suffered, at the hands of Azul.

She looked Keaton in the eyes, and with a fire in her voice she had never heard before, she said four words that she hadn't expected, four words that made her question how far she was really willing to go.

'We make them pay.'

# CHAPTER FOURTEEN

Amelia, Lyall, Deckard, Keaton, and Ealdor all met in The Archive, in order to go over a plan for once they were inside the mirror. Losophos was also present; however, he was only there to help them find documents and offer advice, as he was busy crafting the rings they would need to survive in the outside world.

They sat around the Tablet of Sunt Vitae, while Losophos stepped out of the shadows and laid out a large map on the table, one that Amelia had studied previously in her lessons with him.

The map was crudely sketched in an ink that had begun to fade with age, but it was clear enough for them to read. It was drawn out like a blueprint, showing the outlines of buildings and points of interest, under which was written "Mundus".

'Even the name sounds filthy.' Deckard scoffed.

'Not that it matters,' Amelia interjected. 'Remember why we're here. William needs our help. The longer we sit around complaining about the rats, the more danger he's likely to be in.'

Deckard straightened his back. 'I apologise, Princess. I did not mean to offend.'

'It's okay. Let's just focus on this for now.' She leaned further over the map, inspecting it in detail, pointing to the spot she had been looking for. 'Here,' she said. 'This is where the mirror will put us out.'

The map showed a small, rounded platform, off which a long wall ran towards the much larger fortress.

While everyone inspected that spot on the map, Deckard pointed towards another.

'There's the dungeon,' he said. 'That's likely where they'll be holding Master William. If this map remains accurate, we should have a straight shot across the lakeside, up to the dungeon.'

'*If* it remains accurate?' Lyall asked, with concern in his voice. 'Where did we get this from, anyway?'

'This map was drawn by Azul himself,' Losophos said, 'when he was under our care in The Arbour, before greed turned him into a monster.'

For a few hours, the group studied the map further, pointing out where hidden paths ran alongside cliffs, where guards were likely to be patrolling, and where they were most likely to find Azul.

Once they felt sufficiently prepared for the routes they would each take once in Mundus, they all left The Archive. Each of them agreed to meet up again for a feast in the main hall that would go late into the night, so they could sleep through much of the next day and save their energy for the night-time incursion.

Before they separated, Deckard pulled Lyall aside, shaking his hand.

'Sir, I am honoured to have been chosen for this mission alongside you and your daughter. However, I don't think we've ever been formally introduced. It would assist with communication if I could call you by your name and not refer to you as Amelia's father, or sir, unless that is what you desire.'

Amelia looked to her dad.

'Deckard,' he said, laughing, 'you're right, I'm sorry I didn't introduce myself sooner. You may call me Lyall, both on our mission and after. You have at least earned that right.'

Deckard bowed to him. 'Thank you, Lyall. We shall see you at the feast.' He jumped into his cart, where Keaton was awaiting him, and they hurried off towards the town.

Lyall rejoined Amelia, who was waiting for him in her own cart, and flashed her a smile. 'I guess we can call that meeting the parents.'

Amelia blushed, embarrassed, as Lyall cracked the reins.

\* \* \* \* \*

The tailor rushed out to greet Amelia and Lyall when they pulled up outside his store, causing as much of a commotion as possible, so that passing villagers would see the princess in his shop.

'Good afternoon, Princess, sir,' he said, bowing as low as he could.

'Good afternoon.' Lyall beamed. 'Are you ready for me?'

The tailor looked at Lyall as if to say "Are you kidding me? I've been waiting all day!"

'Of course, sir. Please come in, please, this way.'

Together, Amelia and her father stepped into the tailor's shop, a small room that was filled from floor to ceiling with materials of every kind, including some Amelia had never seen before. The walls were an eclectic rainbow of colours, some vibrant, some dull, with pastels and even a bit of fluoro mixed in.

Amelia sat in a very comfortable chair in the far corner as the tailor pulled Lyall into a curtained section. She giggled loudly, listening to her father's protests and moans of discomfort while the tailor dressed him in his new attire.

When he stepped out from behind the curtain, Lyall looked very much like Amelia did. The bottom layer of his outfit was a fitted bodysuit, black in colour, with hard pieces of wooden armour covering all the important areas, like the knees, groin, chest, and shoulders.

Amelia broke out into laughter at the sight. She had never seen her dad in anything quite so ridiculous, but if it did its job to protect him, then it was worth the strange looks he would get when they stepped out the door.

\* \* \* \* \*

It was well into the night when the whole group was reunited in the main hall of the castle. Amelia felt bad for the matron and her workers, who were putting on the late dinner. However, all of them understood that it was for an important cause.

Before the group dug into the feast that lay before them, Deckard raised a toast.

'Tomorrow, we venture forth into the unknown. It will not be an easy journey; we may not all make it back. However, for now, we are all members of one team, with one purpose in mind. I propose this toast to you, Princess Amelia, and to each member of this group. A group that the townsfolk have chosen to name Amelia's Argonauts!'

He raised his glass high up into the air, followed by every person at the table.

'Amelia's Argonauts!' they all shouted in unison, before bringing their glasses to their mouths.

The adults were sharing in a particularly old drop of wine, which Deckard also allowed Keaton to try. Amelia agreed to share in one sip for the toast, but she still didn't feel quite right about drinking more than that, due to her age and the importance of their mission the next night, politely refusing a refill.

The group ate and drank late into the night, sharing in stories and songs once they had eaten their fill. It must have been the early hours of the next morning when they all agreed to retire to bed, hugging goodnight before they left for their own chambers.

It was an important thing for the group to have done. They had indeed grown into a very close and cohesive unit after sharing so much with each other.

Before Amelia and her parents could make it back to their chamber for the night, Losophos caught them in the hallway, asking to address Amelia in private. Once Amity and Lyall had departed, Losophos reached within his coat and pulled out Amelia's brooch, which gleamed in the glow of the nearest torch.

'Princess, I have completed the additional enchantment as we discussed. There is now no risk of you returning to full size upon leaving Mundus, unless, of course, you want to, at which point all you will have to do is remove the brooch.'

Amelia grabbed the brooch from Losophos' hand and held it close to her chest.

'I must warn you, though, there was not time to include more than the one enchantment, and I'm afraid that it can only be used once. As soon as you choose to remove the brooch, the spell will end forever, so you will have to pick the right time.'

'Thank you, Losophos. I will try to keep that in mind.' She flashed him a grateful smile. 'How goes the work on the rings for Ealdor, Keaton and Deckard?'

Now looking hurried, Losophos said, 'I have what I need. They will be ready before you step through tonight. Now go and rest, I have much to do.'

Without another word, Losophos scuttled along the hallway back from where he had come and left Amelia to join her parents in their room.

As Amelia sat in their window and looked fondly towards Keaton's, she thought on the success of the day. They had a solid plan, each of them had protection of some sort, and they could all call each other a friend.

She smiled as she watched candlelight flicker in Keaton's room, wondering what he was doing, catching the occasional glimpse of him at his desk whenever the breeze nudged his curtains aside. Her room didn't allow such a clear view, but she would've preferred to be there regardless, if the clean-up effort wasn't still underway.

Amelia stared at his window and daydreamed until the first colours of dawn began to spill over the top of the trunk that surrounded them. She closed the curtains, changed into her pyjamas, and lay on William's bed. The dark room caused her to fall asleep very quickly, and she dreamed of her brother, wishing with all her heart that they would find him and he would be okay.

# CHAPTER FIFTEEN

The time had come. The moment that the group had been preparing for was upon them, and as the sun began to set on the world, they rode out of the castle courtyard in a line of horses and carts. Deckard was in pole position, followed by Lyall and Ealdor in his rickety cart. Amelia and Keaton rode at the rear with Samson. They were flanked on all sides by Arbour guards, many of whom were new recruits who had only recently graduated, their first military experiences coming in a time when they would be desperately relied upon.

As the convoy proceeded out of the castle gates and down the town's main street, the people who lined the sides of the road began to cheer, many throwing flowers and confetti, sending their champions off with all the love and support they could afford to show.

Once the convoy had exited the hustle and bustle of the town, they picked up speed drastically, riding towards the outer wall with a noble purpose in mind and heart. Within the hour, they were upon the wall, the mirror-topped spire now in sight, the small bridge dangling between. As each of the five champions traversed its length, they found comfort in the solid stone support of the castle spire.

The round roof was completely surrounded by guards, easily two dozen of them, who clearly expected some sort of retaliatory incursion from the other side, should Ealdor fail to destroy the mirror in time.

Standing before the dark side of the mirror was Losophos, a small wooden box in his hands.

'Good evening, Princess, and her Argonauts,' he said, placing one hand across his stomach and bowing low.

'I still quite like that!' Lyall said enthusiastically, rolling the phrase over in his mouth a few more times. 'Amelia's Argonauts.'

Losophos stepped forward, opening the lid of the box to reveal three rings, each composed of fine white branches and adorned with a single ruby. Amelia did not like seeing her crown butchered and split into several pieces, but for the purpose they were required to perform, the sacrifice was worth it.

Keaton, Deckard and Ealdor all stepped forward, each claiming a ring and placing it on one of their fingers, the rings shrinking or growing to fit them.

'A few notes of warning before I leave you, for I need rest,' Losophos said, clicking the box shut and placing it deep into his robe. 'These rings will allow you to walk the world outside The Arbour, theoretically, for as long as you should like. However, you must be extremely careful. If you take the ring off, damage the ruby, or are killed by other means, your body will disappear as though you have stepped outside the boundary of our tree, and we may never be able to get the ruby back. So please be careful, and don't tarry. I wish you luck.'

With his warning completed, Losophos walked past the group, carefully stepping along the bridge they had only just traversed, leaving them alone with the guards atop the tower. A slight breeze gently nudged the tree's leaves every few seconds, but other than that, the air was quiet. The group stood watching the night sky as they waited for the moon to rise higher and show its face amongst the clouds.

Keaton and Deckard stepped closer to the mirror and turned to face the remaining three.

'Princess,' Deckard began, 'when the portal opens, allow Keaton and I a few seconds to proceed through and take care of any guards.

Once it is clear, I will signal for you through the mirror. It will be safer this way.'

Amelia nodded to Deckard, before moving her gaze to meet Keaton's, whose eyes were only just visible through the small slits in his helm. She knew him well enough to see that he was nervous, although she would be lying if she said she wasn't nervous too.

Before long, the clouds shifted enough that moonlight was allowed to reach the mirror's surface. Unlike the sun portal, which rippled like water when it was activated, the moon portal looked markedly sinister. Its surface appeared to be covered in shifting liquid spikes, reminding Amelia of a science experiment she had done at home in the past, using magnetic ferrofluid.

'On me, Keaton,' Deckard whispered, as though the sound of his voice might travel through the mirror.

Ealdor, Amelia, and Lyall watched on as Keaton and Deckard silently stepped towards the mirror, eventually becoming shrouded in the black liquid and disappearing.

A few seconds passed with no signal, then a few more.

'Do you think they're okay? Maybe the rings didn't work?' Amelia whispered to Ealdor, before the top half of Deckard's body rippled through the mirror, his face appearing above his shoulders, as he beckoned for them to follow him through.

Cautiously, with Amelia leading, the remaining three stepped through the thick, liquid surface of the moon portal, holding their breath as they passed from one world to the next.

The first thing Amelia noticed was the air. It wasn't light and clean like in The Arbour; this air was warm, putrid, and thick, and every breath felt like it required twice the effort she was used to.

Amelia opened her eyes and inspected her surroundings, taking in as much as she could. The sky was dark, the moon barely visible through the tangle of branches and vines that arced high over their heads; only faint columns of light found their way to the mirror's surface on this side, but they were still enough to activate it.

Hearing movement off to her side, Amelia turned to see Keaton struggling to pull a body away from the mirror, its details hidden in the darkness, but its shape undeniably a rat's. Deckard moved over to help, the trail of blood from the side he was on indicating that he had already disposed of his target.

'You did well, boy. Don't lose your nerve,' he whispered to Keaton, who looked up to his father, seeing behind him that Amelia was now here.

He resumed dragging the body as he grunted out the words, 'Yes, sir.'

When the pair had finished hiding the body, they returned to the main group, all five now inspecting the dark cityscape before them. The place wasn't as civilised as The Arbour, nor was it as clean. Hundreds of small houses dotted the landscape, each one appearing to be made from sticks and mud, tiny domes that would do well to shelter more than two full-sized rats each. Far in the distance was a much larger, neater structure, composed of mud and stone, the looming silhouette resembling a fort.

Beyond the structures in every direction, and enveloping the entire area with a confronting darkness, was an enormous dome that stretched from each side of the city, reaching high up above the ledge where the group now stood. Like the smaller houses, the dome appeared to be made from sticks, leaves and other natural debris. The rough composition of the dome meant that there were many gaps that allowed the moonlight to beam down upon the filthy city within.

With much of the outside world blocked from view, it was impossible for any of them to determine where they were currently located in relation to The Arbour. However, given the size of the dome that contained Mundus, it was either somewhere well out of view of the yew tree, or it was exceptionally well hidden.

Each member of the group stood upon the ledge before the mirror, inspecting some dark corner of the world. Deckard was the first to find his bearings, remembering key details from the map, his eyes following the ledge they stood upon, which curved up towards the fort in the distance.

'It seems they weren't expecting us quite so early,' Deckard said, turning to smile at Ealdor, who did not share his optimism, offering a cautious response.

'Or perhaps they were.'

Without responding, Deckard turned back to face the city.

'We've all studied the same map,' he said, pointing towards the fort. 'We must avoid the main halls there, but to the left side is where the dungeon should be, the only place a rat would see fit to imprison one of our own. The quickest way would be through the main streets. However, that would leave us unprotected and easily spotted. I suggest we sneak around the perimeter here...' He motioned towards the outskirts of the city on the left, where it rested on the shore of a murky lake. 'It will take a bit longer, but it should be the quieter and safer route. Are we in agreement?'

The remaining four all nodded, each of them eyeing the dangerous world they were now fugitives in.

As she scanned the horizon in search of the dungeon, Amelia suddenly remembered that she could attempt to find William now that they were through the mirror. Raising her hand to her brooch, she closed her eyes, blocking out all that was around them, focusing on William and the ring that he hopefully still wore.

Her heart raced as she began to feel something. It was small at first, but when she focused on his face, it grew stronger. Relief washed over her as her fears were extinguished. William was still alive. He still had his ring, or at least some living creature did, and now they knew where to go. The mission so far was going as smoothly as they could have hoped.

'He's over there,' Amelia said, pointing in the direction that Deckard had already suggested the dungeon would be in.

'Quickly, then,' Deckard said, stepping off towards the lake. 'Let's get this done before they notice those two are missing.'

Amelia looked into the darkness behind the mirror, the surface of which was still shifting and oozing. She couldn't see the bodies of the guards they had already dispatched, but she knew they were there, the first casualties of their incursion, and hopefully the last, save for Azul.

They killed two of ours, now we've killed two of theirs.

Amelia and her Argonauts silently crept around the lake, keeping as far from the dark mounds that stood on the outskirts of the rat city as they could without falling into the murky waters on their left. The city was extremely dark; the only light was very faint moonlight, whatever managed to pierce the thick brush that blanketed the area.

The darkness made for a slow and treacherous journey, but eventually, they managed to reach the base of a stone outcrop. Its top looked to be a large dirt mound. Where the stone met the dirt, there was a ledge that connected to the main fort structure. On top of the ledge was a large set of double doors.

Amelia once again attempted to reach out to William, the brooch confirming that he was somewhere deep inside the outcrop that stood before them.

'I don't like this,' Deckard whispered. 'There are no guards. In fact, we haven't seen a Malum the whole time we've been here, apart from those two near the mirror. This stinks of a trap!'

'It may not be ideal, but it's all we've got to work with, so let's just get in there and worry about a trap later, if we stumble into it,' Ealdor whispered back. 'We need to hurry.'

Before anybody else had the chance to move, Keaton raced up the cliff face effortlessly, years of exploring the tree having shaped him into an adept climber. Slowly, the remaining four clambered up the cliff, Deckard struggling the most in his heavy armour, but still managing to pull himself over the edge and onto the small plateau.

Keaton had already pried the doors open slightly and was peeking down the corridor that stretched before him. It was so long and dark that he could not tell its true size, but the echoes of his companions' movements rebounded far into the mound, indicating that finding the correct cell might not be as easy as they had hoped.

As Amelia stepped into the corridor, she took a moment to let her eyes adjust. Ahead was nothing but darkness, the walls and ceiling dripping wet mud. Very small holes along the length of the roof allowed for a miniscule amount of moonlight to shine through, which did naught to help them see.

On the wall near her face, Amelia could make out the silhouette of what looked like a wooden torch. The ash-tipped stick was ice-cold to the touch, probably having not been used in centuries, due to the rats' eternal fear of fire, hence why the city was so dark at night.

Amelia pulled the torch free of its holder, handing it to her father, who was confused by the gesture.

'I don't have a lighter,' he whispered.

'No, silly, just hold it still,' she replied.

She concentrated and pictured the torch, whispering, '*Ignis.*'

It came to life in Lyall's hands, the charred tip igniting in a burst of colour, causing him to drop it into the wet mud.

The group stood in silence as the torch sizzled out, the sound of it echoing deep into the darkness. They waited for any signs of movement from deep in the mound, but none came.

'I didn't know you could do that,' Lyall said, finding Amelia's face in the dark.

She smirked, prying the torch from the other side of the wall and handing it to him. 'Don't drop it this time.'

Once again, she spoke the spell and the torch flickered to life, illuminating the corridor that stretched on before them. As far as the light reached, they could see the walls lined with door after door at regular intervals, each featuring a small window filled with bars.

Amelia shuddered to think that her little brother had been imprisoned here for any time at all, let alone a few days. The idea filled her with anger, and she began to walk down the corridor, whispering loudly as she went. 'William! William, where are you?'

The rest of the group followed after her, the taller members poking their heads into the windows of the cell doors, trying to see what each room hid. Ealdor had lit a few more torches, the ambient light spreading and helping them to see the world more clearly.

The tunnel seemed to stretch on for an eternity.

'We'll never find him like this!' Amelia grunted. 'He could be in any one of these cells!'

She leaned against the wall, her arms crossed in frustration. She wasn't sure exactly how long they had been searching, but the dull ache in her legs indicated to her that it had been quite some time. Her fingers played with the brooch on her chest, an idea forming in her head.

'Deckard, place that torch down and carry me,' she ordered.

'Princess, I think it would be more useful if we kept moving,' he replied, continuing to walk from cell to cell.

'Trust me. While you carry me, I will search for him with the brooch and give you a live update of his direction. We can walk or run straight down the corridor without slowing to check every cell, and without fear of missing him.'

Deckard stood still for a moment, before handing his torch over to Keaton. He scooped Amelia up into his arms, nodding to Keaton, who started to walk further into the corridor.

Amelia concentrated on William and the ring as they delved deeper into the dungeon. The connection she felt grew steadily stronger as they twisted and turned through the labyrinthian corridors.

They had been walking down the same corridor for a long time when Amelia started to feel the direction of the ring turning slowly to her left. Up ahead, the light from the torches illuminated a wall, the end of the corridor.

As they reached it, Amelia pointed directly to the cell door on the left side. Deckard placed her back down on the ground and moved forward to inspect it. The door had a large iron locking mechanism, something that was not easily picked. However, the wooden door was compromised by years of rot.

Lyall stepped up to the door. Holding a torch up to the bars, he tried to see into the space, to look for any sign of William, but he could not make anything out. Without a word, he began to kick at the door, breaking rotten chunks off it with ease.

After a few minutes of kicking from Deckard and Lyall, the entire bottom half of the door was gone, having splintered into a thousand pieces. They ducked under the top half, which remained held in place by the iron frame, disappearing into the cell.

'William!' Amelia heard her father call out. 'William, are you okay?'

His footsteps rushed deeper into the cell, and Amelia heard his hushed words as he spoke to William, although she wasn't quite able to make out what he was saying. A pit formed in Amelia's stomach. Then a knot in her throat. Then heat from behind her eyes. Every second without a word from Will coming out of the cell further added to her anxiety. Just one word from the voice she knew to be her brother's would ease every bit of pain she currently felt, but for what seemed to drag on for an eternity, the pains within her grew until she could barely draw breath into her lungs.

Ealdor, Keaton and Amelia stood silently in the corridor, each straining to listen to the events taking place just beyond their sight. The next thing they saw was a pair of legs climbing up the few steps under the door. The legs reached the door, and then Lyall ducked under it once again, this time carrying William in his arms.

Amelia was relieved to see him, but his eyes were closed, surrounded by deep purple circles. He was shivering and terribly pale, despite the warmth and humidity of the atmosphere.

Deckard stepped out of the cell next, the group now reunited, with their prize in hand. The only thing on anybody's mind now was escape.

'Does everyone remember the plan?' Amelia asked. 'Once we get back out of this dungeon, we all split up. Ealdor, you take Dad and William to the mirror and try to get them back through, then destroy it and head for home. Deckard and Keaton, we'll make for Azul's chamber and try to deal with the beast. Any questions?'

Everybody had remembered their tasks, and before they started to navigate their way out of the tunnels, they offered each other a quick pat on the back, and a gentle 'Good luck.'

As they turned towards the way they had come, about to proceed back into the darkness, a noise came from the cell opposite William's, as though someone was leaning on the door, causing it to groan.

All eyes turned to the poorly boarded-up window in the door. From a crack of darkness beneath it, a snout poked out, its lips moving fervently as it spoke in a voice that sent familiar chills down Amelia's spine.

'You'll never make it out.'

# CHAPTER SIXTEEN

Deckard pushed his way to the front of the group, drawing his sword and thrusting it into the black space where the mouth had appeared, narrowly missing Wendelmar's face as he ducked to the side.

'Silence, foul creature!' Deckard shouted, pulling his sword back and sheathing it once more.

The snout appeared through the gap once more, this time in a more cautious fashion.

'You'll never make it without my help,' Wendelmar said. 'That you found this place at all can only be explained by magic. I can smell it on you.'

His nostrils widened as he breathed in deeply, grinning.

'I remember your smell too, little girl. I've thought about it every day since our encounter, since you saved me and set me free.'

Amelia gasped, stepping out from beside her father and approaching the door.

'Are you... the one who tried to kill me in my own home?' she asked.

The snout drooped, a frown forming on its lips.

'I'm afraid I am. My name is Wendelmar,' he said, withdrawing back into the darkness. 'I've had all the time in the world to think about that night since I returned and was imprisoned here, unlucky enough to survive the flames so I could go on to feel Azul's wrath.'

Amelia placed her hand on the door, Deckard pulling his sword partway out of its sheath as she did so. She waved for him to relax, but he continued to stand at the ready.

'Why would Azul punish you?' she asked, peering into the cell window.

'Ah, the naivety of youth,' Wendelmar said from somewhere in the shadows. 'I failed to kill you, the girl who stood between Azul and his prize. A prize whose worth I myself have begun to question.'

Amelia felt sorry for the poor creature. She thought back to the night when she had defended herself in her kitchen while home alone, hitting the rat into the open flames of the hearth, scooping his burnt body off the stone floor and cooling the wounds in the sink before freeing him. Had he really had a change of heart? Or was it all just another game that Azul had created for them?

'What did you mean when you said we wouldn't get out of here without your help?' Amelia asked.

Wendelmar's snout poked through the hole once again. Now that Amelia was closer, she could make out some areas of burnt skin where the hair no longer grew, his remaining whiskers coiled and thinned.

'I'm not sure how you found the little master's cell so easily, but I imagine you weren't clever enough to leave behind a trail. Did you pay attention to the path you were taking as you came deeper into this place?'

Amelia looked up to Deckard, then to Ealdor and her father. They were all glancing at each other and shaking their heads, realising that their best-thought-out plan still had gaps in it.

'Precisely why you will need my help,' Wendelmar continued. 'I know how to get you out of here. In fact, I know a passage that will lead us straight to the outskirts.'

Deckard leaned in close to Amelia, whispering in her ear so that Wendelmar wouldn't hear.

'We can't trust him. He is one of them!'

Amelia thought for a moment, wondering if the best course of action might be to just leave the rat to his fate and attempt to find their own way out of the dungeons. After all, she had already saved him once before.

'Why would you offer to help us?' she asked. 'What do you stand to gain from this?'

Wendelmar's snout was no longer in the crack, but his voice emanated from the gap, reminding Amelia of the night he had hidden in the darkness of her kitchen.

'I wronged you once, yet you saved my life. You may think us to be untrustworthy creatures, but allowing me to return what I owe you would help ease my troubled soul. It would do me well to be rid of this place.'

Amelia thought on his proposal for a time.

'You're not seriously considering this, are you?' Deckard asked, upset at the idea of working with their enemy. 'He will turn his back on us at the first sign of trouble. You can't–'

'Break down the door, Deckard.' Amelia interrupted him mid-sentence, not wanting to hear any more of it.

'But, Princess,' he pleaded with her, as the rest of the group remained silent and watched on.

'Break it down. We have no time. If he leads us into a trap, kill him first.' She walked back towards her father. He was still holding William, who remained unconscious.

Although he hesitated for a moment, Deckard began to beat down the door. The wood was damp, much like William's, so it was an easy task for him, the bottom half quickly disappearing.

'Come out, creature,' he barked. 'You heard the princess. At the first sign of trouble, you will taste my sword.'

Slowly, Wendelmar emerged from the dark cell, his familiar snout appearing first, followed by his face, black eyes peering around at the crowd in the corridor, wincing at the flaming torches.

'Keep the torches at the front of the group,' Amelia ordered. 'They fear fire. And this one has more of a reason to than most.'

Deckard and Keaton followed her command. Once they'd moved away from the cell door, Wendelmar stepped out further, his full body now visible in the flickering light. Amelia inspected him from snout to tail. The extent of his burns was overwhelming. He no longer resembled a rat in the traditional sense. His body was lacking any hair, save for a few strands on his face and snout. Patches of his skin were still red and irritated, weeping in areas that he'd been unable to tend to effectively in the blackness of his cell.

Amelia's eyes became wet with tears as she looked upon the figure she had mutilated.

'I'm so sorry I did this to you,' she croaked, the lump in her throat making it hard to speak.

'This was my own fault. Do not let it weigh so heavily on you, child.'

He stood back on his hind legs, stretching as high up as he could for the first time since being confined to his cell. At his tallest, he stood above Deckard's height, which would've been intimidating, had he not appeared so frail and sickly.

'How long did it take you to get here? We should not tarry. I fear the longer you remain here, the higher your odds are of being detected.'

Ealdor now addressed the rat, speaking in a more kindly fashion than Deckard had.

'We came through the portal a few hours ago. Some of us mean to head back there now, as fast as we can. Will you show us the way?'

Wendelmar inspected each member of the group from head to toe.

'What do you mean, some of you?'

'The boy and his father aim to head back through the portal. I intend to destroy it once they are safely through.'

'A wise choice for your people... and what of the other three in your group?'

Ealdor looked to Amelia for approval to speak of their secondary mission, and she nodded.

'The others intend to eliminate Azul.'

Wendelmar's expression changed to one of confusion.

'And how exactly do the three of you plan to kill Azul?'

'With fire,' Amelia said, the coldness returning to her voice as she thought back to his attack on The Arbour.

Wendelmar sat back on his hind legs, itching at a scarred spot on his thigh.

'Has any one of you ever seen a Rat King before? Even heard about them?'

Deckard and Ealdor looked to each other, Keaton and Amelia doing the same.

'Well, it's just a normal rat, isn't it?' Keaton asked. 'Maybe one that's bigger than the rest?'

At this, Wendelmar scoffed.

'I fear you may not be adequately prepared for the task you are about to undertake.' He leaned forward, his arms and face close to the ground in front of him as he began to etch a picture into the mud.

'A Rat King is not just one single rat, one larger, stronger rat, as you suggest...' His claws drew the outline of a rat, its long tail twisting far behind it. 'A Rat King starts to form when multiple rats become intertwined with each other, the tangle of their tails proving too much for them to get out of.'

Wendelmar sketched another rat, then another, and another, until there were eight of them in a circle, their tails all reaching into the centre, where they tangled together in a messy clump. 'One by one, they start to die off.' He drew crosses through the silhouettes, one at a time. 'Some may die of starvation, some may die of wounds inflicted as they fought. Some simply can't handle the boredom of being forever attached to the corpses of those who died before them, opting to end their own lives...'

At this point, Wendelmar had struck out seven of the eight rats. 'When there is only one left alive, he is crowned the Rat King. He regains whatever strength he lost, as others begin to respect him and bring him food, water, comforts. This Rat King is blessed with power, but cursed to remain attached to the rotting corpses of those who weren't strong enough to beat him.'

The group looked sickened by the story that had been shown to them in the dirt.

'Disgusting creatures,' Deckard whispered.

Keaton stepped closer to the drawing, placing his torch carefully on the ground before approaching the rat.

'But what if another Rat King begins to form while there is already one in power?'

Wendelmar drew another collection of rats to the side of the original one.

'Should that happen, the new tangle will be taken to the current king and their tails are entwined into his. Should they outlast him, they will be crowned the new king. However, by this point, the king will have gained a following, so people tend to support him more than the usurpers.'

'So, you're saying it's likely Azul isn't alone?' Amelia asked.

'Precisely,' he said. 'You will be safer at a distance. Azul's reach is limited by the length of his tail; he's stuck in that tangle whether he likes it or not, only able to step as far as his balcony. Behind the balcony is a large curtain, and behind that curtain lies the pile of rats who didn't make it. Some newer additions were still barely clinging to life the last time I saw it.'

'Then we set fire to the curtain and let it fall on them. Give them no chance for escape,' Deckard added.

Wendelmar nodded.

'That would be your safest option. A word of warning, however. Although you now know what a Rat King truly is, most people don't have the stomach for that sort of thing. I would not recommend peering through the curtain. The sight that awaits you is not one that is easily erased from the mind.'

'Very well,' Amelia said. 'Let us keep moving for now. Once we escape these corridors, we will go our separate ways.'

Keaton returned to the front of the pack, collecting his still-flaming torch from the ground as they began to move at speed through the winding corridors, Wendelmar directing them at every turn. Eventually, they reached the long, dark corridor they had entered through. As they began to see the faint glow of moonlight through the still-open doors, they threw the remaining torches down into the mud, the sticks extinguishing with a *hiss*!

Pushing back out into the quiet night, the group halted on the ledge outside the dungeon.

'This is where we part ways,' Amelia said, walking over to her dad and giving him and William a long hug. 'Be careful.'

'You too, my sweet. We'll see you back at home,' he replied, before striding up to Deckard. 'Look after her. If she doesn't make it back, neither do you.'

Deckard straightened his back, meeting Lyall's gaze.

'From one father to another, you have my word.'

They nodded at each other, before Lyall returned to his position near Ealdor.

Wendelmar remained by himself, resting on all fours. He looked to his left, where Amelia, Keaton and Deckard stood. He raised himself to rest on his hind legs, addressing them as a group.

'Tread lightly, friends. It comforts me to be on your side of this battle. Should you manage to start the fire, I would not recommend dawdling. Forgive the pun, but there will be an army on your tail, and they will be determined for revenge.'

Amelia stepped up to Wendelmar, resting a hand on his snout.

'Thank you for your help, Wendelmar. You kept your promise and saw us safely out of the dungeons. You owe us nothing further, but I would ask you one favour.'

He stared into Amelia's eyes.

'What would you ask of me, child?' he whispered.

'That night you attacked me, you found your way home in the darkness, did you not?'

Wendelmar shifted his gaze to the thickets of branches that arched high above the city, the moon still piercing through in scattered places. He knew what she was going to ask before she said it.

'Should the mirror be closed when you all arrive, would you guide my father and brother safely back to the tree? I would owe you a debt, which I intend to pay in full when I return.'

Wendelmar turned to look at the group who were bound for the mirror. Lyall was clearly growing fatigued from carrying William for so long.

'I will,' he said, turning back to Amelia. 'You rescued me from my prison. I will see to it that your family is returned safely.'

With that, Wendelmar joined Lyall, catching one last glance at Deckard, who raised his sword from its sheath slightly, to warn Wendelmar what would happen should he betray them.

'If you hear the mirror shatter before you have lit the fire in Azul's chamber, run for your lives,' Ealdor added, before turning away and heading off with his group in the direction of the mirror.

Amelia watched for a brief time as half of her Argonauts, along with an unexpected new companion, proceeded down the cliff and along the banks of the lake. She drew in one deep breath before turning away and re-joining Keaton and Deckard, who were already sneaking further up the plateau, towards the heart of the fortress.

# CHAPTER SEVENTEEN

Lyall, Ealdor, William and Wendelmar were most of the way around the bank of the lake when Lyall began to stumble. The exhaustion of carrying William's unconscious body for so long had begun to set in, and his pride was now the only thing pushing him forward.

As they trotted along mushy dirt that sloshed under their feet, Lyall's steps began to fall shorter, his heels sinking further into the mud the longer he stayed in one spot. Finally, his body gave way, and he fell to his knees, still holding William in his arms, which now rested on his thighs.

Ealdor and Wendelmar heard Lyall fall.

'You needn't carry him on your own. I can share the load,' Ealdor said, moving towards the pair with his arms outstretched.

'No,' Lyall said, panting, 'you need to save your energy for the task you still have yet to do. I only need a moment.'

'Perhaps I may be of assistance,' Wendelmar said. 'We are not far from the mirror. If you place the young one across my back, you will be able to rest, and as a group we can move faster.'

Lyall thought on this proposal for a moment, eyeing Wendelmar from head to toe.

'I still don't know if I can trust you,' he said. 'I only just found out that you tried to kill my daughter. How do I know you won't do the same with my son?'

Wendelmar nodded, before retreating slightly and sitting on his hind legs.

'Perhaps you are right to not trust me. It is true I attempted to kill your daughter. However, I believe that there may have been other powers at play behind that decision.'

Lyall looked into Wendelmar's eyes, confused.

'What do you mean by that?' he asked.

'Well, as I said to your daughter in the dungeons, I have had the curse of time to think on my mistakes while I sat in the darkness of my cell. I've wondered time and time again what it was that convinced me to accept Azul's mission, yet when I think back to the days before my attempt on her life, I cannot remember much, only bits and pieces. You see, like you, I am also a father, and I would do anything to protect my children. With that comes the mutual responsibility to protect the children of others, including those from other species.'

Wendelmar turned his head away from the water, peering towards the mess of stick-and-mud houses that sprouted up from the ground in the distance.

'I believe there were darker powers behind my decision, and I do not believe it was my own. I am of the opinion that Oscuro, the king's right hand, and a dark magic user, played with my thoughts in order to fulfil Azul's plan.'

Ealdor crouched in the mud, entranced by Wendelmar's story. 'I'd heard rumours of Malum magic users, but never have I seen evidence to support those claims. If what you say is true, The Arbour may be in greater danger than we thought.'

Ealdor got to his feet again, looking towards the mirror. There was still no sign of movement in the darkness that surrounded it.

'You can be sure there is magic in this place,' Wendelmar said, addressing Ealdor directly. 'It's what is currently draining the young master of all energy. Check him for yourself.' Wendelmar waved his hand towards William.

Ealdor cautiously approached Lyall, who gave him a nod of approval before he placed his hand on William's head, closing his eyes and his mind as he searched inside the boy's own.

After a few moments, Ealdor shouted and jumped backwards, falling on his back in the mud.

'It's true,' he gasped. 'Master William's mind is swirling with dark magic. We must get him home so I can begin to undo the damage. Quickly now.' He grabbed Lyall's wrist and pulled him towards Wendelmar, encouraging him to use the rat to their advantage. 'Quickly, we haven't much time, and I fear that Oscuro now knows of our presence here.'

Lyall groaned as he lay William across Wendelmar's back and hurriedly wiped the mud from his legs.

As the trio began to run the last distance that separated them from the mirror, a bright flash of green light exploded in the air high above the city. The trail it left behind indicated that it had originated from high up in the fortress.

'Oscuro,' Wendelmar said. 'We must hurry. Their entire army will be upon us soon.' He pushed through the ache in his frail limbs and his run increased to a shocking speed.

Ealdor and Lyall began to lag behind, but using as much energy as they could muster, they maintained a steady distance between themselves and Wendelmar.

'Sorry,' Lyall shouted, 'did you say *army*?'

Before Wendelmar could reply, he was cut off by several spears landing in the mud to his side. Wave after wave of spears flew through the air from within the dark city behind them, narrowly missing them as they ran and dodged their way up the last small hills before they reached the wall that the mirror was built on.

Wendelmar leapt up the wall in one quick movement, careful not to lose William off his back in the process. Ealdor used his magic to rise the entire height of the wall effortlessly. Lyall was left alone on the ground below them, quickly scaling the wall, finding this relatively easy due to its rough construction.

When they had regrouped at the top, Lyall was relieved to see the mirror remained open. Grabbing William from Wendelmar's back, he ran towards the mirror, stopping just before it to address Ealdor one last time.

'Thank you, Ealdor. Wendelmar.' He gave them both a nod before stepping through the vibrating black liquid and disappearing from sight.

Ealdor took a step back from the mirror, facing it head on.

'You heard the plan,' he said. 'Once I destroy this foul instrument, we run!'

Wendelmar called, 'You focus on that, but make it quick. I'll hold them off for as long as I can!'

He ran towards the opposite end of the wall, where there was a series of small barricades and worn-out guard posts. As he climbed the few steps to the top of the guard post, he could see a mass of black, writhing shadows approaching from the fortress.

'My God,' he whispered to himself, 'there's thousands of them.'

Thinking quickly, he began to chew holes into a few barrels that were stored below the guard post. Dark liquid poured out onto the stone wall as he backed up towards the mirror.

When he was only a few metres from where Ealdor stood, he threw the barrels down on the ground and watched them roll back along the wall. He stood in silence, listening to Ealdor whisper magic words to the mirror, as he stared along the bridge into the darkness, waiting for the mass of warrior rats to approach their now-trapped victims.

Ealdor had no idea of the danger that was headed their way, focusing on the mirror with every fibre of his body and mind, reaching out into the gloom around him and feeling its magic touch. He blocked out all sound, as spears continued to connect with the wall they stood upon, splintering on its hard surface.

Reaching out to the life within the plants and trees surrounding the area, Ealdor directed all of his energy, and what little he could borrow from the flora, into the mirror's surface.

'Aduersus praecipio tuis,' he whispered. 'Aduersus praecipio tuis.'

With each incantation, his voice grew louder, chanting again and again until he was screaming at the top of his lungs. Though he was howling with a deafening level of volume, his words were drowned out by thousands of footsteps, thundering all around him.

He continued despite his inevitable demise moving in closer and closer, roaring the words one last time, a smile forming on his lips as he watched a crack appear in one of the corners of the mirror.

* * * * *

Amelia, Keaton and Deckard had been sneaking along the many narrow ledges and parapets of the fortress for some time, drawing closer to their secondary mission. From the height they had achieved in their climb, they were afforded an ideal vantage point over the rat city, trying as hard as they could at regular intervals to spot where the other half of their group were, unable to see in the darkness.

As they neared the largest section of the fortress, looking down into the courtyard below to see a few patrolling guards, they were surprised by a blinding flash of green light that seemed to come from the very walls behind them. The light spread out over the entire city, and for a split second, they were able to see the other four members of their group, very near to the mirror, but still treading through the muddy banks of the lake.

They stood in silence, watching as the light faded, until they could no longer make out the shadowy figures. Ducking down below the edge of the railing they were following, they heard the footsteps of many thousands of creatures rushing out into the city from what must have been a barracks to the side of the fort.

Seizing the opportunity to move about the area without fear of being heard, the trio ran the last length of the parapet, before dropping down onto a balcony that jutted out of the side of the main hall.

As they walked through the hall's dark entrance, they were overwhelmed by a stench that neither Keaton nor Amelia had ever had the displeasure of smelling before.

'What is that?' Keaton whispered in disgust, waving his hands in front of his nose.

Deckard held his finger up to his lips, before pulling Amelia and Keaton in close to him.

'That is the stench of death,' he whispered. 'Tread carefully.'

The three would-be assassins crept deeper into the hall, examining the carved walls and floors, making sure not to bump into or trip on anything.

'There it is,' Amelia whispered, pointing above them to the far end of the hall. Halfway up the wall, there was a balcony that ran the width of the whole room. A large, tattered curtain shielded whatever was behind it from view.

But they already knew what was behind it; they had at least that advantage. They knew what to expect from the Rat King, and they knew the limitations it placed on Azul's freedom of movement.

With all the courage they could muster, they quickly tiptoed to the end of the room, where the balcony ran above them. Casting each other one last glance, they began to scale the wall. Keaton and Amelia climbed up a length of stone carved in a spiral from floor to ceiling, providing them ledges to grab with their hands and supports for their feet. Deckard found a length of rope off towards the centre, using it to pull himself up the wall, walking sideways slowly so as to not make any noise.

Keaton and Amelia reached the balcony first. Hauling themselves over the banister, they rested on the ground for a moment to catch their breath and allow Deckard to regroup with them.

As they peered into the balcony, they could now see the curtain in greater detail. There were many holes in its surface, each revealing a deep black darkness behind, which seemed to shift and move ever so slowly in some places. The curtain was secured along the roof by a length of rope so thick that it may have been larger than even Deckard's torso.

Once he had made it to the balcony and joined Amelia and Keaton in the dark corner, Deckard used hand signals to motion that Keaton was to keep a look out along the left side of the curtain, while he watched the right.

When they were in position, Amelia stood from her hiding spot and walked to the centre of the balcony, facing the curtain. She raised her hand to her brooch, and searched for William, to ensure that they had made it through before she triggered any further alarms. Unable to feel even the slightest tingle, she smiled to herself. She gave Keaton and Deckard two enthusiastic thumbs-up to indicate that she was about to start.

Once again, she closed her eyes, although this time she pictured the curtain that stood only a stone's throw away. She focused on the two ends of the thick ceiling rope, seeing the dry, frayed bundles in her mind, and whispered her magic word.

'*Ignis*.'

She waited for a moment, before opening her eyes. The room remained dark; no flame had sprouted from the rope. She closed her eyes once more and tried again, whispering her word and opening her eyes. The result was the same.

*I'm too far away*, she thought, embarrassed that she was being watched by Deckard and Keaton as she failed to do the job she had volunteered for. She took a few steps forward, Deckard raising his hand for her to stop once he thought she was getting too close.

As she closed her eyes and focused on the rope once more, the silence that had surrounded them was pierced by an unearthly noise like the shattering of glass, although amplified a hundred times over. A few seconds later, once the shattering had stopped echoing throughout the world, there was the sound of a large explosion, and a flash of orange light glowed into the room from the balcony door they had entered.

Behind the curtain, something began to move. The fabric waved and rippled about as though it was being touched from the other side. Deckard and Keaton simultaneously ran away from the curtain, reaching Amelia together.

'We have to leave!' Deckard hissed, grabbing Amelia's arm and yanking her towards the balcony.

'Stop!' Amelia shouted, causing Deckard to release her and halt in his tracks. 'I have to finish this.'

Deckard's eyes darted from Amelia to Keaton to the exit, his mind conflicted, but as he recalled Lyall's warning that if Amelia didn't make it home, neither would he, he stood in front of her and braced for what was inevitably going to appear.

'Well... well... well...'

The voice came from behind the curtain. It had a deeply sinister tone, and filled every space in the hall, bouncing from one wall to the next.

'I was wondering how long it would take you to mount a retaliation, though I never once thought you might be foolish enough to come here yourself... Princess...'

# CHAPTER EIGHTEEN

The voice hissed the last letters of the word princess, so that the "s" sound carried on for some time, as though it came from the jaws of a huge serpent.

As Keaton, Deckard and Amelia watched the curtain, from the centre the fabric began to jut out, as though something was pointing into it and continuing to move forward.

The figure's legs were revealed first, followed by his long, hairy snout, an evil grin sprouting below it that revealed few teeth, and copious amounts of drool, which dampened the fabric as it dragged over his face. The wetness also caused the crown atop his head to glimmer in what little light there was. It wasn't anywhere near as beautiful as Amelia's had been, and it was so small that it almost looked comical on Azul's giant head, but it was a crown nonetheless.

'I suppose that if you want a job done right, you have to do it yourself,' he continued, his whole body now revealed before the curtain, which fell back into place behind him. Only his tail continued on beyond it, a tail that Amelia thought must be exceptionally long, as it still wasn't being pulled taut at the distance it had already covered.

Keaton shuffled across so that he was now beside Amelia. Reaching out his hand, he grabbed hers and held it tight, squeezing it to remind her that whatever they were about to do, they would do it together.

'How romantic,' Azul whispered. 'Which one shall I kill first? Who would suffer the most by watching the other die?'

Deckard ripped his sword from its sheath in a spectacular fashion and charged towards the beast, sword raised high above his head, screaming.

'Why don't you start with me, you foul creature!'

When he was only a few steps away, Deckard swung the sword sideways at the height of Azul's head, hoping to cleave it from his shoulders. However, at the last moment, Azul ducked out of the way, causing Deckard's sword to miss him completely, and instead slice a great cut right through the fabric that hung behind him.

With a movement too quick for Deckard to react to, Azul slammed his body forward into Deckard's, sending him flying backwards, landing hard on the ground in front of Amelia and Keaton, skidding almost to their feet.

Faster than Amelia could blink, Keaton unsheathed his own sword and ran at the king. Again, Azul lunged towards Keaton as he drew nearer, though he was nimbler than Deckard. Using his size as an advantage, he ducked under Azul's front legs and slid along the floor, guiding his sword so that it traced along the rat's chest while he passed under.

Amelia watched the creature, expecting him to recoil in pain, or howl in agony, or give some other sort of reaction, any reaction at all, but by the time Keaton had returned to Amelia's side, none had come.

Azul chuckled and inspected the thin red line that had appeared within his fur.

'You think this hurts me?' he bellowed, resting on his hind legs as he wiped a paw over the trickle of blood. 'I have endured pain which none of you could ever imagine. I have beaten more powerful foes than any of you. You are but babes, and I am a king. I doubt you have the stomach to do what it takes to rule; I doubt you truly understand the price of power. Once I defeat you, you will take your place under my feet, a further reminder of my strength.'

Azul reached for the curtain draped over his back. With a mighty pull, he ripped it from its stitching. It fell to the ground as silently as a leaf in autumn, kicking up a cloud of dust, which briefly obscured the vision of all within its vicinity.

As the dust cleared, Amelia could see that Azul remained standing at full height, studying the faces of the three insurgents as they began to take in what was revealed beyond the curtain.

Wendelmar had warned the group that looking upon the Rat King would be something they would never be able to forget, but this had done nothing to prepare them for the reality of the image now burning into their memories.

Amelia's eyes followed the king's tail where it ran under the curtain and continued on into the space behind. After what must have been a whole metre, it began to discolour from pinkish brown, and became a pale, fleshy lump where it was trapped, intertwined amongst the knotted and rotting tails of the rest of the Rat King.

The mound behind Azul was an image of true horror. There were dozens upon dozens of rats, all in various states of decomposition. At the bottom of the pile were the oldest, and the first to join with the Rat King, now nothing more than hollow grey shells, as though they had been mummified. There were distinct layers above the initial pile of corpses, where Azul had been challenged by brave or foolish champions who thought they could best him. At the very top of the heap were a few rats who looked to be only a couple of days dead. The chests of two or three could be seen rising and falling ever so slowly, as they clung to the last of their life.

Amongst them was a clear hollow, a depression in the pile of corpses that appeared to be just large enough for Azul to curl up and lie upon. A literal deathbed.

A grin of pure evil spread across Azul's features as Amelia's eyes shifted back to him. To her left, she could hear Keaton retching. She too was close to that point, but thought it best to not show any weakness before such an unpredictable and resilient enemy.

'As you can see,' Azul sneered, 'I have indeed proven my strength over the years. It has cost me much, including my ability to use magic, but where that emptiness grew, my strength flourished.'

He drew himself up, stretching to his full height.

'So, I challenge you now, little girl. Come at me with a weapon, strike me down with your best jab. If you defeat me, I will give you my crown, and you can rule Mundus as you claim to rule over that tree. However' – he raised one finger in warning – 'if I beat you, the deal is reversed. You must give me your crown, and I will rule over both cities however I wish.'

'I'll never let you!' Amelia shouted. 'We came here to kill you, and I intend to do just that. Not only for the two soldiers your men killed the other night, nor even the attempt on my life, but for thinking I would just allow you to take my brother and receive no punishment. You may be strong, you may be powerful, you may be one of the most hideous things I have ever seen in my life, but I am not scared of you, and I am much more than just a little girl.'

As Amelia spoke, Deckard, the brave fool, ran at Azul again. This time, Azul didn't rush at Deckard, nor shy from his swinging sword. Instead, he took the full force of the blade in his left arm. It sliced through as though Azul's flesh were not there, but met with a hollow *thud* as it stuck itself in the bones of his very arm. As this happened, Azul grabbed Deckard by the throat with his other arm and held him high in the air. The ease with which he did this made it appear that Deckard weighed no more than the sword itself.

'Well, now we have another choice to make,' Azul said, with gleeful energy. 'Submit to me, or watch this old fool suffocate.'

Amelia couldn't see Deckard's face, as his back was to her, but she could see him struggling at the clawed hand around his throat, trying with all his might to get another breath of air.

From her side, Amelia felt a rush of moving air as Keaton lunged forward towards the rat with his sword pointed straight at the monster's torso. As Keaton ran ever closer to his target, Azul flailed his free arm, which still had Deckard's sword protruding from it. It was a flurry of hair, blood and metal.

Keaton feinted to the side when he took his penultimate step and leapt up as Azul's arm swept the ground under his feet. With a ringing sound that shocked the ears, Keaton's sword connected with Deckard's, knocking it free of Azul's arm, the length of the sword clattering to the ground at Azul's feet. Several globs of blood followed and landed on the tarnished blade.

This time, a flash of pain showed on Azul's face. And he fumbled, dropping Deckard to the ground in front of Amelia.

A thought came to her as she watched Keaton cautiously backing away from Azul, towards Deckard. She remembered a battle that Losophos had described to her during one of their lessons, one that involved no weapons, no blood, no physical prowess. It was a battle of the minds, a fight to overpower your enemies' thought, to bend them to your will through mental suggestion and, if needed, cause them to destroy themselves.

Not knowing how to initiate this, Amelia acted on instinct alone. She dove deep into her mind, to the same place she found her power when using her words of magic. Using that seemingly infinite pool of energy, she pushed it towards Azul with all the hostile intent she could manage. For just a moment, one tiny, fleeting moment, she felt the touch of his mind. It was enormous, powerful, and hungry for more.

As she tried to cling to the feeling of his mind, a tidal wave of thought sloshed through her head. Azul had turned her weapon against her. She trembled as the energy filled her head and fought with her limbs, Azul's thought manipulating her brain into betraying its own body.

'Give me the crown.'

The words ricocheted between Amelia's ears. Azul's mouth hadn't moved. His voice was now in her head. He had control. She stepped forward, though she hadn't meant to.

'Give me the crown.' The voice in her head spoke with more force and desperation.

Again, she stepped forward. She was trying with all her might to stop her body acting independently of her own conscious thought, but Azul was too strong. As she took another step, her hand raised up to her chest height, to where her brooch took pride of place. She was going to hand Azul her jewel, and with it, her power, though she did not want to.

It had been quiet since Keaton's attack. He had reached Deckard and helped back him away from Azul's feet, and now he was noticing the change in Amelia, who was gazing doe-eyed at the king. He saw her continue to step forward, now reaching for her brooch, and he knew something wasn't right.

Keaton glanced at Deckard, who gave him a knowing look, and together they rushed at Azul, Keaton with his sword, and Deckard with his bare hands.

Keaton swung his sword over his head and brought it crashing down into Azul's side. The thick fur blocked most of the damage from Keaton's attack, his sword bouncing off the Malum and connecting with the stone floor, sending a shower of sparks high into the air. Though it didn't appear to have damaged him, the attack had served its purpose. Azul's concentration broke, and Amelia's body woke from its trance.

She had made a decision before she could even weigh up her options. Their lives were in grave danger, and she couldn't afford to be entranced again. She raised her hands high above her head and closed her eyes.

'Surrendering so easily?' Azul exclaimed, chuckling deeply as he swiped at Deckard, who was ripping chunks of hair from his side. 'You're as pathetic as I had hoped. Now give me the crown.' He sounded slightly desperate, stepping towards Amelia in anticipation of his reward.

Amelia blocked out everything beyond her own body, focusing once more on the rope above the curtain, and on the shrouded pile of the Rat King. Mustering all the anger she had suppressed, she let it flow through her now, feeling every part of her body tingle and burn.

When she opened her eyes, they were no longer filled with fear. They were angry. Her usually green eyes had been transformed into swirling fireballs. Azul's face changed from a sneer into a look of horror, as his focus was broken by the swirling flames.

'You want your crown?' she screamed towards Azul. 'I'll give you a crown of fire!'

Without having to speak the word, Amelia pushed her hands forward, and exactly how she'd pictured, at both ends of the rope, and in the darkness behind the fallen curtain, three flames sparked to life.

From the Rat King came the sickening screams of burning Malum, as the last living competitors attached to the pile were scorched where they lay. Azul tried to run at Amelia, his coiled tail stopping him as he lunged for her.

She stood and watched him coldly, as the rope on the ceiling burnt all the way through, and the flaming chunks fell down to the ground like fiery meteors, covering Azul's body. He screamed, an unearthly sound, as the smouldering clumps stuck to his filthy fur and begun to blaze wildly.

In a sheer panic, the king looked all around himself for a means of escape. His eyes settled on his tail, and without another thought, he threw himself to the floor and began to chew through it in an attempt to free himself.

Amelia could feel herself losing consciousness as the energy she used to light the flames pulled her further away from the waking world. The last thing she saw was one of Azul's clawed hands reaching for her through the smoke and flames.

# CHAPTER NINETEEN

The rat city sprung to life as Keaton and Deckard carried Amelia out of the fortress. Peering over towards the mirror, all they could see was fire. A long row of flames spread from the very end of the wall, where the mirror once stood, now a withered frame with no swirling liquid within its boundary.

At the closest end of the wall was an army of dark shadows. Many, covered in flame, ran against the crowd, desperately trying to extinguish themselves before they were burnt to a crisp. This of course only added to the chaos, as any unfortunate body they brushed against would also begin to squirm in pain when the transferred flames licked at their flammable, furry skin.

There was no sign of Ealdor, and they could not tell Wendelmar apart from any of the other hundreds, if not thousands, of rats from this far away. They turned towards the back of the fortress and ran towards the city boundary, hoping to get out unnoticed, as they would never be able to outrun an angry rat.

When they reached the perimeter of the domed world, they looked back on the fortress. The structure remained solid; however, from its highest windows spilled a black, putrid-smelling smoke that contained the ashes of many dead rats, including Azul's.

Deckard placed Amelia down for a moment, resting her head on Keaton's lap. He unsheathed his sword, and began to swing wildly at the thick layer of branches and bush that separated them from the outside. The cacophony from the other side of the city did well to cover the *snap* and *crack* of breaking sticks, although Deckard did not relax even the smallest bit, as any ears close enough would easily come upon the desperate party.

Once he had carved a hole large enough for the three of them to slide through one at a time, he sheathed his sword, ushered Keaton through and pushed Amelia out of the dome, before crawling through himself.

Upon leaving the barrier of the tree, Keaton and Deckard both felt a painful tingle in the fingers they wore the protective rings on. Their mortality was now painfully clear, and they knew that they were no longer under the protective spell of The Arbour, the connections between both worlds having been shattered with the mirror, and the magic of Mundus deserting them as soon as they left its walls.

'We can't stop yet,' Deckard groaned, picking Amelia up and placing her over his shoulder once more. 'We must get some ground between us and Mundus, then we can figure out which direction to head in.'

The pair ran for as long as they could, barely able to see where they were headed. The faint moonlight did little more than offer faint silhouettes of the surrounding landscape as they pushed through thick layers of branches, grass, and leaves, not able to differentiate one tuft of grass from any other they had passed.

Keaton was ahead of Deckard when he tripped on the end of a root that was sticking out of the ground, landing heavily in the dirt, his helmet bouncing off his head and disintegrating into nothing.

Deckard and Keaton looked at each other, the rare expression of fear returning to Deckard's face.

'Be careful, boy,' he whispered. 'Anything that separates from our body appears to suffer the effects of leaving the boundary, just as was described to us. Take each step as though your life depends on it.'

They pushed on through the darkness for what felt like an eternity, before they came upon a large tree that shot up into the night sky, higher even than the home they were used to, The Arbour. The tree had small holes amongst its writhing roots, one of which was large enough for all three of the fleeing insurgents to comfortably lie in, covered on all sides but one in thick mounds of dirt.

Deckard sat awake after he had placed Amelia down, allowing Keaton to lie next to her and keep her warm. Now that they had left the rat city, the air was as cold as they had ever felt it.

Keaton fell asleep quickly. He had never experienced such a long night. After many minutes passed, and Deckard was satisfied that they had not been followed, he too gave in to the sleep that forced itself upon him.

\* \* \* \* \*

Several hours had passed since the party had journeyed through the mirror, bound for the rat city. Lyall stepped back through the portal, this time with William in his arms, much to the surprise of the patrolling guards. They jumped at him with weapons drawn, before realising who he was, and apologising profusely.

He did not even stop to speak with them, opting instead to run straight across the bridge to the inner wall of the tree, carefully treading down the spiralling staircases that took him to the bottom, where he knew transport would still be waiting.

Relief came quickly when he spotted it. Amelia's cart was there, the spectacular white horse still hitched to the post, its nose buried in the feeding trough.

Lyall placed William gently down on the passenger side of the cart, secured the horse to its front, and with a loud *crack* of the reins, urged the cart forward, turning it around and heading along the outer road to The Archive.

It was no speed record, but he arrived as quickly as he could, guiding the cart past the small body of water and right up to the tree wall. He remembered that the entrance was somewhere around here, hidden amongst the cascading vines, but he could not see it.

He leapt down from the cart, pushing aside vines in search of a door, but still there was none. He grew frustrated, kicking the trunk with all his might. The sound of his boot connecting with the thick wood changed as he moved from spot to spot, becoming hollow, as though there was a void behind where he last kicked.

Paying particular attention to the spot that sounded hollow, he kicked it again and again, until finally, it swung open, Losophos appearing from within the shadows behind the door.

'You made it back, Master Blackwood?' Losophos said, still groggy from sleep.

'I have William with me. He needs your help!' Lyall shouted back. He ran to the cart and once again carried William in his arms, taking care not to hit the unconscious child's head on the doorway as he stepped through.

He followed Losophos down the dark staircase into the equally dark chamber of The Archive. Losophos hurried down a row of shelves that disappeared to the right, Lyall keeping up as well as he could.

'Place him down over here,' Losophos said, pointing to a small nook carved into the wall. A basic mattress and some blankets made it appear quite comfortable.

Lyall did as he was told, placing William down on top of the makeshift bed, stepping back as Losophos moved in to inspect the child. He watched in silence as Losophos looked over William's body, clicking his tongue and mumbling quietly to himself. When he finally stood up again, he walked quietly over to Lyall, who was sitting on the ground, leaning on a bookshelf, half asleep.

'Ealdor detected a dark magic in his mind. I couldn't think where else to take him. Is there anything you can do?' The words fell from Lyall's mouth without thought, between his raspy breaths. Now that he was safe, the adrenaline from the night was beginning to wear off, and it left him feeling exhausted.

'He will be alright, but it will take time. Best to leave him here.' Losophos bent over and grabbed Lyall's arm, helping him get to his feet. Lyall looked back towards William. He felt relieved that his son was back in the safety of The Arbour, but now his worry turned to Amelia.

Losophos ushered Lyall to the double doors at the base of the stairs.

'Your wife needs you now, Master Blackwood. She must be unimaginably terrified, wondering in the lonely darkness who, if any, of her family will return. Go to her and rest, if you can.'

The hidden door closed behind Lyall after he stepped out of it, and he jumped back onto the cart, once more following the road back towards the castle, where Amity would be awaiting his return.

As he passed the stairs that came down from the mirror, he saw that all the guards who were supposed to be up on the tower, guarding the portal, were now walking down, not far from the base of the tree.

Lyall pulled the cart to a stop, the wooden wheels grinding to a halt on the dirt road.

'Why have you left your post?' he shouted to them.

The guard closest to the bottom hurried his descent, running towards the cart once he had reached the ground.

'Sir,' he said, panting as he caught his breath, 'the portal is closed. The surface has cracked.'

Lyall turned towards the spire.

'Very well. Carry on,' he said, and he cracked the reins again, the cart moving forward once more.

When he entered the courtyard of the castle, Lyall removed the restraints from Samson, allowing him to roam freely within the stables, before running up the stairs into the main hall and navigating the passages that led to their room.

He quietly pushed through the door, the aged wooden frame creaking loudly. Amity sat up in the window, where she had been staring into the night, wondering, waiting. Seeing Lyall's face smiling at her, she threw the blanket that covered her legs to the side, running towards him, where they embraced for a time.

Amity withdrew first, holding Lyall at arm's length and looking deep into his eyes.

'Tell me the children are alright,' she pleaded, tears rolling down her face in silent desperation.

'They're going to be fine,' he whispered, moving one hand to wipe the tears from under her eyes and resting it on her cheek. 'William is with Losophos in The Archive, being seen to as we speak. He isn't injured physically, but he needs rest. I can take you to him once I receive word that he is awake.'

'And Amelia?' she asked, nuzzling her face further into his hand.

At this, he withdrew slightly. Not truly knowing himself where she was, or if she was okay, but not wanting to burden Amity with more worry.

'She's on her way back with Keaton and Deckard. They had to take the long route, but I promise she is safe with those two in her company.'

He felt Amity tense up in his arms as she considered what he'd said, her body relaxing again after a short time, knowing that there was nothing she could do to change the situation. The two of them remained in a silent embrace, barely awake, on the very edge of consciousness.

To quiet her bellowing thoughts, Amity turned her attention to the welfare of the one person still within her grasp. Her husband, who had proven his dedication as a father by risking his life to save their son and help their daughter.

Pulling back from their lengthy embrace, she offered him a pained smile.

'You're filthy,' she said, 'and you smell. I'll run a bath for you, and you can tell me all about what happened.'

She let him go, vanishing into the bathroom behind him. He moved to the fireplace, warming his body as he removed the armour from his limbs.

When he could hear that the tap had stopped running, he stepped carefully into the bathroom, where Amity was sitting on a chair beside the water, tending to it. He stripped out of the last layers of his underclothes, before climbing into the bath, exhaling deeply as the warm liquid surrounded him and soothed his aching muscles.

Lyall recounted the events of the night as Amity dabbed his face and chest with a damp cloth, before washing the filth from his hair. He told her of the journey through the dungeon, of finding William, and of enlisting the help of Wendelmar, omitting the part about him trying to kill Amelia previously, knowing this would only cause her worry to deepen.

When he had finished speaking, and was sufficiently dry after his bath, they returned to bed. Neither of them had slept since the morning prior, and as quickly as they placed their heads on their pillows, they both fell into a deep sleep, hands intertwined, while the slowly rising sun began to creep through the window of their room.

# CHAPTER TWENTY

Wendelmar reeled as he began to regain consciousness, quickly leaping to his feet and backing away from the burning wall. He inspected his surroundings, making sure to always keep one eye on the fire.

He strained to recall what had happened, thinking back to Ealdor chanting at the mirror while it slowly grew cracks in its surface, before splintering into a countless number of pieces, causing the loudest noise and the largest flash of light he had ever experienced.

His ears were still ringing now, which made stumbling through the thickets very difficult, throwing off his sense of balance. He'd still been half-blinded when Ealdor lit the trail of flammable liquid he'd poured along the wall's length in anticipation of the arriving army.

*But where is the old man?* he thought, taking his eye off the fire long enough to turn around and spot the human.

He raced to Ealdor's side. He was face down in the mud, doubled over a thick root.

'Wake up!' Wendelmar said as he nudged Ealdor's side, although he couldn't be sure if he spoke or shouted, as his ears still weren't working properly.

There was no response from Ealdor, and Wendelmar turned his attention back to the army at the end of the wall, who still appeared as though they were far too busy dealing with the resulting fire and casualties to have even started searching for the pair.

Wendelmar picked Ealdor up and threw him over his shoulder, struggling to walk on his hind legs as quickly and quietly as he could, further into the thickets, towards the perimeter wall of Mundus. He carried Ealdor for several minutes, forcing his way through layers of branches, leaves and reeds, his hearing gradually returning as he went. From behind him, the sounds of pained screams and crackling fire became clearer. There were no pursuing footsteps as of yet, but he continued to listen intently as he carried on closer to freedom.

Exhausted, Wendelmar reached the perimeter wall, with Ealdor still on his back. The space between where he stood and where the makeshift stick wall sprouted from the ground was minimal, no more than a few body lengths. He pushed himself forward one last time, eager to be free of Mundus.

From where he had just come, Wendelmar heard a new sound. It wasn't crackling fire, screams of pain, nor pursuing footsteps. It was more otherworldly, an unnatural noise that caused the remaining hairs on his body to stand on end. It was the sound of magic.

The perfectly pitched gust of wind hit Wendelmar hard in the centre of his back, throwing him forward. He landed in the mud, sliding towards the wall, which he impacted with enough force to stun him momentarily.

As he regained his senses, he turned around, seeing Ealdor had been knocked clear of him, far off to the side. Peering desperately into the path he had just traversed, Wendelmar could see nothing of the magic's source, so he relied on his ears once more, listening for the slightest bit of movement.

There was nothing. For a moment it seemed as though all sound was gone from the world, save for the beating of his own heart, and the raspy breath from his lungs, until suddenly, from above, that same perfectly pitched *whooshing* sound flew towards him. He instinctively dodged out of the way, rolling in the mud to his left as the gust of air hit the wall behind him, causing many of the branches to blow out and splinter.

Crouched in the mud, Wendelmar turned his attention to the sky above, and what he saw made him instantly feel sick.

Hovering in the air, in perfect silence, was Oscuro. His eyes were glowing green, and a pale green aura radiated from his body as he grinned wickedly at Wendelmar and began to float down towards the earth.

'Very clever, Wendelmar,' Oscuro sneered, his voice still the only thing Wendelmar could hear. 'I'm surprised you were able to convince them to let you out. You, the one who was sent to kill their beloved princess. Perhaps I underestimated you, or perhaps they are stupider than I thought.' He spat the last few words with particular aggression.

Wendelmar forced himself to his feet, now almost level with Oscuro, who was about to finish his descent.

'Shouldn't you be aiding your precious king?' Wendelmar shot back with exceptional bitterness. 'If the girl has succeeded, he might be lying in a pool of his own blood as we speak.'

Oscuro seemed to consider this for a moment before replying to Wendelmar with evil excitement in his voice.

'She's still here, is she?' He laughed loudly, his glowing green eyes showing the insanity in his mind. 'This may all end better than I had planned.' As he finished speaking, he raised his hand towards Wendelmar and curled his long fingers into a fist.

Wendelmar could no longer move his own body. His limbs were stretched out as far as they could go, and he was hovering very slightly off the ground.

'What do you mean?' he asked, struggling to get the words out as the magical grip compressed him.

Oscuro was now very close to Wendelmar, the tips of their snouts almost touching as he began to reveal his scheme.

'You think this just happened coincidentally?' he asked. 'You think I placed you in that exact cell for no reason other than it was furthest away?' He snickered to himself and started to pace back and forth before Wendelmar. 'Oh, you underestimate me, just as the king does. I knew the girl would come through the mirror in retaliation. I knew her human pride would drive her to act with bravery, a word that could easily be given the same definition as stupidity. Humans are predictable. And now, she will reach the height of her bravery, and not only rescue her dear brother, but take care of Azul for me in the same stroke!'

Wendelmar had not anticipated that this was all a trap, yet the series of events that had led him here and had seemed to present themselves to him in such an opportunistic fashion now, in hindsight, were clearly planned.

'But he is your king,' Wendelmar said, still confused by Oscuro's treachery towards their monarch, as someone who always respected the hierarchy and knew his place.

Again, Oscuro smiled.

'You really think he is in charge? Certainly, there was a time when he may have been, just after he returned from their kingdom. An injured traitor, nursed back to health by the kind people of The Arbour, weak in the knees for their beloved queen, and growing stronger with the use of magic, which changed the way our people saw him. Now a hero, a prodigal son of Mundus.' He spat on the ground beside them. 'I cut that off very quickly!'

Oscuro was growing angry, and Wendelmar was trying to buy time, any advantage he could use to escape, so he went along with the conversation, willing the evil rat to reveal more of his plan.

'So, you were behind his change in motivations?' Wendelmar asked.

'Of course I was,' Oscuro spat back. 'When Azul returned to us, he was weak. He had grown a heart for those people and wanted to be friends. Of course, once I got in his ear, I was able to convince him otherwise, with a little help from my powers... but you know all about that already, don't you, Wendelmar?'

Wendelmar was confused. 'I've never heard whispers of this before now. We all thought the king wanted power. Nobody knew that he was under your control, especially not me.'

Oscuro stopped pacing and faced Wendelmar once more.

'Don't be so sure, old fool. You've had time to think. Now, tell me, do you remember ever coming before the king and volunteering to take the girl's life?'

Wendelmar's heart sank. 'You don't mean...'

'Yes. It was me controlling you the whole time, as I have controlled Azul, as I have controlled the princess's dearest little brother. Perfectly normal one moment, my willing puppet the next.'

Oscuro took pleasure from the pain on Wendelmar's face as he revealed that Wendelmar was simply one of many pawns in his cruel game.

'Now the plan has come to an end, dear Wendelmar. The girl will have killed Azul by now, and will soon be reunited with her dear brother, my final puppet, who will help me conquer that tree from within. I will take your head to present before the army for conspiring with the enemy, who will in turn place me in power, and then' – he sneered, as he pulled a dagger from his belt and held it to Wendelmar's throat – 'then, I will be unstoppable.'

As Oscuro drew the blade back slightly, ready to lunge forward and take the life from Wendelmar, a sound came from the side that took them both by surprise. Oscuro turned. Wendelmar, still unable to move his body, could only look ahead at the evil wizard.

There was a familiar sound, a perfectly pitched gust of wind, flying through the air towards Wendelmar. This time, however, it struck Oscuro, and with such force that he was thrown far off into the lake on Wendelmar's left. Oscuro's magic lost its grip on Wendelmar's body, whose feet fell to the ground as he turned his head to the right and saw Ealdor standing in the mud where he had fallen.

'Welcome back,' Wendelmar said to Ealdor, who was now upon him, supporting his body as he hunched to the side.

Ealdor, seeing that Wendelmar was exhausted, and lacking in

energy himself, guided the towering rat further into the dense reeds. He uttered several different incantations, explaining that they would be obscured from sight as they recovered their energy and waited to head home.

'There's much we need to discuss. Your people are in danger,' Wendelmar said hurriedly.

'I know,' Ealdor whispered, 'but for now, we need to regain our strength, otherwise we may never make it there to warn them.'

'There's no time!' he shouted. 'The little one–'

Before Wendelmar could finish his sentence, Ealdor had waved an arm over his face, and cast him into a deep sleep.

\* \* \* \* \*

Light was beaming in when Keaton began to stir, causing Amelia and Deckard to also wake from their slumber. The sun was clearly up outside, ambient light reflecting into the gap amongst the roots where they slept, allowing them to take in their surroundings with more certainty.

Amelia shot upright, looking from Keaton to Deckard.

'What happened? Where are we?'

Keaton sat up next to her, placing his arm around her shoulder to support her, as she still appeared groggy and lethargic from expending her energy hours before.

'We escaped the rat city. We ran for a while and found shelter in the roots of this old tree, and we thought it best to wait until morning to get our bearings.' He leaned forward to get a better look at her face. 'How are you, Amelia? You had me worried for a while there. You're lucky Dad was with me; I don't think I would've been able to carry you out on my own.'

Amelia smiled gently at Deckard.

'Thank you,' she said, her voice quiet.

Deckard said nothing back, only offering a small nod of the head in response.

'And what of Ealdor? Did he make it out?' she asked.

Deckard grunted, shifting to lean more comfortably against a protruding root. 'We don't know yet. Before we left, we saw the mirror in the distance. It appeared as though he was able to destroy it, but the entire place was on fire and swarming with Malum.'

That familiar lump formed in Amelia's throat once more.

'On fire? Did I do that?' she asked groggily.

'No, I don't think so,' Deckard replied. 'The fire you started was perfect, something only magic can produce. The flames that consumed the mirror were messy, like fuel burning. Best not to dwell on it until we return home.'

Amelia reached up to her brooch, concentrating on William. After a few minutes with no signs of the ring, she lowered her hand.

'We're too far from home. I can't see him.'

'There are other ways, Amelia,' Deckard said, getting to his feet and stepping out of the nook.

Keaton and Amelia followed him, wincing as their eyes adjusted to the sun, which was high in the sky, closer to midday than it was to sunrise.

Deckard stopped after taking a few steps out of the tree and turned back to face it, placing his hands on his hips as he looked up the entire length of it.

'What do you say, boy? Think you can climb that?'

Keaton turned around to take in the tree, now that the light of day showed it in detail. It was a dead tree, of that he was sure. It was lacking any green foliage, and the remaining bark and branches were grey with age. He scrutinised its trunk, identifying a few different paths he may be able to climb up.

'I think I can,' he said enthusiastically, 'but I would need to remove my armour. It's too heavy to climb that height in.'

Amelia placed her arms around him. 'I don't know if you should do this,' she said, pulling her head back and looking him in the eyes. 'You could die.'

He smiled at her, returning her embrace.

'I could have died any number of times last night. I could lose my ring finger and die, I could wander around out here for days and die of starvation, or I could die climbing this tree, trying to find us a way home. Is any one option really worse than another?'

Amelia buried her face in his collarbone, feeling her own warm breath as it heated his chest.

'I suppose you're right,' she whispered. 'Please just be extra careful.'

'I will,' he said, flashing her another smile before kissing her on the forehead and breaking the embrace.

He stepped up onto a higher root and started to untie his armour, starting with his shin coverings. As he finished undoing the last lace, he let it fall to the ground, where it vanished without a trace. Once he had finished with his legs, he moved on to his torso, followed by his arms. The only things left on him now were his dirty underclothes, which would do little against the cold of the night.

He gave Amelia and Deckard one last smile, waving a goodbye, before he leapt up onto the nearest bit of the trunk, climbing with shocking speed and confidence, the bark cracking as he pulled his way up each piece.

Amelia and Deckard sat on a tuft of grass, watching Keaton as he got higher and higher into the tree, both of them internally cheering him on.

'He might not see it yet,' Deckard began, his eyes remaining focused on Keaton, 'but I am proud of my boy.'

'I'm glad to hear it,' she said warmly, 'but you should tell him that.'

Deckard hummed in acceptance.

'Yes. I should. I will.' He removed his gaze from Keaton, looking at Amelia and smiling.

Amelia wasn't sure if she was still dreaming or not, but seeing Deckard express a happy emotion meant that things had definitely changed within him. He was not the same man she had met when she first entered the tree; his cold, demeaning exterior had slowly changed to one of warmth and compassion.

'Once we get back and have had the chance to relax for a moment, I'll tell him. His mother would be proud too.' Deckard choked on the last few words, quickly clearing his throat and resuming his watch over Keaton, who was still steadily scaling the tree.

For what felt like hours, the pair sat and watched Keaton as he ascended, losing sight of him in the glare of the sun once it reached the peak of its arc across the sky. Deckard began to walk the perimeter of the trunk, ensuring no spies or threats had followed them out, or were waiting in ambush.

Amelia dozed in the shade of some tall grass, taking the opportunity to regain more of her strength. It wasn't until she heard the cracking of bark again that she woke up, rubbing her eyes, to see Keaton racing back down, not far from the base of the trunk.

She jumped to her feet, climbing up a few roots until she reached the ground just below where Keaton would be landing, looking around eagerly for Deckard, who was just finishing up one of his perimeter walks. He joined Amelia at the base of the tree, and together, they stood patiently waiting for Keaton to finish the last few minutes of his descent. When his feet made it back to the dirt, Keaton was dripping with sweat, his body red and burnt from the hours of exposure to the sun, but he shared a smile.

'I know where home is,' he managed to get out between breaths. 'It's that way.' He pointed into the distance behind Amelia and Deckard. 'A stream runs right by it. If we keep going in the direction we were running last night, just past this tree, we should find ourselves on the river's banks, and then it's a straight shot.'

'Well done, boy.' Deckard grunted.

Amelia picked up a piece of a leaf that was lying in the dirt near them, using it to fan Keaton's overheated body.

'How far do you think it is?' she asked.

Keaton made a thinking sound in his throat.

'Hard to say when we're this small,' he said. 'Probably about a day's walk, maybe less if we run. Unfortunately, the stream flows in the other direction, so we can't use that to our advantage.'

'Very well,' Deckard said, getting to his feet. 'We fortify here for tonight, and leave before dawn. It should be fairly warm in our burrow if we cover the entrance.'

Keaton returned to the hole, resting for much of the afternoon out of the piercing heat of the sun. Amelia and Deckard worked together to collect enough sticks and leaves to cover the entrance, ensuring they would be protected through the night, not only from the cold, but from any stray visitors.

Once the sun had started to set, the area around the base of the tree grew very cold, very quickly. The trio sealed up the entrance once they were all inside, relaxing within their small but warm hole, safe for another night.

Deckard fell asleep first. He was good at hiding it, but the last twenty-four hours had worn him out completely, and the longer sleep would ensure he woke early, hopefully before the sun, so they could start their return journey.

Keaton and Amelia talked into the night, speaking at length about William, what they had learned about magic users amongst the rats, and how relatively easy it seemed to be to dispatch Azul. The thought had stuck with her, gently nudging at her waking mind at every opportunity. She had only *injured* a Malum before. Now she had *killed* one. She had taken life from a creature, and although he had meant her deathly harm, the thought did nothing to soothe her internal conflict. They both agreed that even though they had taken care of Azul, the army of rats they had seen would surely be out for revenge. Perhaps they would be even more dangerous now, if Oscuro was chosen to lead them.

The Arbour would have time to prepare, at least, with the mirror seemingly destroyed from within the rats' own home. If they were to mount an attack on the tree, it would take time to arrange such an endeavour. Plus, a force that large would not go unnoticed as they travelled across the land. Keaton and Amelia also assumed that it would take time for the rats to choose a new leader, and while they were not ignorant, they hoped that the new leader might at least have less destructive ambitions than the last.

Amelia had been talking for a while about what she planned to do in preparation once they returned to The Arbour when she looked at Keaton, whose shoulder she had been lying on. He too was fast asleep, his chest rising and falling gently as he dreamed.

She wondered for a while what he was dreaming about, watching his eyes move from side to side under his eyelids, and before long, she too closed hers, welcoming the comfort of sleep.

* * * * *

When Deckard shook Amelia and Keaton awake, it was still very dark, though when they left the safety of their burrow, they could see dawn's first light spreading across the horizon. They had nothing to carry, other than what they wore, so without a moment of hesitation, they began their journey beyond the tree. They would walk until they reached the stream, before turning left and following it all the way to the stone wall that Amelia knew well.

While it remained dark, they walked at a steady pace. By the time they reached the stream, however, the sun was over the mountains in the distance and the world around them was lit up in detail. They each took the opportunity to have a drink from the freshwater stream, before continuing on their way, following the winding body of water, which seemed like an ocean compared to their size.

They ran when they could, ducking under the shelter of roots and grass whenever they spotted birds flying nearby, not wanting to become a small snack for some swooping animal. By late afternoon, Amelia could see the stone wall in the distance, an indication that they were almost within the perimeter of her family's land.

When they reached the arch in the stone wall that the stream ran under, they clung to its side, stepping carefully along ledges that jutted out over the flowing torrent of water below them. The water was moving at such speed that if any of them were to fall in now, they would be whisked away before they could even blink, setting the journey back by hours, and there was still the mammoth task of climbing the wall, which was the only way they would be able to cross to the other side of the stream.

Once they had stepped out of the far side of the stone wall, they found themselves amongst the green grass of Amelia's family property. Looking behind, she could just see the tip of the roof over the large hedge, which was looking less lush than usual, suffering in the early morning frosts that were frequenting the valley.

She felt sad for a moment, realising how long it had been since she stepped foot out of The Arbour and spent a day in the house, something she wanted to do once everyone was safely returned home.

After a brief break, Amelia, Deckard and Keaton began to climb up the wall, taking their time and helping each other jump from stone to stone. The venture took them more than a few hours to complete safely, as they opted for the safest path, rather than the quickest.

Keaton climbed over the edge of the wall first, leaning back down to assist Amelia, who was passed up to him by Deckard. Once Amelia and Keaton were on top of the wall, Deckard pulled himself over the edge, rolling onto his side as he breathed a sigh of relief.

After they had regained their breath, the three of them sat together, facing the direction of The Arbour, seeing its green leaves jutting out over the top of the surrounding bushes and trees, a welcoming sign that they were nearly home. They chose to take one last brief rest before the sprint to the finish line.

# CHAPTER TWENTY-ONE

When Oscuro regained consciousness, he found himself lying in his own chamber. His body was painfully sore as he pushed himself out of his bed and limped over to the balcony.

He looked down upon Mundus. The far wall with the Moon Portal was scorched black along its entire length. To his left, the king's own hall had been reduced to large chunks of rubble. The flames had subsided, but small wisps of black smoke still trailed their way from smouldering piles of ash and high into the domed sky.

He pulled a small length of rope that hung from the ceiling, causing a bell outside his door to ring, and sat in his large chair as he waited for his servant to arrive.

She entered the room carrying a small wooden plank with food and water and placed it on the table in front of him, bowing as she began to retreat backwards towards the door.

'Wait,' he hissed.

She stopped in place as she waited for his command, fearing that he would be in a foul mood.

'Well?' he asked. 'What news of the intruders?'

She kept her gaze on the floor, not wanting to look Oscuro in the face.

'My lord... it's been a whole day and night, and there's still no sign of them, although patrols continue to sweep the area outside Mundus.'

Oscuro pretended to get frustrated at this, although in his own mind, he was pleased that the plan was going so well.

'And what of the king?' he asked, beginning to shove handfuls of food into his mouth.

'The... the king is dead, my lord.'

At this, Oscuro stopped eating, waving a hand at the slave, indicating for her to get out.

When she had closed the door, he waited a few moments until he was sure she would be far enough away, and allowed himself to laugh out loud, quietly at first, but getting louder as it continued.

When he had filled his empty stomach, Oscuro walked back to the balcony, retrieving a tiny black feather from a shelf on the way, which hung near his bed. He stood in the open air, basking in the small pillars of early sunlight that pierced the branched dome above.

He smiled to himself. His plan had worked; he would soon be named king, and there was nothing to stop him. His scheme to take The Arbour was now only days from fruition. Then, his army would be unstoppable.

He raised the feather close to his face, whispered a few words and cast it up into the air, where it flew straight up, finding its way between the branches of their dome and disappearing into the morning sky.

'Let's see how you like those.' He sneered to himself, before returning into his room to change, ready to be seen amongst who were now *his* people.

* * * * *

It was early morning when Lyall and Amity woke up, though they both felt so well rested that they concluded they must have slept through an entire day. The fireplace was extinguished, having not been tended to since the night before, and there was a cold bitterness to the air in their room.

It had been more than twenty-four hours since Lyall had dropped

William off at The Archive, and both he and Amity were anxious to check up on his progress and see if there was any word from Amelia yet.

As they went to leave the castle, they came across the matron, who was busy preparing food for the day, but suggested they take a moment and eat something. They realised that their stomachs were indeed empty and gurgling at the prospect of a warm meal.

Amity and Lyall sat and ate a healthy helping of porridge and fruit, quickly polishing clean the bowls that sat before them. From the pantry, Tilly came to clear the dirty crockery off the table.

'Please forgive me for asking,' she said, curtseying before them, 'is Master William back? Is he okay?'

Amity smiled at Tilly, knowing that she and William had grown close in the days after his birthday.

'Sweet little girl, please don't apologise,' Amity said. 'William is indeed back. He's been resting and should be his usual self again soon. I'll let you know as soon as he's well enough for visitors. In fact, we're on our way to see him right now. Would you like me to tell him you said hello?'

Tilly lowered her head shyly, collecting the last of the cutlery from the table.

'Yes, please,' she said, before retreating back into the passages of the pantry.

With bellies full and spirits growing higher, Lyall and Amity retrieved Samson from the stable and attached him back to the cart, waving and smiling at various townsfolk as they made their way out of the town and across the plains that led to The Archive. Leaving the horse and cart by the water, they walked over the small hill, hand in hand, until Lyall found the same hollow spot in the trunk where he had knocked two nights previously, once again beating on its surface and waiting for Losophos to climb the staircase and open it.

Once Losophos did so, he greeted the pair, beckoning them to follow him down into The Archive, where William was sitting up at a table, reading an old book in the sunlight that shone through the water-filled roof. When he heard the footsteps enter, he looked up to the doorway, seeing his parents' smiling faces. He dropped the book on the table and ran across the room to meet them, hugging both of their legs, as they threw their arms around each other and him, forming a three-way embrace.

'How do you feel?' Amity asked, kissing William on the forehead before watching his face for a response.

'I feel good,' he said, smiling, something that they hadn't seen him do wholeheartedly in a few weeks.

'Your little girlfriend sends her regards,' Lyall said, jokingly nudging William's arm.

He pouted, his cheeks filling with red as he blushed.

'She's not my girlfriend,' he said, crossing his arms and frowning at his father, who laughed in response, messing William's hair with his hand and apologising.

'Where's Mealy?' William asked, peeking around his parents as though expecting her to walk down the stairs behind them.

Lyall knelt in front of William, placing his hands on both of his shoulders and looking into his eyes.

'Your sister led the party that came through to rescue you from the rats. Getting you and I out was the most important job, but she had another to do, so she stayed behind with Keaton and Deckard.'

William felt guilty at the peril Amelia was in because of him and wrapped his arms around Lyall's neck, sobbing quietly into it.

'It's okay, buddy,' Lyall said, patting William on the back. 'She can look after herself. That sister of yours is strong; I bet she'll be back before long, maybe even by the end of the day.'

William slowed his sobbing, an idea beginning to form in his head.

'Can we go look for her, Dad?' he asked, pulling his head out of Lyall's neck and looking into his face.

Lyall looked up to Losophos, who had been standing silently in the background as the family reunited.

'What do you say? Is he well enough to come and sit in the branches for a while?'

Losophos nodded. 'I'm sure that will do him well. But before you go, may I have a word with you in private, Master Blackwood?' Losophos waved a hand at Lyall, motioning for him to follow down a nearby aisle.

'I'll be back in a moment, buddy,' he said to William, handing him over to Amity and giving her a kiss on the forehead. 'I'll meet you at the cart.'

Lyall walked over to where Losophos had headed, seeing him waiting as he rounded the corner.

'What is it? Is there something wrong?' he asked.

'There still appear to be remnants of dark magic inside the young master's head. I would not recommend keeping him out beyond sunset. I think it would be best if he spent his nights here with me for a time, either until we can be rid of the magic completely, or until he learns to block it out.'

Lyall thought on these words for a while. Only one question kept reappearing in his mind.

'What happens if he doesn't learn to block it?' he asked.

'I can't be sure,' Losophos began, 'but it's best I try and help him learn how. If he chooses to embrace the darkness, it could prove extremely dangerous not only to him, but to all that we hold dear. There are wards and barriers around The Archive that will protect him through the night, when the power of dark magic is at its strongest, so rest assured he will be safe in my care.'

'Very well,' Lyall whispered, looking through the glass ceiling to see where the sun was in the sky. 'I will ensure he is back here before dark.'

Lyall left The Archive, smiling as he saw William and Amity playfully sitting on the cart in wait of his arrival. They appeared to be acting as though they were people of great importance, maybe even a princess and her advisor. Tilly was sitting up as straight as she could, with her chin high in the air, while Will, also sitting straighter than usual, struggled to reach for the reins.

Lyall jumped aboard, and together they trotted off towards a section of the trunk that would allow them to sit on some of the lowest branches. This spot would also allow them the best view of the tree's surrounding area, for they were still unsure as to what direction the party would be returning from.

Once they chose the staircase they were to climb up, they hitched the horse and started the steep ascent into the foliage, stepping off at the first available branch and walking out halfway along it, before taking a seat together and eagerly searching the landscape for any sign of movement. They sat and watched for hours, playing games of "I spy" and at one point even performing charades, much to William's amusement.

The sun was just about to start its descent behind the surrounding hills, and Lyall was ready to return William to The Archive, when Amity spotted something moving quickly within the fence that surrounded the tree.

All three of them looked intently in that direction, eventually spotting the object in motion. It was indeed moving fast, so fast it appeared only as a blur, but Lyall was sure that he knew what it was.

'A rat,' he whispered. 'Quick, we have to warn the guards.' He started to run back along the length of the branch, until William's voice stopped him.

'There's someone on its back!' he shouted, pointing.

Lyall and Amity moved closer to the edge of the branch, leaning over it to get a better look at the creature. William was right; there did appear to be someone riding the rat, someone whose cloak was flailing wildly behind them in the breeze.

'Is that Ealdor?' Amity asked.

'I think you might be right,' Lyall replied. 'Which means that's Wendelmar. I suppose he could be trusted after all.'

They continued to watch as Ealdor and Wendelmar reached the base of the trunk, the rat's claws serving him well as he began to scale the tree with ease. As they got closer, Lyall shouted to them, getting the attention of Ealdor, who spoke something into the rat's ear that caused him to change direction and head for the group.

Wendelmar leapt onto the branch from the nearby trunk, reducing speed and eventually stopping just before the trio who awaited them.

'I'm glad to see you both made it,' Lyall said, offering them a smile. 'Whatever you did to the mirror worked. The guards reported it closed, the surface cracked.'

'We were lucky to get out of there,' Ealdor said as he stepped off Wendelmar's back, producing his pipe and sparking it up. 'Once I had destroyed the mirror, I regrouped with Wendelmar, who was just behind me, and what we saw made me question the likelihood of us getting out of there alive. A swarm of Malum like I have never seen, thousands of them, clad in makeshift armour and weapons. Wendelmar had been clever enough to lay a trap, and when I lit a flame, the whole wall exploded into an inferno, throwing us from its height, deep into the shadows.'

He took a long breath through his pipe, holding it for a few seconds as he considered whether he should inform them of the encounter with Oscuro, before releasing the large cloud of smoke into the air.

'We waited in the shadows through an entire day, watching as the army regrouped, salvaging what it could from the attack. It seems that Amelia may have completed her task also. For most of the time we were there, the fortress billowed black smoke from its windows, before they got it under control. It was enough of a distraction for us to sneak out when the sun set again, and we made for home.'

He took a second long puff. He could feel Wendelmar's eyes inspecting him, wondering why he had omitted the near-deadly encounter. This time, he blew the cloud of smoke into the shape of a rat running, the figure of a man on its back.

'Where is Amelia? Resting, I suppose?' he asked, looking around the branch.

Lyall cleared his throat, stepping forward. 'The second group haven't made it back yet.'

Ealdor coughed up smoke as he heard the words that he hadn't expected. 'We thought that surely they would beat us back, with our delay. Something must be holding them up also,' he said. 'Worry not, though; if anything had happened to her, this ruby would no longer be set within the ring on my finger. It would've hidden itself to be found by the next successor, so they could prove themselves worthy of the crown.'

This brought further relief to Amity and Lyall.

Wendelmar stood on his two hind legs, his height scaring William, who cowered behind his mum's legs, visions of his interrogation in the king's chamber flashing in his mind.

'You stay here and rest,' Wendelmar said to Ealdor. 'I will go and search. Perhaps I can help them once more.'

Without another word, Wendelmar launched himself from the branch, clinging onto the trunk as he ran back down it. Ealdor, Amity, Lyall and William all watched him scurry across the mossy ground under the tree, scaling the fence effortlessly and disappearing from view once more.

Movement caught Ealdor's eye as he looked out over the surrounding landscape, though it wasn't on the ground. High in the sky, circling between the farmhouse and the tree, was a flock of seven or eight black ravens. A pit formed in his stomach as he worried that perhaps they had found themselves three tasty little treats, who were no doubt exhausted, starving, and defenceless.

# CHAPTER TWENTY-TWO

K eaton, Deckard and Amelia were now so close to home that
they ignored the pain in their muscles and the growling of their
stomachs, picking themselves up and running along the stone
wall that would take them close to the shrubbery surrounding the yew
tree.

The sky was slowly changing from blue to the oranges and pinks
that the serene countryside offered each night when the sun lowered
into the mountains. Their attention, however, was not focused on the
sky, but on ensuring that they stepped carefully along the stone wall,
avoiding the larger cracks that ran between rocks, which would mean
broken bones for sure if they were unlucky enough to fall down one.

The stone wall was getting steeper, running up the small hill that led
from the stream to the shrubs and trees of the protected area. It was
the ideal path for them, allowing them to run in a straight line, rather
than dodging clumps of grass and hilly terrain on the ground.

The group froze in place as a large shadow sailed over them,
vanishing again as quickly as it had appeared. It was followed by
another darting shadow, and another, and another.

When they looked up into the sky, through the gaps in their fingers,
they could see a few black objects flying high above them. A couple
had darted down to get a closer look at them, obscuring the sun as
they glided past.

The next shadow to fly over them came far closer than the previous ones. The downward force of its wings flapping knocked them over, as it swooped back up into the sky.

'We need to get off the wall!' Amelia screamed. Beginning to scope out a path to the ground, she lowered herself down.

Keaton and Deckard followed suit quickly. Gliding shadows continued to shoot past them as the birds searched for their location.

When a force of wind almost blew them clear of the wall, Amelia, Keaton and Deckard looked up to where they had been running. A large raven had now landed there, peering over the side as it hunted for its meal with its unnaturally glowing green eyes.

Deckard was the highest up the wall, moving slower than Amelia and Keaton, who had lighter or no armour on. The raven reached down and pecked at Deckard, narrowly missing him and chipping off a piece of stone, which sprung out near him. Again, the raven pecked at him, this time finding its mark. Its beak connected with his armour with a hollow *thud*. The armour held up and did its job of protecting him, though he was now held tightly within the tip of the creature's beak.

He let go of the stone with one hand and reached down for his sword, which he swung at the bird's face, annoying it enough that it let go of his torso. He used the opportunity to scurry further down the wall until the raven had recovered and went to peck him again.

Its beak shot down in his direction, and met with the swing of his sword, the two connecting. However, the bird's strength knocked the sword from his hand. It fell for a second before vanishing, having been separated from his touch.

Amelia and Keaton had reached the ground and were running towards the bushes that surrounded the yew tree when they heard Deckard scream. They turned just in time to see him fall from the wall, landing in a clump of grass.

They moved to head in his direction, but a second raven swooped down between them and Deckard, causing them to turn back the other way and continue their desperate race for the tree.

'We have to get through the fence!' Amelia shouted as they ran. 'I'll be able to grow back to full size and scare away the birds!'

They pushed through the outer layer of low-growing shrubs, darting left and right as they dodged branches and leaves, the white fence appearing through thinner sections of foliage.

At last, they were upon it. Now only a small gap stood between the bush they were sheltering under and its wooden panels. Keaton began to run forward, but Amelia grabbed his arm at the last moment, holding him back.

'Look,' she said, pointing towards the grassy gap. It was an eclectic scene of light and dark as the ravens flew directly above it, blocking out the sun for seconds at a time as they glided round the fence.

'We have to take the chance!' Keaton shouted. 'Dad could be injured!'

Without saying anything further, he pulled free of Amelia's grasp and ran out into the corridor that separated them from the fence. She froze in place for a moment, watching as Keaton dodged round after round of swooping claws and beaks.

He was almost at the fence when he tripped on a stick, his eyes busy watching the sky, not concerned with the ground. Amelia instinctively ran for him, not concerned for her own safety, hoping to pull him beyond the fence.

She had just reached Keaton when a large raven swooped down above them. The wind that its wings generated caused her to fly forward, hitting the fence with reasonable force.

Jumping to her feet as quickly as she could, she ran towards Keaton again, unable to see him behind the looming figure of the predatory bird. The raven pecked again and again. Amelia could hear Keaton's gurgling screams and see blood dripping from the tip of the crow's beak, and spattered around its eyes, which were also notably green, instead of the usual black. Tears poured down her face as she stood against the fence. She felt a gap between the pickets and followed her hands through it, spotting the familiar mossy surface that grew only inside the fence.

She placed a foot down on the moss, and closed her eyes, waiting for the magic of The Arbour to return her to full size.

When she opened her eyes, nothing had changed. She was still tiny and helpless.

*What's happening?* she shouted in her mind, and then it came to her, as though she had run straight into a wall. *The brooch. Losophos added the extra enchantment to prevent me growing unexpectedly.*

Reaching down to her chest, Amelia ripped the brooch from where it was pinned and threw it to the ground. Suddenly, the familiar dizziness filled her head, and she fell forward as she returned to normal size. When she opened her eyes again, the world didn't seem quite so large anymore. Picking herself up, she looked at the fence, which was now no higher than her shoulders. With a running start, she leapt over it, using her arms to swing her body high over the fence.

She landed just behind where the raven stood over Keaton. Quickly turning towards it, she kicked out with her right foot, connecting with the bird's body as it tried to fly away.

She fell to her knees. Keaton lay motionless in a pool of blood. The damage appeared bad. Each peck had met no resistance, without his armour to protect him.

As she tried to pick him up, a rustling from the bush beside her caught her attention. She prepared to fight off more of the ravens, but the figure who appeared was Wendelmar. He was carrying Deckard on his back, who saw Keaton struggling for breath on the ground, jumping down and rushing to his side.

Deckard picked Keaton up and carried him over to Wendelmar, leaping onto his back once more, this time with his son in his arms. It looked like he tried to yell something at Amelia, but she couldn't hear him over the gurgling croaks of the circling birds, who were still hoping for something to eat.

Wendelmar lunged forward, quickly scaling the fence even with the two packages he was carrying. When he had disappeared from view, Amelia continued around the side of the fence, finding the latched gate that led into the clearing. She saw a brief flash of movement as Wendelmar's tail disappeared into one of the larger branch openings on the tree.

Amelia was now alone. Not even the ravens had hung around long enough to see her fall into a heap on the soft, mossy ground. She lay on her back, staring up into the branches above her, hoping with all the love in her heart that Keaton would be okay, and that Ealdor and Losophos would be able to heal him.

For the first time in as long as she could remember, Amelia just cried. She curled into the foetal position, hugging her knees to her chest, and let out all that she could. Keaton's injuries weren't even the only thing that affected her. A wave of memories pooled in her head, and she cried her way through each of them as they left her body through tears.

She let go of all her frustrations and doubts about her ability to be an effective and compassionate leader. She let go of all the bitter feelings she'd held onto against the rats. She let go of the resentment she felt towards herself after murdering every member of the Rat King, even though it was something that she really didn't have much of a choice in.

As she cried, Amelia began to feel the cold night air creep in. Since she had lain down under the tree, the sun had set behind it, covering the valley in a dark shroud that sucked any warmth from the earth.

She slowly got to her feet and moved towards the gate. In the corner of her eye, something flashed on the ground. She looked over to see her brooch gleaming in the sunset, now full-sized. She retrieved it, placing it back into her chest piece, and continued to the gate, stopping as her hand reached the latch and turning back towards the tree.

'Tell him I love him,' she said into the evening air, hoping that someone in the tree was watching her and would pass on the message.

She unlatched the gate, stepping out of the clearing and pulling it closed behind her. As she followed the fence, she spotted the dark stain on the ground where Keaton's blood had seeped into the soil, kicking some extra dirt over it so she wouldn't have to see it again.

The path home was quiet. Amelia concentrated on the clouds that formed as she breathed out into the biting air. Each step on the grass emitted a satisfying crunch as the blades began to freeze in the winter frost.

She trod her way up to the front of the house. The large ornate wooden doors still hung ominously below the weeping windows, although the amount of greenery sprouting from the vines had greatly diminished in the cooler weather.

The doors were locked, as she expected, and she located the key that was carefully placed behind one of the many potted plants dotting the stairs.

Amelia turned the large key in its lock, which clicked loudly. She pushed the door open and entered the freezing room that she remembered with such fondness from the first time she walked through it. Her hand reached for the light switch on the wall to her left, and the dozens of small lightbulbs adorning the root-like chandelier came to life, filling the room with a warm orange glow.

Heading to the pantry first, Amelia grabbed a packet of biscuits stashed on a high shelf, opening it and taking several with her as she went upstairs to her bedroom. She found the acorn-shaped handle and twisted it, the door opening to reveal her room, which was bathed in a rainbow of colours. The moonlight shining through her window scattered itself on every surface, refracted by the stained-glass tree.

Raising her hand to her brooch, she felt its edge with her fingernail, prying it from the carapace of her fitted armour. After placing the brooch on her pillow, she fished through her drawers for a change of clothes, opting for her long winter pyjamas. She held them under her arm as she headed to the bathroom.

She finished the last of her biscuits as she threw her pyjamas onto the floor. Leaning into the shower, she turned on the hot water, letting it fill the air with steam, fogging the window and mirror. As she stepped into the shower, her skin was shocked at the touch of the scalding hot water, but the armour helped to absorb most of it. She adjusted the temperature of the water until it was much more comfortable, and dismantled her armour piece by piece, watching each part disappear into nothing when she threw it away.

In her frustration, she began to throw the pieces harder, screaming and hurling them at the wall opposite her. The pieces, of course, never made it to the wall, which only added to her exasperation. As she removed the last of her armour, and, finally, her bodysuit, she threw it as hard as she could, wailing as the material vanished. She slipped in her anger, remaining on the ground as she cried.

Once the water began to run cold, Amelia reached up and turned off the taps, finding her towel and drying herself off before she climbed into her pyjamas.

Amelia crawled into her bed. The blankets were cold at first, but as she lay under them, they quickly warmed up from her residual body heat, returning what she gave to them.

She tried to fall asleep as quickly as she could, knowing that the sooner she did, the sooner she would awaken and be able to see Keaton.

Long into the night, she thought about him. Wondering if he was doing okay, if she would be able to see him when she stepped through the mirror in the morning. She couldn't stop seeing the blood. His blood was everywhere, so much of it spilled in the dirt, too much.

The hours came and went as she was plagued by anxious thoughts. Her attempts at clearing her mind only served to add more fuel to her already overactive brain.

Eventually, she fell asleep, late into the night when the world outside her room was at its darkest, the only sounds around her belonging to the wind and the trees, and her gentle sobbing.

# CHAPTER TWENTY-THREE

The gentle rays of the morning sun caressed Amelia's skin as they trickled in through her room's large windows. Through her closed eyelids, the orange light still found its mark, waking her from the short sleep she had been afforded. It wasn't quite on the mirror yet, and she used the time she had remaining to change from her pyjamas into something more appropriate, opting for overalls and a long-sleeved shirt.

She sat on the foot of her bed and waited, the minutes stretching on into what felt like hours, until a familiar voice called to her.

'Amelia, darling, are you coming through?'

Amelia opened her eyes once more. She had fallen asleep in her long wait, her mother's voice returning her to the waking world. She stood, walking towards her mother, who had receded back into the mirror.

When she stepped through, the first thing she saw was her mother standing directly before her, arms outstretched, pulling her into a tight embrace.

Although she didn't want it, the hug made Amelia feel better. Her mother always gave the best hugs. They had a strange way of making her feel protected and warm, even in moments like this when she didn't want the attention.

'I'm so sorry we couldn't come to be with you last night, my darling.

By the time we got William back to The Archive, it was very dark, and whatever those rats did to him was causing him distress. Losophos was having a hard time trying to inspect his mind and he asked us to remain, as our voices were soothing to William.'

'How is he?' Amelia asked, whispering into her mother's ear as she looked around the top of the spire, seeing nobody else around.

'We managed to keep him calm through the night, and–'

'No,' Amelia spat in frustration, 'how is Keaton?'

Amity released Amelia from her embrace, holding Amelia's shoulders at arm's length as she looked into her daughter's face. There was a deep emotion in Amity's eyes. It didn't look like the worry she had worn like a mask since William's kidnapping. It looked more like pain.

'Ealdor tended to his wounds as best he could. The last thing I heard was that Keaton had asked to be taken to the bird's nest,' she said, taking Amelia by the hand and leading her along the rickety bridge that led to the trunk's inner wall.

They walked together, neither one saying a word for a long time, passing from corridor to corridor on their way to the nest, a pathway Amelia knew like the back of her hand.

*He must be alright,* she thought. *Why else would he be at the nest? If he was unwell, he would surely remain under the care of Ealdor or Losophos.*

She picked up her pace, slipping out of the hold Amity had on her hand and leaving her to fall behind, wanting to see him as quickly as she could and tell him how much she loved him, how sick she had been with worry as she tried to rest through the night, and how thankful she was for his part in returning William safe and sound.

She rushed out onto the familiar branch, spotting the nest through the ever-thinning leaf layer that usually concealed its whereabouts. Climbing along the safety rope, she pushed through the leaves, seeing a pair of guards by the nest, each of them standing at attention upon spotting her.

Amelia couldn't contain her excitement. She ran to the nest, jumping up to its edge and pulling herself up high enough to see over the side.

Keaton was there, lying in the middle of the nest, although he wasn't in the condition Amelia had been hoping for. Her stomach tightened into a tangled mess of knots as she saw the tapestry that covered his body from his feet to his waist. His arms were crossed over his chest, and over his eyes were two wooden discs, finely carved from the smallest of branches.

Her arms gave way as the sickness in her stomach grew. She heard her mother push through the leaves, and she tried to maintain her dignity in front of the three people nearby, but her attempts failed as she leaned over the side of the branch and threw up the biscuits she had eaten the night before, quickly emptying her stomach of all its contents.

'Amelia, are you alright?' Her mother ran to her side, patting her on the back. However, it only fuelled the fire that was growing in her heart.

'Leave me...' she whispered, wiping the bile from her lips.

She turned to face her mother and the guards who still stood vigil beside the nest, none of them yet moving to depart.

'Leave me! All of you!' she screamed.

The guards responded first, marching off along the branch towards the tree at the command of their princess. Amity, however, remained behind. Peeking over the edge of the nest, she saw Keaton's lifeless body. Her hands moved to cover her mouth as she gasped at the sight and quickly tried to comfort Amelia.

'Amelia, please, it'll be alright...' She moved towards Amelia, arms outstretched, wanting to grab her and hold her tight.

Looking into her mother's eyes, Amelia retreated towards the nest, hugging herself tightly.

'Please,' she said, her voice shaking, her already irritated eyes beginning to fill with tears once more, 'just go.'

Amity, although wanting to comfort her daughter, knew that it was probably best to leave her alone as she had asked, not wanting to exacerbate her already heightened emotional state. Amity nodded, slowly stepping backwards along the branch.

'I'll be over here if you need me,' she said, pointing towards the opening in the tree, where the guards had moved.

Once her mother had left, Amelia looked back towards the bird's nest, climbing the side with all the courage her heart could muster, trying her best not to look at Keaton's body until she had stepped down into the middle of the nest, coming to a rest on her knees beside him.

She looked down at his face, which appeared pale. Leaning forward, she placed a hand on his forehead. It was ice cold. He had been dead for a while, and she hadn't been around to comfort him.

Tears flowed from her eyes as though they were rivers running down her cheeks. For countless minutes she sat, kneeling over Keaton, living only in her mind for the longest time. The world around the nest faded. There was no sound, no movement, no hope. The possibility of him being seriously injured, she had mentally prepared for. But dead... she hadn't dared to imagine.

Her body buckled. She fell gently beside Keaton. Lying down in the nest beside him, close to his body, she placed her arm around his torso and nestled her head in the curve of his neck. Her mind was as tumultuous as the untamed sea, swirling with thoughts and anger. Like a whirlpool in that same sea sucks in and destroys everything, she could feel her mind falling ever further into the dark place beyond the maelstrom.

Taking her time, she worked through each chaotic thought, one by one, ensuring she could maintain some semblance of calm. Time was no worry today. This time was hers, his, theirs. As the hours passed, she began to replace the negative thoughts with positive ones, something her parents had taught her long ago. She remained by Keaton's side, staring with unseeing eyes up into the leaves above them. With great effort, she could feel her mind clawing its way out of the pull of the tide, and into calmer waters.

'Keaton,' she whispered, her voice raspy from the hours without use, 'I'm sorry I wasn't there. I wish I could have been with you at the end, like you've been with me for so long. I know you can't hear me, but there's things I need to say, words that need to be spoken. Who knows, maybe they'll find you in the next life, wherever that may be.'

She took a deep breath in, holding it for as long as she could, before she released it again, whimpering softly as she spoke.

'I thought I knew love before I met you. My family showed me love my whole life, but it was nothing compared to what you made me feel.'

Her tears once again started to escape from her eyes, which were glazed and red at the corners. With one shaky hand, she wiped the wetness from her face, before taking a deep, trembling breath and continuing to speak from her heart.

'I knew I loved you that morning when I came through the mirror after first escaping Beersheba. You were sitting on the edge of the tower, waiting for me to return, even though you barely knew me. I could see something in your eyes when you turned to me, a spark that warmed my heart and made me feel special.'

She ran her fingers through his hair, her head remaining close to his, as she whispered lovingly into his ear.

'You opened up to me so quickly, and you never asked me to change who I was. On the contrary, you encouraged me to keep fighting and to believe in myself. Keaton, you made me the person I am right now. I only wish we had time to say goodbye. You should know, Deckard is proud of you. We all are. Your name will be celebrated until long after I'm gone; I will make sure of that.'

Amelia lifted her head above Keaton's, looking at his face for a moment, before placing her lips on his forehead and gently kissing him for as long as she could.

She had been lying with Keaton for much of the morning when she was interrupted by the sound of someone else climbing into the bird's nest.

When she turned, she saw Losophos. His usually emotionless face looked pained. Below his eyes were purple bags. He too had been unable to sleep properly through the night, between caring for William and expending great levels of magic in trying to save Keaton with Ealdor.

'Amelia,' he said, taking a seat against the nest wall, respectfully keeping his distance from the grieving princess, 'I do not offer my sympathy. I know you well enough to know that you don't want that. Instead, I offer you some advice.'

He shuffled a little further down the side of the nest, now within reach of Keaton's body, placing a hand on his leg.

'Losing someone you love is hard; I know this. Most people you will meet know this.'

Amelia thought that perhaps she had seen his eyes begin to fill with tears, but when he noticed her looking at him, he quickly turned his head away, continuing his thought.

'But losing someone who loved you, that is so much harder. I would like to tell you that everything will be okay, and it will, eventually, but it will take time and patience. This pain will stay with you for a while. Even when you think you have completely healed, it will find a way to creep back into your head when you least expect it. This is the nature of love. This is the price we pay.'

He wiped his face, turning now to look upon Amelia. His eyes were red. He had indeed been crying, whether he chose to show it or not.

'The price of love is always worth it, Amelia. It matters not if it is a lifetime's worth, or a fleeting moment's; love is what makes us human. It is what separates us from those who seek to destroy us. Love will always prevail.'

Reaching into his chest pocket, Losophos produced the Crown of Queen Elinora, placing it atop Amelia's head, before excusing himself and departing the nest.

Amelia had been looking forward to wearing her crown again since giving it up in the days prior, but now the longing she had felt meant nothing. Her desire to reunite with it was overshadowed completely by the pain she was experiencing. She would have given her crown up a hundred times over, if it meant that she could have Keaton back.

She remained beside Keaton as the morning turned to afternoon. Her wish to stay beside him didn't make sense; it wasn't like he would even know she was there, but just being around him comforted her. This was something she had grown accustomed to at their old house with William. Even when he didn't want to play with her, or wanted to do his own thing, it would comfort her to just be in the same room as him, whether he acknowledged her or not.

So, Amelia remained, silently mourning the one she had loved, the one she still loved, the one who loved her.

It wasn't until dusk that she could no longer ignore the complaints of her stomach. Aside from a few biscuits the night before, which were now scattered on the ground far below the tree, Amelia hadn't really eaten anything in days. It was making her weaker as time went on, and the loud rumblings of her vacant belly disrupted the serenity of the world she wanted to remain in.

She placed one last kiss on Keaton's forehead before she left. She lowered herself over the side of the nest, placing her feet on the branch. She breathed in deeply, holding it inside her lungs for a few seconds, before taking the first of many steps away from him.

When she reached the inner wall of the tree, Amelia was greeted by two guards, different to the ones she had encountered at the nest earlier that morning. Given how long it had been, the watches had no doubt changed to allow them rest.

'Princess,' one said, as they both bowed before her, 'your mother asked us to tell you that she and your father will be at The Archive with Master William, waiting for you to come and see him when you are, of course, ready.'

'Thank you,' Amelia said, turning away from them and descending the nearest staircase towards the ground.

It wasn't long before she reached The Archive. The stairs put her out just on the far side of the pond, which she walked around with haste, eager to see her brother and her parents, not wanting to be alone anymore, but ready for human contact.

She felt ashamed for the way she had spoken to Amity that morning, but knew that she would understand. She always did. Even if Amelia didn't feel like explaining what was happening in her head, her mother seemed to know what she was thinking, always seeing the reasons behind her behaviour.

It was one of the traits that Amelia admired most about Amity, her empathy. Although she never understood why such an important word had such a negative name. There was nothing pathetic about being empathetic; in fact, the opposite was true. The greatest people, and many of Amelia's idols, became such fantastic role models through their empathy, their ability to understand and connect with others.

Lost in thought, Amelia found herself before the entrance to The Archive. She stepped up to the door and it opened before her, sensing the crown that she once again had in her possession. She walked down the dim staircase, trying not to let herself think of her memories with Keaton in the very same place, at least not for now.

When she entered The Archive, it was noticeably quiet. Her parents, Losophos, Ealdor and William all sat around the table to the side, none of them speaking, sharing in food.

All hearing the creak of the doors, they turned their heads to see Amelia enter. William leapt from his chair and ran towards her.

'Mealy!' he shouted, throwing his arms around her waist.

'Hey there,' she said, her voice raspy from a day of sobbing, lowering herself to her knees and hugging him close. 'How are you feeling, little guy?'

He pulled his head back and flashed her a grin.

'Better!' he said, nuzzling into her shoulder.

The two of them remained on the floor as the rest of the group continued to eat, respecting their space while they took some time to catch up.

For the first time since returning, Amelia felt at least a small bit of normality. Within the shortest time, she had lost one great love of her life, but regained another. With William back, she once again had someone to confide in, someone to speak to and laugh with when she couldn't sleep, someone who knew everything about her and loved her anyway.

When they were satisfied that they had spent enough time alone together, they joined the group at the table, where Amelia ate her fill, before excusing herself and saying her goodbyes.

Ealdor requested a moment of her time to speak in private. The two of them stepped off to the side, just out of the others' earshot.

'I'm sure you know what is to come tomorrow, Amelia,' he whispered.

Amelia nodded, understanding that tomorrow would be the day The Arbour gave Keaton a fitting send-off, one that she would ensure was worthy of the mightiest hero.

'It's customary within these walls to offer up gifts to the dead, something that might aid them on their journey into what lies beyond. Yours will be the last gift offered before we light the pyre. Usually, it would be a task reserved for me, but I thought, since you two were close, perhaps you would want to do it.'

She thought on the prospect for a few moments, when something else occurred to her. 'What about Deckard? Should it not be his right to send off his son?'

Ealdor's head lowered so that his chin rested on top of his chest. 'Normally, yes, but I fear Deckard is a broken man. He may not have the strength.'

'I'll do it,' she replied, answering so quickly that Ealdor stumbled on his next words.

'Ve... very well. I will have the tailor put together some appropriate mourning attire for you.' He placed a hand on her shoulder, offering a kind, pained smile.

'We did try to save him, Amelia. We tried so hard.' Ealdor struggled to get the words out as his eyes grew wet with tears. 'Everything will be right again. Just give it time.'

# CHAPTER TWENTY-FOUR

The sky was dark when Amelia returned to the castle with her parents. She wasted no time in saying goodnight to them before heading up to her room, which she hadn't visited since the break-in.

She walked in, expecting to see the place was still a mess. However, it looked just as she had left it. Her bed was neatly made, the curtains carefully tied on either side of the large window, which was sparklingly polished, without a speck of dust or smudge on its surface. If she hadn't been told that it had been destroyed, she would've had no idea. It was flawless.

The room was cold; there was no fire smouldering in its hearth. This was not the fault of the staff, however. They did not know when she was to return. Logs sat in a bundle in the centre of the fireplace, and with no effort at all, Amelia waved her arm towards them, thinking the word in her mind and watching as they became consumed by flames.

She smirked to herself as the wall of warmth passed through her, radiating outwards from the fire. Her powers had indeed continued growing over the past few days. The smirk turned to a frown as she remembered her inability to help Keaton, not for lack of trying.

Amelia approached the window, where she stared out over The Arbour. Winter had truly come now; the night air was thick with frost, even within the trunk, making it hard to see much further than the edge of town.

She looked longingly towards Keaton's window, hoping, beyond reason, that she had dreamed everything up until now, and that he would show himself, smiling back at her.

To her disbelief, she saw something moving in the darkness of his room. Her heart began to race, and her thoughts quickened as she rushed to discover the truth behind what she had seen.

It was late in the evening, so the castle halls were deserted. She did not see another face between her room and Keaton's, a journey that would usually find her pausing several times to share in conversation with the many workers and residents within the building's walls.

As she approached Keaton's door, she noticed that it was ajar. She listened at the door for a few seconds, hearing something shuffling around inside. She quietly peered into the room. It was dark, with only small bits of moonlight spilling in through the window. She couldn't locate the figure; however, she noticed candles hanging from the walls. She pushed through the door quickly, igniting them as she went.

Deckard's hulking figure appeared in the flickering candlelight, his new sword pointed directly at Amelia.

'Forgive me, Princess,' he said, sheathing it and turning away from her. 'You startled me.'

Amelia looked around the room, seeing that Deckard had been packing Keaton's things. He hadn't accumulated much during his time in the castle. She felt ashamed that she had interrupted Deckard during such a personal moment.

'Deckard, I'm sorry.' It was all that she could think to say. She hadn't seen him since they had returned, since his son had died.

He stepped over towards Amelia without a word, standing directly before her for a few seconds, before crouching down and hugging her.

Amelia froze for a moment. She had never seen Deckard hug anyone; the only time she'd seen him happy was when he told her how proud he was of Keaton. She reciprocated the hug, although her arms barely extended halfway around his hulking frame.

'Do not be sorry for me, Amelia,' he whispered. 'I had my chance with him, and I wasted it, which is my burden to bear. I will mourn him in my own way, as I know you will.'

He pulled away from the hug and walked over to the fireplace, picking something up from the mantle.

'I found this amongst his things,' he said, as he turned back to Amelia. 'It has your name on it.'

Deckard placed the letter into Amelia's outstretched hand, continuing to walk away, pausing as he reached the door.

'I'm sure that you're being given advice from every person with a voice at the moment.' Deckard looked at Amelia over his shoulder, his eyes growing red and watery as he collected himself. 'I would not recommend opening that until after tomorrow's service. It'll only make it harder to say goodbye. Trust me, I've been there.'

Without another word, he faced the door and stepped through it, disappearing into the darkness beyond, the sound of his footsteps gradually fading.

Amelia walked to the foot of Keaton's bed, taking a seat on its very edge, her fingers playing with the letter in her hands. She turned it over again and again, inspecting the fine lines on the front that formed her name, written in Keaton's handwriting. The back was sealed with a small lump of wax, which bore the advisor's mark, a role that she had chosen him for.

The silence was tortuous. Amelia placed the letter into the front pocket of her denim overalls, hoping that the old saying "out of sight, out of mind" would help her curious brain resist the urge to rip it open.

Amelia lay back on the bed, her arms stretched high above her head, and closed her eyes. She pictured what the room was like when Keaton was moving around inside it, when the space was warm and filled with positive emotions.

The bed still smelled of him. She liked that, following the scent up to his pillows. She rested her head on the pillow that had an indentation in it, a reminder of where he'd slept, inhaling deeply and reminiscing on his smell.

She became lost in her thoughts, in every memory she had with him, from when she first met him while blindfolded as a prisoner, to the last time she saw him, lying in a pool of his own blood.

Amelia didn't want to end her reminiscing on such a negative image, instead beginning to dream on what the future could have been, playing with different outcomes in her mind, seeing wedding dresses, children, the both of them old and happy, the things she didn't know she wanted before now.

* * * * *

When Amelia awoke, it was bright outside. She rubbed her eyes and went to the window. The fog from the previous night had cleared, and the town below her was a hive of activity. The market square had been cleared of its many stalls and displays. Now, only a few figures walked around the space, setting up for the ceremony to come.

It was a cruel reminder of what today would bring, the ceremony where she was to say goodbye to her love in front of all her people.

In no particular hurry, she walked to the door. Pausing for a moment, she took in the space for one last time, the space that mirrored her room almost identically. She said the first of many goodbyes in her head, before stepping over the threshold and pulling the door shut behind her.

Amelia roamed the hallways once more, this time in the direction of her room, passing several workers, who acknowledged her as they went.

Her door was open wide, her mother sitting by the window, looking upon the world. Amelia stepped in loudly, so as not to frighten her. Amity turned and saw her daughter, who offered a pained smile.

'Good morning, my love,' Amity said, rising from her chair and meeting Amelia in the middle of the room, where they hugged. 'I expected you would return soon to get ready for the service. I wanted to be with you.'

Amelia had lost a big love, but she knew that she was still loved, which made everything seem a bit less dire.

'Where are Dad and William?' Amelia asked.

'They're getting ready downstairs; they'll be up soon to see you.'

Amity let go of the hug first, keeping her arm over Amelia's shoulder as they walked over to the wardrobe.

'If you recall, the tailor was going to make us some matching winter dresses. Ealdor suggested that he make them appropriate for an occasion such as today.'

Hanging over the doors was an elegant gown, its main body black, with green highlights. It looked thick and warm, yet delicate. Amity stepped forward and pulled the dress from its hanger, turning to Amelia with a smile.

'Here, let me help you.'

Together, Amity and Amelia helped each other into their new gowns. It was simple; they were made to fit perfectly, and they did.

'Beautiful,' Amity said, as she buttoned up Amelia's gown and turned her around to inspect it in the mirror. 'A dress fit for a queen.'

Amelia didn't say anything out loud, not wanting to upset her mother, but in her head, she scoffed at the prospect of being a queen. Her chance to marry Keaton and make him her king was long gone, and it would be a very long time before somebody else would be able to fill those shoes.

The thought of Keaton reminded her of the envelope. Finding her overalls, she produced the letter, which she slid into a pocket on her new gown.

Amity and Amelia remained before the mirror for a while, doing each other's hair and not saying much. The weight of saying goodbye was starting to affect them both.

Lyall and William joined them in Amelia's room as they finalised their preparations. The four of them stood in the window and hugged one another once they were all ready.

'I suppose we had best head down,' Lyall said, holding Amity by the hand and leading her out the door.

'I just want a moment with William,' Amelia called out after them. 'We'll be right behind you.'

Once their footsteps had stopped echoing up the hall, Amelia sat with her brother on the foot of her bed and pulled his hand into hers.

'How are you, William? I imagine this room is no longer your favourite place.'

He looked to the window, its colours reflecting in his eyes.

'It's not the room that was my favourite place.' He smiled, laying his arm over Amelia's shoulder. 'Wherever you are is my favourite place.'

Amelia hadn't expected such kind words from William, and it caught her completely off-guard. She began to sob.

'I miss him so much, Will.'

'I know you do, Mealy.' He rubbed her back as she cried into his shoulder. 'I'd like to tell you... the way he spoke about you, the feelings he described to me, he truly loved you. I mean truly.'

Amelia cried harder and louder as William told her of the conversation they had shared in his cart one evening, recalling the emotion that Keaton showed on his face.

As her sobbing slowed, Amelia eased her head up from William's shoulder. He looked into her eyes as she wiped away tears.

'Are you ready to go say goodbye?' He flashed her a sympathetic smile, which she responded to with a teary nod.

'I am.'

William stood and grabbed Amelia's hand, as they began the long walk down to the service in the market square.

* * * * *

The ceremony went as smoothly as could be expected. Many of the townsfolk offered up exceptional gifts to aid Keaton in the afterlife, something that Amelia wasn't so sure really existed. However, this wasn't the correct time nor place to bring up such topics.

At last, the time came for her to offer up her parting gift to Keaton, and she approached the pyre where his lifeless body lay, dressed in his finest clothes, surrounded by gifts.

She leaned over him, her mouth resting in the air just beside his ear as she whispered, 'Keaton, my love. I have already given you my greatest gift, my heart.' She began to tear up, trying her hardest to at least maintain her composure in front of all who watched. 'I wish there was something else I could give you, something worth more than that, but there isn't. All I can give you today is my thanks. Thank you for helping us save William; you brought back the second biggest love in my life at the cost of your own. I wish there was another way. I love you.'

Her hand brushed his hair, before moving down his face, where it rested on his chin. She moved her face in close to his and gave him one last kiss on his cheek.

It was not the rush of blood and fireworks that she usually experienced when she kissed him. His skin was cold and dry. Unresponsive. Dead.

She took one final look at him, before turning away and walking back up to the podium, where she sat and watched over the square.

Ealdor addressed the crowd, as was customary, preparing them for the last part of the ceremony, which would be burning Keaton's body. Losophos appeared beside Amelia, placing a hand on her shoulder, and ducking down to her level.

'Princess Amelia,' he said, reaching into a pocket in his jacket, 'I thought perhaps this would help you in your healing.'

His hand reappeared, the long pale fingers holding a small red ruby, although it wasn't carved in the same shape as those in Amelia's crown. This one was a perfect circle.

Amelia reached for the gem, not even looking at Losophos.

'Is this what I think it is?' she said, her fingers caressing the cool surface of the ruby.

'It is indeed. I knew this would be a hard loss for you to mourn, so I used the old magic and transfused what remained of Keaton's lifeblood into this gem for you, to do with as you please.'

Amelia clenched the gem in her hand, throwing her arm around Losophos in thanks, just as Ealdor called her forth to light the flame.

She stood and walked to the edge of the balcony that overlooked the market. The sea of faces all looked up at her, hundreds of them. Every soul inside the tree was here today, honouring a fallen hero.

Amelia raised her empty hand and pointed it towards the pyre. Closing her eyes, she concentrated on the feeling of the gem in her other hand, which helped to calm her mind. She pictured the pyre before her, the body of her first true love in the middle of it, and when she was ready, she spoke the word in her mind. Seconds later, she felt the heat radiating from the courtyard below her.

After lowering her empty hand, Amelia brought her other hand into view before her and opened her fingers, seeing the ruby lying in her palm.

Choosing not to watch the fire directly, she instead stared into the gem, watching as the flickering flames reflected onto its many carved faces, making it look alive. She did this for a few minutes, wishing that Keaton's soul would somehow find its way into the gem and remain with her forever.

# CHAPTER TWENTY-FIVE

Amelia did not hang around after the ceremony. In The Arbour, funerals were followed by celebrations that often carried on for days. People broke bread, shared food and drinks that they might have been saving for such a special occasion, danced and played games.

Her family wanted to stay behind and participate, and Amelia gave them her blessing to do so. She wished to mourn Keaton in her own way, and being alone was precisely what she wanted.

She walked to the stables and gathered Samson, whose demeanour had also changed, as though he knew his master was gone. She didn't want to take the whole cart, so she just climbed up onto his back and wrapped her arms around his neck, hoping that somehow, he would know to be gentle with her.

The trot from the stables to the edge of town started uncomfortably, until Amelia began to settle into the rhythm of Samson's movements, bouncing her body at the right times so as not to hurt her legs too much. Once they were in the fields, she allowed him to take off at whatever speed he desired, adjusting her bouncing to match the tempo of his rise and fall, guiding him by turning his head with her hands.

When they arrived at The Archive, Amelia jumped off his back, and left him by the water, hoping he wouldn't wander too far before she returned. She ran down the dark staircase and raced through the rows of artefacts and books, reading their spines until she found the one she wanted.

Amelia returned to Samson, climbed onto him and wrapped one arm around his neck, using the other to secure the book against her torso. They galloped back through the fields towards the town, turning off the road just before entering its perimeter.

They reached the place they had set out for, the place where she had planned to spend the day while the rest of the town gave Keaton a fitting send-off. She slid down from Samson's back once more, placing the book carefully on the ground before smacking his behind and allowing him to run off wherever he wanted.

The air was warm and quiet at the small pond where Keaton and Amelia had previously spent a few afternoons relaxing, following in the footsteps of Keaton's parents. She walked around to where they had chosen to plant the apple seed. The first green shoot had sprouted from the brown dirt. With her back to the water, she knelt beside the sprout and reached into her pocket, producing Keaton's ruby and the envelope he had left for her.

Holding the ruby in her hand, Amelia opened the envelope, cracking the wax seal as she pulled open the back flap. Inside was a piece of paper with writing on it. She pulled it free of the envelope and unfolded it, bracing herself to read his message.

*Amelia,*

*Tomorrow, we venture through the mirror to rescue Will. As part of my preparations, I thought it best to write this letter, so that should I be unable to tell you how I feel, you would at least know.*

*You have been the best thing to ever happen to me. You helped me know my father, helped me know my mother's face, and helped me know love.*

*I thought that love was just something parents made up so they could guilt their children into caring for them when they were older. I was so wrong.*

*I know what love is now. Love is wanting to make someone happy without the expectation of receiving anything in return. Love is wanting to spend every moment of every day with someone, no matter where they are or what they are doing. Love is scary and beautiful. Love is all the feelings you have never understood wrapped up into a little bundle and thrown right into the middle of your heart.*

*Love hurts and love heals. It makes us wiser and, at the same time, makes us crazier. It makes us want to do things even if it means getting hurt.*

*I love you, Amelia. I know that now.*

*Keaton*

Amelia read the words again and again. He had loved her, he had been in love with her as he wrote this letter, and she was in love with him.

She began to cry, slipping the letter back into the envelope, as well as the ruby. She used her hands to dig gently around the sprout, until the hole was deep enough to put the letter in. Kissing the envelope, Amelia placed it in the ground and covered it with dirt. Once the hole had been filled in, she smoothed the earth and leaned into it.

As she began to sob louder, sadness and frustration grew inside her heart. Her tears fell and her hands formed fists that pounded the ground around her. She pictured the letter and the ruby and continued to hit the ground and cry uncontrollably, feeling her emotion move through her veins as though it were blood.

As her emotions heightened, the dirt beneath her began to tremble, but she didn't pay attention to it, her mind still focused on the objects buried below her. She continued to unleash all of her energy into the dirt, pushing out all of her anger and her sorrow, hearing rumbling and creaking around her.

Through her closed eyelids, she noticed that something had blocked out the sun from above her, her body now cool in the shade. She began to calm herself and rub her eyes free of any remaining tears, and when she opened them, a trunk was right in front of her face.

Looking down to the ground, Amelia could not see the patch where she had buried the letter and the ruby. It was now below an elaborate root system, which she followed upwards with her eyes. The root system joined with the twisting brown trunk that shot up before her. High above her head, it split into many branches, each one laden with emerald-green leaves and deep red apples, as though the fruit had taken their colour from the surface of the ruby itself.

Amelia remained kneeling in silent confusion, inspecting the tree that stood before her. She wasn't sure how it had happened, or where the power had come from, but she had caused the tree to grow instantaneously.

After a moment of reflection, Amelia walked to the place where she had left the book, and carried it over to the apple tree, sitting in a comfortable bunch of roots that formed a smooth seat. She opened the book, turning the pages until she found the correct spot. On the left page was the picture of Keaton's face when he was born, as well as the date and his parentage written below. On the right, the page remained blank.

Amelia produced her pencils from within her gown and began to sketch the face that she inspected hours earlier, the face of the boy she loved. She sketched into the afternoon, taking the occasional break to look over the town on the horizon, the quiet winter air ringing every now and then with the cheers of the townsfolk.

When Amelia had finished Keaton's portrait, she closed the book and let it lie on the ground next to her, resting one hand on its cover. She smiled to herself as she peered up into the branches of the apple tree, looking at the red fruit that Keaton loved so much.

'I'll need you with me now, more than ever.' She spoke to the open air, picturing Keaton sitting next to her amongst the roots. 'This next part won't be easy without you, so I need you to be with me. With us.'

As she finished speaking, a single apple fell from the tree and landed with a *thud* right next to her. She picked it up and held it close to her face, inspecting the flawless red surface, catching her own reflection smiling back at her.

She cuddled the apple close to her chest and smiled into the sky. Her spirits were getting higher as she thought of what it all meant, hoping that this was a sign from her lost love, a symbol that he would be with her in the battle that was to come, and that, perhaps, he would be waiting there for her in the end.

# EPILOGUE

Mundus was a hive of activity in the days after Amelia and her Argonauts snuck in. Wounded Malum were tended to on the shores of the lake, the only area big enough to house so many burnt bodies. Most of the injuries had come from the explosion on the wall where the mirror once stood. Those unfortunate enough to have been standing on the wall, or in the guard post at its end, had suffered the worst wounds, ranging from minor burns to broken limbs.

Other injuries had come from smoke inhalation, which was worst nearest the fortress, the location of the second major fire that took place within their nest that night. The fortress had been reduced completely to rubble. The flames continued well into the next night, and the search for survivors was looking more futile as the days continued.

Oscuro had assumed control after the fortress collapsed. The entire city had witnessed the pained screams that filled the air around the building as it burnt the members of the Rat King that remained alive. Being Azul's right-hand man, Oscuro was naturally the next in line, until they had the time and resources to start the next Rat King.

The focus of his first command was to dismantle the old fortress and raise a newer, stronger building where it had once stood, a symbol of power and fear to all those who dared question his authority. It had only been two days since the fire, and already the ground was almost reduced to a flat starting block.

As a pair of rats focused on clearing the last charred remains of the stone foundations, they heard a wheezing from beneath the pile before them.

'Survivors?' one said to the other, who was already frantically digging through the rubble with his front paws.

'Hello?' he called out to the pile as he moved large portions of it to the side. 'Can you hear us?'

As they cleared more and more of the heap away, it began to shift and move without them touching it. The two rats backed away slowly, watching while it appeared to rise on its own, chunks of stone and sand spilling off it.

Their mouths dropped open, and they fell to their knees as they witnessed the emergence of the figure before them.

There, in the painful light of day, stood a rat covered from head to tail in burns. Much of his hair was gone, save for a few patches that were curled and burnt. His tail was a stump that looked as though it had been chewed through, the edges torn and uneven. Atop his head was not a gold crown, but the remnants of one. It had melted in the heat of the inferno, fusing itself permanently with what remained of his flesh.

He flashed the two rats a disgusting smile. Many of his teeth were missing, and drool began to spill from the gaps between them as he spoke in a raspy, painful voice.

'Prepare the army.'

Shawline Publishing Group Pty Ltd
www.shawlinepublishing.com.au